CASCADE

A NOVEL

JANICE BOEKHOFF

CASCADE Published by:
Lost Canyon Press
P.O. Box 624
Bettendorf, IA 52722

For Riley,
May your courageous spirit help you to climb to amazing heights
with God.

CHAPTER 1

*A*s volcanologist Lenaia Talavera bounced up and down, waving frantically at the family, the friable ground underneath her feet popped and groaned. She stopped bouncing but kept motioning for them to leave. Only trained professionals were allowed in this part of Hawaii's Kilauea volcano, and even for them, the risk was high.

The family of three walked on about a hundred yards away, stumbling over the uneven lava rock, and wandering into dangerous territory. *Why do people go on vacation and leave their common sense at home?* Lenaia flattened her hands in front of her, making an X in the air, hoping they would get the message.

In response, a redheaded girl, maybe six or seven years old, waved at her and continued walking. Her parents followed blindly behind.

Lenaia squinted at them, sensing something familiar about them both, but she couldn't determine what. "No! Stay back."

The trio kept coming. Couldn't they hear her? They obviously hadn't paid attention to the warning signs telling them to stay off of this part of the volcano. She secured the gas meter in her back pocket, then moved to intercept them.

Her trained eyes scanned the dark rocks for fissures, steam vents or depressions. The rock might look stable, but lava tubes ran under this area. At any minute, the seemingly solid ground could cave in, opening a skylight into the tube and exposing a turbulent river of molten rock. And if they were standing there when it happened—instant incineration.

Off to the right, Lenaia detected a tiny column of steam, barely visible as it distorted the backdrop of the sky before dissipating in the island breeze. It was a vent for the roiling mass of liquid rock underneath. A sign of the unstable ground in this area.

The redheaded girl skipped ahead of her parents. She tripped once, then got up. After brushing black dust off her jeans, she continued at a slow run. The closer she came, the more uneasy Lenaia felt, and not just because of the peril. This girl looked oddly familiar too.

"Go back," Lenaia yelled and pointed at the steam vent dusting the air at a right angle between them. They were thirty yards away and seemed to have heard her. The three of them turned their attention to the steam, but then moved toward it like curious toddlers. Dread coiled in the pit of her stomach. What were they thinking?

"No." She ran forward, her fire-retardant boots scraping along the rough rocks. A broken up section of lava tripped her up. She caught herself before she fell and resumed running.

The father stopped for a second and gave Lenaia a confused look. As their eyes met, the years disappeared between them, and she recognized her ex-boyfriend's brother, Dan. That meant the woman was probably his wife, Summer. Their little girl's name escaped her since the girl would have been young when Lenaia last saw her. But why would they be out here?

The little girl glanced over at Lenaia, let out a squeal, and began running again, bolting for the steam column. She thought this was a race. Lenaia had to get to her before it was too late. She pushed her legs faster.

A loud popping noise rose over the crunching sound of her boots. It came from the ground to her right. Two more steam vents opened next to the first, the wispy plumes swirling upward like white pinwheels.

Lenaia swallowed the fear rising up in her throat. As she ran past Dan, his feet seemed rooted to the ground, but Summer began to run behind Lenaia. Within ten feet of the girl, a louder, more terrifying sound reached Lenaia's ears—the sharp crack of breaking rock.

No, please, God. Don't take this little girl's life.

Still running, Lenaia ignored the sharp pulse of heat burning through her boots. Just a few more steps.

She jumped and reached for the girl with both arms.

The ground fell away beneath her feet.

Wrapping the girl's small body in her arms, Lenaia held on as they flew through the air in a football tackle. Lenaia's left shoulder took the full force of the landing. She kept the girl tight to her chest.

The turbulent rush of fast-moving liquid filled the air. Lenaia looked down at the ground from where she'd jumped. It was gone, replaced by a gaping hole in the lava tube.

Heat smothered her legs like a smoldering blanket and pain seared through her left ankle, probably burned from the steam. She drew her knees under her and tugged the girl away from the churning chasm. The girl clung to her neck.

Twenty yards away, she laid the girl down as gently as she could on the sharp rocks. "Are you okay?"

The girl nodded with tears running down her cheeks and wetting her touristy red-dirt Hawaiian T-shirt. Lenaia blew out a deep breath and spun around. Summer was crab-walking away from the skylight. She must have jumped at the same moment.

"What were you thinking?" Lenaia pointed to the girl. "None of you should be out here."

Even as she scolded the woman, her subconscious prodded

her. A heavy feeling in her chest insisted something was still wrong. Wiping dirt from her forehead, she took another deep breath, trying to get her nerves to settle down.

Then she saw it.

Another skylight had opened up farther along the length of the lava tube. Thick drops of melted rock shot up from the molten river, splattering in wide arcs. Dan was nowhere in sight.

From behind, she heard the little girl's mousy voice. "Daddy?"

CHAPTER 2

 ne month later ...

"Don't answer that." Travis Perego snatched the ringing cell phone off the bed.

Lenaia stopped in the midst of unpacking to glare at her boyfriend. At least, as much glare as she could pull off while staring into his cornflower blue eyes. She held out her hand. "Give it back."

"Not if this call is going to take you out of town again." He flopped onto her bed and looked at the caller ID. "It's Jayna. Probably with another assignment."

She put her hands on her hips. Did he really think she'd stop working if he confiscated her phone? Under her stern gaze, he relented, but she'd already missed the call. "It might not be for work. Maybe she's calling to talk. We haven't been on a girl's weekend since she had Melanie."

"I'd rather not take the chance." He moved over until he sat next to her suitcase.

She slipped a pair of jeans into a drawer, then returned to grab a sweatshirt, glancing at him out of the corner of her eye. He ran his fingers through his hair, making it stick up like tawny bundles of wheat. How could a man look so good without trying?

"I'll have to call her back, you know. She's my boss." She lifted the corner of her mouth. "*Our* boss, actually."

Travis rubbed at the day-old stubble on his chin. Her grin fell. He must have something on his mind, but she didn't dare to ask. If it was about their future, she couldn't handle that subject right now.

He stood and moved behind her as she continued to pull the remaining clothes from the suitcase to toss them across the room into her hamper. His warm hands slid down her arms. She stopped throwing clothes long enough to enjoy the tingles racing along her skin. Her senses melted into the familiar scent of his cologne, like the outdoors after a cleansing rain.

"Please," he whispered in her ear. "Don't go out in the field again for a while. You've been gone for a month straight, ever since ... " His hands stilled. "Since the incident in Hawaii."

She bit her lip. The incident. That was one way to put it. Why not make it sound like a sprained ankle, rather than a lost life? A life she might have saved.

"Work has been busy lately." A wave of shame coursed through her. Travis didn't know that after each assignment, she called Jayna begging for another one. Being out in the field was easier than sitting around thinking about what she could have done differently. Easier than remembering the agony on Summer's face when she realized she'd lost her husband. Or the blank look of shock in their daughter's eyes as she tried to process why daddy wasn't standing there.

"You said you wanted to see your mother this weekend."

Ugh. He knew what would get to her. It had been a month since she'd visited her mom in the nursing home. She still liked to see her mother, but neither one of them got much else out of the visits. Her mom had stopped participating in life years ago, after her dad died, long before an attempted suicide left her with permanent brain damage and in need of constant care.

With a soft sigh, Travis moved his hands up to rub her shoulders. "I talked to Dr. Hill. He can see you as early as tomorrow, if you'll go."

The muscles in her back stiffened. Using all of her willpower, she pulled away and went into the bathroom. She set her electric toothbrush in the holder, hoping it would have enough time to fully charge before she left again. She took a few more minutes to sweep her hair into a messy bun and wash her face. Maybe Travis would forget the question by the time she came back.

When she returned, he was leaning against the headboard with one leg on the floor, the other angled on the mattress. The concern etched into his face gave him an intense look, which coupled with the pose, created an image straight from the cover of *GQ*. When he looked at her like that, she had such a hard time saying no to him.

His eyebrows lifted in hope. "Will you go?"

She grabbed a few shirts from the suitcase and threw them at the hamper. On the way, they hit the top of her dresser, sending her rock samples—a geode, rough opal and tourmaline—rocking and probably scratching the wood. She turned to meet his gaze, holding it for a moment. Her stalling tactics hadn't fazed him. She knew he meant well, but she'd have to be more direct. "I prefer to work on emotional stuff myself—*by* myself."

"I know and I respect that. But with your uncle's death and then the ... " He paused to swallow, as if the words *lava tube* might send her over the edge. "With what happened in Hawaii, you could use a little help. And you don't want to talk to me about it."

"Because I'm fine."

He leaned forward. "Then what's the harm in talking to somebody?"

"No harm. Just a waste of time." She rifled through the receipts she'd stuck at the bottom of her bag. When he didn't say anything more, she glanced over at him. His eyes pleaded with her, melting her resolve. Besides, if she didn't get him to back off soon, he'd keep pressing until he found out everything. And she didn't want to talk about how she knew Dan. She sighed. "All right. I'll go see the doctor tomorrow, unless Jayna has a new assignment for me." Hopefully, Jayna would come through for her.

Travis turned his lips down in a mock pout. "Well, thanks for that."

"Speaking of assignments, has Jayna gotten *you* another one?" Jayna, owner of Rowan Geologic Consulting, had hired Travis after the university fired him for his beliefs on creation. Even though he had saved the college by exposing another professor's fraudulent claims, a paleontology professor who wouldn't teach evolution was still an embarrassment to the college.

"Yes. I'm reworking parts of the stratigraphic column using microfossils. Not as exciting as dinosaurs, but at least I'm doing paleontology."

"Good. I'm glad you've got something to do for a while." She went to the hamper, picked up the clothes from the floor, then yawned and stretched her arms. "Now, I'm sorry, but you must go home. I've got to call the boss back and get to bed."

He rose and crossed the room in two strides, until he stood towering over her. "I'll go." His finger traced her jawline. "But now that I'm getting some steady work, you and I need to talk."

"About what?" As if she didn't know. He'd been hinting for months. Ever since she'd moved to an apartment in Mt. Holly, North Carolina, to be closer to his house.

"The future." He placed a palm on her cheek. "More specifically, our future."

Spikes of anticipation shot through her stomach, along with knife-edged stabs of fear. The anticipation she understood— Travis was the most generous and caring man she'd ever met. He would lay down his life for her, and she'd do the same for him. It was the fear she couldn't understand. She pushed down the confusing swell of emotions. "Can we talk later?"

He bent down, bringing his lips to hers in a gentle kiss. "Soon," he said, as he pulled away.

She sucked in a breath, drawing the air deep into her lungs, and shivered from the lingering pleasure of his kiss. Travis could overwhelm all her senses. If only that was enough to quell the fear swirling inside her.

"JAYNA, I'm glad I finally caught you." Lenaia plopped down on the couch in her living room. She'd left her boss a message last night then tried again this morning.

"Sorry, I meant to call you first thing, but Melanie has a fever and she's not sleeping, which means my schedule is up in the air. She can't go to day care again until the fever breaks."

Which was exactly why Lenaia wasn't ready to have kids yet. Last year, she'd envied Jayna as she carried her first child, but now she saw the conflict that hounded her boss every day. The guilt of not doing the job the way she used to, together with the guilt of not spending enough time with Melanie, wore Jayna down to the point of exhaustion. Lenaia already had enough guilt in her life.

"Anyway, enough about my sick kid." Jayna paused and the sound of shuffling papers filled the noise in the background. "I've got an assignment for you. A personal request, in fact."

Lenaia hopped up from the couch and went to the bedroom. Another assignment was just what she needed. "Where to?"

"Your old stomping grounds. How do you feel about visiting Mt. Rainier again?"

Not Rainier. Normally, she'd jump at the chance. Mt. Rainier held a special place in her heart. The forested slopes, the quaint town of Mayim, the massive peak of fire and ice—all beautiful echoes of a life she'd left behind. Still, she couldn't bring herself to agree. In Mayim, she'd be haunted by what happened in Hawaii. But Jayna had no way of knowing what she was asking. "What do they need?"

"Somebody who can figure out their mystery."

Lenaia's specialty. She could determine the problem with just about any natural system. If only her superpower worked while trying to figure out her own future. A year ago, she'd been praying to meet the man God had planned for her. Then, Travis had appeared out of nowhere to rescue her in the jungle. Despite his heroics, she'd dismissed his interest because he was struggling spiritually. She'd been down that road before with Zayden, her ex-boyfriend. He'd been far from God and had pushed her away too. Their relationship had almost cost her faith.

Thankfully, Travis had overcome his doubts, but now Lenaia was drowning in a sea of her own fears. Every time Travis talked about the future, her heart would race and her chest would tighten, making her short of breath and dizzy.

Maybe some time on Mt. Rainier would give her space to think about it. But visiting the mountain would also force her to confront her guilt from Hawaii. She hadn't seen Summer since Dan's death. Would Summer be angry if Lenaia came to town? Then again, going there might help clear out some of her emotions without seeing a counselor, like a reset button of sorts.

Unless Zayden still lived there.

"Did someone from the Washington Department of Natural Resources ask for me?" She went to the closet, pulled out her medium sized, hard-shelled suitcase and threw it onto the bed. At least, spring at high-altitude with the lovely carpets of wildflowers was a perfect time to visit.

"Sort of. They recommended you. The government has been shut down for a week now because the budget bill failed in Congress and they ran out of extensions. Well, the shutdown includes the U.S. Geological Survey. The few geoscientists holding things together up there—and working for free I might add—don't need more work to do. When your old boss at the Washington State DNR reminded them of all the work you did on the mountain, they wanted you to come out."

"Great." Lenaia chuckled. "Does that mean I'm working for free too?"

"No, I've got you covered until the government gets back up and running again. Then, they'll get a bill from me."

"So, what's the problem?"

"Their tiltmeters are flaking out once in a while, measuring a large degree of tilt, almost like the mountain is swelling. But it's not clear what the problem is. Plus, they're concerned the lahar sensors might be a problem."

"I installed the tiltmeters when I worked there. They've been solid for years." The tiltmeters measured upward movement of the mountain, like intruding lava, and the lahar sensors warned of mudflows coming down the river channels. Both systems were essential to protecting the people who lived in the area, especially the town of Mayim right at the base of the volcano. "Do the geologists out there have any ideas?"

"Not right now. The geologist they've got on the mountain is pretty new on the job. Another reason why they asked for you."

Lenaia yanked open a drawer and threw a couple of sweatshirts in the suitcase, excitement for the challenge leaving her restless. "I'll catch a flight today."

"No hurry. Friday would be fine."

Her hands stopped in the middle of folding a pair of jeans. She flipped the top of the suitcase closed and plopped onto the bed. When she spoke again, her voice sounded quiet and meek to her ears, but it was from barely controlled anger. "Travis told you to work around Dr. Hill's schedule, didn't he?"

Jayna didn't answer for a long moment. "He might have mentioned it when I called to check on his job assignment."

Lenaia blew out a trapped breath and stomped her foot. "This is why it's hard to mix business and personal life."

"Lenaia, you know that's not my philosophy on business. We're friends and coworkers. And Travis is just worried about you."

She shifted the phone to her other ear, pushed off the bed, and went to the dresser, searching for her compass to throw in the bag. "I don't need to see a doctor."

"Because?"

Why did she constantly have to explain herself? No matter how much Jayna and Travis cared, they needed to back off a little. "Because talking about it won't change anything."

"Lenaia, I know what it's like to shut everything up inside and hope it goes away, but that never works. You've experienced a lot of tragedy recently. Believe me, bottling up those emotions will only make them explode later."

What could she say to that? Jayna had experienced more than her fair share of tragedy and had come out on the other side as a shining example of peace. But Lenaia didn't handle things like Jayna. How could she explain that talking made everything worse? Putting words to tragedy didn't make it go away; it made the pain more real.

"I'll think about it."

"There's one more thing."

"What's that?"

"It's about Rainier," Jayna continued. "My contact at the DNR says the strange readings are too large to be a random thing."

Lenaia furrowed her brow. "What do you think that means?"

"I honestly don't know."

"Non-random means it's not likely a computer glitch. Could be a systemic equipment failure."

A squeaking noise came through the phone. Lenaia imagined her friend absently running her hand over her cell phone's rubber casing, a habit Jayna had when tense. "Or it could be something happening on the ground."

"Sounds like you're saying someone might be causing this."

A long pause. "I'm just saying be extra cautious while you're out there."

She hesitated at Jayna's serious tone but then answered in her usual manner. "Always, boss."

CHAPTER 3

*A*fter a two-hour drive from the airport, Lenaia turned off at Mt. Rainier National Park and stopped at the closed gate. Hard to believe the federal government couldn't agree on a budget—again. But what did it matter to the politicians? The lost revenue from closing the parks would only hurt the National Park System.

She got out and pushed the long arm of the gate open, then got back in the car and drove through. On the other side, she got out of the car again and had just reached for the gate to close it when the whir of tires signaled the approach of another vehicle. Lenaia walked toward the car. She'd have to tell the other driver to turn back because only park staff members were allowed to go any farther.

As the vehicle drew closer, she recognized the symbol painted on the door, barely visible in the fading sunlight. A set of wavy lines inside a box with the letters USGS next to it. She hadn't anticipated seeing someone from the U.S. Geological Survey at this time of the evening.

The door squeaked open as a slender man, a few inches taller and a few years younger than her, stepped out onto the asphalt.

His dark hair and skin set off bright hazel eyes the color of green jasper. He might be attractive if he weren't scowling at her.

The man slammed the car door shut. "I thought I might find you out here. I've been waiting for you."

She raised her eyebrows. "Excuse me?"

"I'm Griffin Wall. They told me to come meet you. You're Lenaia Talavera, right?"

"Yes." She hadn't planned on seeing anyone out here until tomorrow, but he must be the on-site geologist, and he was working late. "Uh, did you say Griffin?"

He pressed his lips together before answering. "It's a family name from my mother's side."

She folded her arms across her chest. "Just making sure I got it right. I wasn't told to meet anyone. Who sent you out here?"

"Sherry McCrea. Otherwise known as my boss."

"Oh, okay." Lenaia had known Sherry during the time when Lenaia served as a liaison between the USGS and the Washington Department of Natural Resources. They had similar philosophies on life—be the best at whatever you did and never compromise. Sherry had even pushed to have Lenaia promoted, despite the fact Lenaia worked for the State of Washington, not the USGS. But that was all before Lenaia became consumed with questions. When Lenaia told Sherry she had doubts about evolution, Sherry had gone to Lenaia's boss and asked to have her replaced. It had been a shock at the time, but Lenaia couldn't blame Sherry for acting on her convictions. It was something she would have done if their positions were reversed. Besides, leaving Mayim allowed her to meet Travis. She could never be sorry about that, no matter how God had to orchestrate it.

Griffin circled one finger in the air. "You'll have to turn around. My office isn't at the Sunrise Visitor's Center. It's at Jackson." He shoved his hands in the back pockets of his jeans. "Since I'm the low man on the ladder, I get to work for free right now." He turned and walked back to the vehicle.

Nice to meet you, too. She climbed into her rental car, made a U-turn and followed him out of the gate. After stopping to close the gate, she jumped back in and steered the car onto the highway that led around the southern side of the mountain.

The road twisted along the steep volcanic contours, clinging tight to the fractured rock faces. She tried to focus on the panoramic views around each corner, but the argument she had with Travis last night kept pushing to the forefront of her mind. They had danced around the truth, discussing her schedule and obsession with work, while the real problem had been left unsaid. Travis thought a counselor could change her back into the woman he'd met last year in the jungle. If that were possible, Lenaia might have welcomed the sessions, but the woman she used to be was no longer in reach. She was different now and there was no going back.

By the time she parked at the Henry M. Jackson Visitor's Center, Griffin had already disappeared inside. This could be a rough assignment if the guy didn't want to work with her. Maybe she could convince him to go home and let her handle things alone for the next several days.

She climbed out of the car and looked around. With its sloped metal roof and wood-plank siding, the visitor's center mirrored the rustic atmosphere created by the forested wilderness surrounding it. The full-length windows on all sides had huge dormers sticking out like moth's wings, which would be closed in the winter to keep the glass from breaking under the weight of the mountain's massive snowfalls.

Behind the center, the mountain rose like a snow-capped finger pointing to heaven. A wispy mist circled the summit, wrapping most of the peak in a cottony cocoon. Dark ridges of lava ran the length of the slopes, standing out in contrast against patches of pale glaciers. Emerald green forest encroached a third of the way up the mountain, but the rest was a barren landscape of gray basalt rock and bright, white ice.

On the far side of the parking lot were two other buildings: the park rangers' station and the lodge, a hotel from the early days of the national park. If only the hotel staff wasn't on furlough, she would have stayed there instead of in Mayim. The small town had been a great place to live five years ago, but now it felt as uncomfortable as a too-small pair of threadbare jeans—a place where the fragile seams keeping her past contained might burst apart at any moment.

With the extra elevation and the retreating sun, the temperature had dropped into the upper sixties, but she still felt warm in her jeans and cotton shirt. She pulled open the thick wooden entrance door and noted the escape of heat from the interior. The air conditioning must not have been running during the warmer parts of the day due to the shutdown.

A bright glow shone down from the two-story hanging lights above. At least, they hadn't turned off the electricity, which probably meant the air conditioning still worked as well. Maybe Griffin didn't want to waste the energy since no one else was out here.

She passed the empty information desk and climbed the stairs to the second level. Exhibits on plants and animals of the area, along with the mountain's history, dotted the second floor. She avoided them all and opened the door to the back staff area.

A familiar hallway stretched out in front of her. She walked to the end and entered the main office. They'd changed the layout of the room since her last trip here. Two large desks topped with computers took up most of the center of the room. A third, smaller desk sat against the wall to her right, holding a laptop. Griffin perched on the edge of a chair at one of the larger desks, staring intently at the computer screen, his back to her. He checked a printed sheet in his hand, then looked back at the screen.

Lenaia dropped her backpack on the floor and got right to

business. "What's going on with the tiltmeters and lahar sensors up here?"

Griffin kept his head buried in his work.

Odd that he would come find her and then ignore her once she got here. "Help me out."

He tossed the paper on the desk. "We've had tiltmeter problems, yes. I don't know about the lahar sensors. Those are run by the county. I remember hearing about some problems, but I'm sure they've got it fixed by now." He narrowed his eyes at her. "I don't know why they called you in. I've got everything covered." He said it matter-of-factly without any bitterness, although maybe a hint of irritation.

Now she understood his bristly attitude. He felt threatened. She put both hands up in mock surrender. "I'm just here to help. Sherry must have thought you already had enough work on your plate. You know, with the shutdown."

Griffin shrugged. "Not really. My project is on hold, thanks to the shutdown."

"What project is that?" Maybe if she took an interest in his work, Griffin would realize she wasn't here to take over his job.

"Ice coring on the Puyallup Glacier. I've drilled twenty, out of the thirty, holes I'm supposed to complete, but the money is currently in congressional limbo."

"That's typical. Hopefully, things will get back to normal soon. Okay, you don't think I have to worry about the lahar sensors." Relieved, she moved to lean against the desk. No photographs, paper or even a decorative rock on top. Didn't Griffin have a life outside of work? Not that it mattered to her. She didn't need to befriend him, just be cordial long enough to figure out the problem. She touched the side of the screen. "Do these computers still send signals to the base computers at the Cascade Volcano Observatory in Vancouver?"

Griffin leaned back in his chair. "Yes, CVO gets a copy of the data, along with the Pacific Northwest Seismic Network in Seattle."

She nodded. The system was similar to when she'd worked here. "How did you discover the tiltmeter failure?"

"The geologists at CVO noticed. They have more time to look at the data than I do. When the Brainiacs find a problem, they call me to fix it." He crossed his arms over his chest. "And I always fix it. So why did Sherry call you, as if I can't do my job?"

"Nobody is saying that." She wouldn't take his defensive attitude personally. Other geologists often felt threatened by her consulting role, especially the newbies. He looked at her and seemed to be deciding whether to make an answering comment or not. When he dipped his head back down, she continued. "I used to make trips onto this mountain, and back then, only one geologist and about a dozen park rangers were stationed here. Is that still the case?"

He tilted his head and stared at her. "When were *you* here?"

"Five years ago, I worked for the Geology Division of the Department of Natural Resources. I coordinated the State's volcano activities with those of the USGS."

"So you weren't a field geologist."

"Not so much then, but now all I do is field geology."

Griffin looked her up and down and gave a curt nod, his idea of a compliment she supposed.

"You didn't answer my question." She pushed off the desk and dropped into one of the rolling chairs. "How many geologists and rangers are usually up here? You know, on a day when the government has decided to function."

He actually gave a crooked smile. "It's just me. No other geologists come out here. Plus, about twenty park rangers, all of whom are on furlough, except for one."

"Which ranger is still working?"

"Randy Turnbuckle. He comes out once a day."

She nodded. "I know him. He's been here a long time. Good

guy." Randy was like a fatherly Boy Scout. Whenever she used to run into him, Randy would make sure she had her pepper gas canister, her compass, and plenty of food and water. "So, *you* haven't noticed any problems with the monitoring stations?"

"Not stations. Just one station. And only the guys in Vancouver noticed. They send me to check out random things all the time. Turns out, they were right to question this one. The tiltmeter angle increased by two hundred microradians."

Her mouth dropped open. That volume of lava could be as large as twenty football stadiums intruding into the rock. "How could it increase by that much?"

He shrugged and looked to the carpet, avoiding her gaze.

She rolled the chair over and stared at him until he met her eyes. "Come on, Griffin. Were those readings real data?"

He shook his head. "I don't know. From looking at the numbers, CVO thinks there might be a lava dome forming on the western flank, but I'm not convinced."

"You found a lava dome *here*?"

His eyes widened, as if he couldn't believe she'd know lava domes were rare on Mt. Rainier. The magma under the mountain held less silica, which made it a more fluid, andesite magma that flowed like Kool-Aid. On other nearby mountains, like Mt. St. Helens, the magma was a thicker, dacite magma that flowed like molasses and sometimes built up a dome under the surface rock. Rainier's Kool-Aid magma was much less likely to form a dome. Finding one would make volcanic history in the area, but more importantly, it could mean danger for adjacent towns. She imagined a buried pool of lava straining under the superficial cap of rocks—a fragile dam holding back a fiery tidal wave.

"But you're skeptical?" she asked.

"The degree of tilt is wrong." Griffin flicked his gaze to the computer. "If pressure from a lava dome caused a tilt like that, we'd see other signs. Physical indications and probably more earthquakes." He returned his gaze to her, blinking a few times.

"I've been on the mountain almost every day for the last month and I haven't seen any other signs."

She shook her head. "Earthquakes would likely increase, but Mt. Rainier is heavily glaciated. The signs you're looking for might be happening under the ice. And even though you can't confirm the lava dome in the field, you shouldn't ignore the readings."

Griffin stood, towering over her, with his hands on his hips. "I'm not ignoring them, but I haven't been able to confirm them either. The equipment is registering nothing now."

"Nothing at all?"

"Nope."

She pushed her ponytail over her shoulder. "Strange." She hated to ask the next question, given how sensitive he seemed, but she had to do her job. "Do the other geologists at CVO have any theories?"

He twisted his mouth and blinked again. "Yeah. The thing is broken. Without coming up here, how would the office jockeys formulate a different theory?"

She didn't blame Griffin for his frustration. Those geologists who analyzed data and made assumptions but couldn't back them up with real fieldwork irritated her as well. Signing up for a career in geology meant signing up for the physical demands of the job, not sitting behind a desk. A queasy swirl of guilt ran through her stomach. That was part of the reason why having a family with Travis could cause many problems. Balancing a family with a demanding and dangerous career like volcanology sounded like a recipe for failure.

She took a deep breath. "Unless you've added some recently, Mt. Rainier has two tiltmeters and half a dozen GPS monitoring stations. Which tiltmeter is causing the problem?"

"St. Andrews Rock, the STAR station."

That was one of the tiltmeters she'd helped put in. "Isn't there also a GPS monitoring station there?" A GPS station used satellites to track the position of the mountain and could confirm the presence of a magma intrusion.

Griffin plopped down into his chair, his shoulders slumped. "Yes, but it's damaged."

She raised her eyebrows. "Damaged how?"

He sighed. "It was an accident. When I was flying in some of my ice coring equipment, I whacked the receiver with the helicopter treads."

"That's inconvenient." She tapped one finger on the desk. "And no other stations have picked up evidence of a lava dome?"

"No. Like I said, I'm not sure it exists."

She frowned and spun her chair away from him. Maybe Sherry had brought her in because of Griffin's dismissive attitude. When dealing with volcanoes, it was always better to be safe than sorry. She turned back around to face him. "At least tell me you're committed to finding out."

He opened his mouth and closed it. "Of course."

"Good." She didn't quite believe Griffin, but he'd come around. As for her, the idea of going onto the mountain again had her legs twitching. "Let's hike up there tomorrow morning."

He settled his fingers on the keyboard. She'd take that as a yes. He might not like her presence, but he needed to get over it. She stood, grabbed her backpack and left him to his brooding.

As she came out of the heavy double doors, she stood for a second in the empty parking lot, her gaze rising. The clouds had momentarily cleared off the summit and she caught her breath at the beauty before her. The massive white peak appeared cold, and yet a hot fire radiated within its core. It was rock-solid on the outside, a turbulent mess on the inside. A little too much like her.

CHAPTER 4

*S*harp rays of sunlight, like yellow daggers, sliced through the gauze curtains of Lenaia's room at Wild-flower's Bed and Breakfast. She rolled onto her stomach and buried her face in the plush queen-sized bed, but duty tugged her eyes open. Daylight was ticking by and she had a long hike ahead of her.

"Breakfast is ready," a singsong voice called from the main level.

Probably Marge Blumer, the owner. Marge had taken over the bed and breakfast three years ago when the previous owner had died. Funny, Lenaia always thought of a bed and breakfast as something retired couples did together, and yet Marge had told her last night that she'd never been married. Lenaia tried to fast forward to an image of her and Travis married, maybe even with kids. Nothing came. Only the familiar fear, which slithered into her heart like a constrictor, squeezing until her chest hurt. Too many men around her had died. She didn't know how to envision a happy ending.

She pressed against her rib cage until the tension eased. Then she got out of bed and washed her face in the pedestal sink. As she came out of the bathroom, the smell of biscuits drifted up from the lower level. She dressed quickly and rushed down the stairs.

She selected a table by the open window, breathing in the clean mountain air with a hint of wild herbs. Marge placed a steaming plate of sausage and biscuits in front of her and she dug in, finishing half of it before Marge came back with a glass of orange juice.

"Delicious, Marge." She looked up into the woman's sweet, round face.

"I'm glad you like it. So many folks nowadays don't appreciate a meal with meat. We get a lot of vegans from the city and the poor things look half dead. I love fruit and all, especially the seasonal ones we get around here, but a girl needs some meat on her bones." Marge gave Lenaia's arm a squeeze. "You could use some more on you, but at least you look healthy. And absolutely gorgeous with your dark skin. Where are you from, dear?"

"I live in North Carolina, but my dad was from Brazil."

Marge nodded. "Well, you sure are lovely. You watch yourself out there on that mountain alone. There's a great many lonely guys around here who'd love to get their hands on a young thing like you."

Lenaia stuffed the last bite of sausage into her mouth. "Thanks for the warning." Marge needn't worry. Nobody should be in the park right now anyway.

"You've heard about the tragedy we've had around here?"

Even though it happened far away, Marge had to mean Dan. His gruesome death would still be the talk of the town. Fortunately, no one here would know she'd been there when it happened.

"Such a shame, a girl from town going missing. There have been too many, of course, but the others were mostly from Seattle and the towns around the big city. Not from sleepy little Mayim."

"What missing girl?"

"Oh, dear. You haven't heard. Summer Planke disappeared three days ago."

Not Summer. Lenaia's chest squeezed tight again, the pressure cinching like a rope around her heart. One month after Dan's death, his widow was missing. "What happened?"

"She didn't show up to get her daughter from school. Like she just vanished."

"And her daughter?"

"Poor thing. Arielle is doing about as good as she possibly can with her mama gone. Her uncle is her guardian, but she's staying with friends right now because Zayden is spending so much time looking for Summer."

Zayden. Her ex-boyfriend. Just his name brought up waves of emotion. Guilt. Nostalgia. And maybe just a little bit of longing. He was the first guy she'd ever thought of marrying and half of the reason she'd left Mayim five years ago. For the last month, she'd wondered how he was dealing with his brother's death and now this. He had to be a wreck.

"Do you want some more, dear?" Marge pointed at Lenaia's empty plate.

"No, thanks."

Lenaia's cell phone sang her familiar ring tone, "My Lighthouse." She checked the screen. Griffin. She looked back at Marge. "Excuse me. This is my appointment for the day." She stood as she pushed the answer button. "Hey, are you ready to check on the tiltmeter?"

"Sorry, change in plans for today. A possible missing hiker. I'll be helping with the search, so I won't be able to hike out to the monitoring station today."

Her shoulder's dropped at the thought of another missing person. "Is it a man or woman?"

"A thirty-year-old mother."

Five years ago, she'd helped in a missing person's search that didn't turn out well. A young girl. The memory of that failure still haunted Lenaia. Now there were two women gone in the span of a few days. She couldn't imagine how distraught Arielle would be if she lost both parents, and this new missing woman was a mother as well. Lenaia's hand trembled, but she suppressed the tremors. Getting emotional wouldn't help whoever was missing now. "I'll come search, too."

"Okay. The more eyes searching the better. I'm gathering the volunteers at the Jackson Visitor's Center."

"I'll meet you there in half an hour." Lenaia ran upstairs to grab her hiking pack. As she darted out the door to her car, she breathed out a quick prayer for the missing woman and her family.

IN THE PARKING lot of the visitor's center, a group of about twenty people—mostly men—congregated in one corner. She grabbed her backpack, swung the car door open and strode toward the group.

Griffin stood on a log, peering at the search team as if he was disappointed with their numbers. The wood and steel visitor's center rose behind him with its steep roof designed to allow snow to slide off easily. At least the missing hiker wouldn't have to worry about snow in April, unless she'd gone above 8,000 feet.

"Rachel Marshall went missing twenty-four hours ago. And as you all know, Summer Planke has been gone for three days. We're looking for evidence of both women." Griffin swept a hand over his shoulder at the imposing volcano. "We don't know for sure if they are on the mountain, but the last thing Rachel talked about to her husband was a long hike on Rainier, and Summer is also fond of hiking these trails. Either one of them may have gotten lost or been injured. We've all experienced how unreliable cell phone coverage can be out here and how easy it is to get lost." Many in the group nodded their heads. "Let's go look for them or any evidence of them, but be sure to stay with your partner and stay safe. No accidents today."

Griffin called out a few names and target search areas, mainly along the western section of the Wonderland Trail. She wasn't surprised to see the volunteers treat this as routine. Several hikers went missing every year, almost all of them found alive. The bulk of the group moved off to their assigned grid. The few volunteers who were left stared at Griffin expectantly.

"Summer's mom said she preferred the western side of the mountain for hiking, but if she's lost or turned around, she might try to hike her way out across the east side. I need two people to go down to Box Canyon and cover the Wonderland Trail all the way to White River. How about Lenaia Talavera and Zayden Planke?"

Lenaia sucked in a sharp breath. Zayden was here? She stood on her tiptoes, scanning the half-dozen faces and caught one looking at her over the others. Her breath held tight in her lungs as his dark eyes met hers. A shock of chestnut hair fell across his pale forehead. His dark hair against his light skin gave him a fragile look, but she knew better. In many ways, he was as tough as they came.

As the crowd dispersed, Zayden strolled over to her with his hands in the back pockets of his jeans. His dark blue Henley shirt stretched across his wide shoulders. He didn't carry a jacket. Probably wouldn't need one. His body temperature had always been higher than most, like a furnace with a stuck thermostat.

She pulled up the zipper on her jacket, even though she wasn't cold. If only she could zip up the past as easily. "How have you been?" She cleared her throat. Stupid question. His brother had died a month ago and now his sister-in-law was missing. "I mean, how are you doing?"

Zayden stopped a few feet in front of her. "Fine." The lie was obvious as tortured emotions flashed through his eyes. He pointed over his shoulder. "We can take my truck down to Box Canyon." He turned on his heels and walked away.

Two minutes in and Zayden had already shut her out. Some things didn't change. Maybe that had been part of their problem all along. They were too much alike. She grabbed her pack off the ground and followed him.

Zayden got in the same dark red truck he'd always owned. After climbing into the passenger seat, she tossed her pack on the floor of the cab and stowed her car keys in the open compartment in front of her.

He turned to look at her, one eyebrow raised. "Make yourself at home."

She felt her face grow hot at the edge to his voice. "Sorry. Habit, I guess."

He turned the key in the ignition, put the truck in reverse and looked over his shoulder out the back window. "We had a lot of habits together, didn't we?"

Flashes of their two-year relationship flipped through her mind like a slide show. Mostly happy times, except for the ending, when she'd left him. Definitely not a topic she wanted to discuss today.

She glanced over at him. His face held a flat expression, like a storefront mannequin. Was he still angry with her over how she had left things? Or would he blame her for his brother's horrible death? Surely, Summer had told him she was there. Lenaia opened her mouth to tell him she was sorry about Dan but thought better of it. Her words might not be welcome, especially since he was now dealing with Summer's disappearance. Instead, she turned to face the window.

They made the drive to the trailhead at Box Canyon in silence. Zayden parked the truck at the far end. Lenaia turned from the window to see him reaching toward her, his hand close to her knee. She held her breath. Was he going to touch her?

His hand passed over her lap to retrieve his pistol from the glove compartment. She released the trapped breath, relief flooding over her like cool water.

Zayden squinted at her. Had he read the confusion on her face? Without a word, he stuffed his pistol in his pack and got out. She grabbed her backpack and followed.

He headed down the trail at a fast pace, tossing his words back at her. "This is going to be a long day. We'd better get started."

She knew he was serious. On this part of the trail, they had to traverse close to fifteen miles and span thousands of feet in elevation. It was still early, but they'd have to hustle to search along the trail in order to get to the campground before dark. If they didn't make it, hiking in the dark would bring new dangers, like nocturnal predators and the risk of falling off the trail.

She did her best to match his pace. Although his long legs had quite the advantage over hers, there was no way she would ask him to slow down. The more area they covered, the more likely they'd find Summer or Rachel. If either of them were out here.

"Do you know what to look for?" he asked.

"Lost clothing, wrappers or trash of any kind, and evidence of campfires. I've done this before, remember?" Her voice took on a somber tone. "We searched for Lindy Strothers together."

He glanced back, and she caught the hint of sadness in his eyes. "Yeah. This won't turn out like that."

Eight-year-old Lindy had run off into the woods after fighting with her brother on a family excursion. Zayden and Lenaia found her in a ravine two days later. The little girl had died from exposure due to the cold temperatures. The day before they found her, they had walked right past the ravine. They didn't see or hear anything that day. The coroner said Lindy would have still been alive, although probably unconscious. Lenaia swallowed through the sudden lump in her throat. If they'd have found Lindy the day before, she might have had a chance. Instead, she'd died all alone, probably praying for rescue. Why hadn't God led them to her?

Lindy was the first failure in a string of deaths that looped back to Lenaia like the cord from a noose. She shook her head to clear it. Maybe she could help this time. She needed to keep focused, for Summer and Rachel.

Zayden walked with determined strides but slumped shoulders. What would it mean to him if they found Summer too late? He'd have to raise his orphan niece alone. She had no doubt he'd do it, but it wouldn't be easy.

As she walked behind, she swept her eyes from near—taking in the fallen leaves and rocks on the forest floor—to far—the dense rows of standing trees like commuters packed on the subway. Nature stretched for miles but nothing man-made.

Stringy pine needles brushed over her coat from the tight row of pine trees flanking the trail. Now warm from the miles of hiking, she slipped her jacked off and put it in her pack, leaving her in a long-sleeved cotton shirt.

Ahead, Zayden cocked his head as if listening. Then, she heard it too. The bubbly sound of water came from the trail ahead. He disappeared around the bend, and she heard, "Just great."

She caught up with him and leaned out to look around. Nickel Creek was swollen with snowmelt, but the log bridge normally used to cross it had fallen into the water. The thick portion on the near side had sunk into the rocks and mud on the bottom of the creek.

Lenaia shrugged. "It looks safe to cross without the bridge." Despite the rushing water, the creek ran at about a foot deep.

Zayden agreed and entered the water first. It came up mid-calf-high on his boots. He took a few slow steps.

Lenaia followed behind, treading carefully on the slippery rock bottom. The frigid water cooled her feet through the leather hide of her boots. They navigated around a large boulder that split the current and sped up the water.

On the other side, her boot slid sideways on a moss covered rock. She lost her footing and fell backward. A startled cry escaped from her lips. If she hit the large boulder, it would probably knock her out. She gasped, reaching out to grab Zayden's shirt.

Before she could make contact, he spun around, swung one arm around her back, and the other behind her legs to lift her out of the water. He held her tight for a step, then climbed the bank. Her heart beat fast from her close call. She buried her head in his chest and took a steadying breath. The faint scent of his after-shave swirled around her, stirring memories with it. She shifted to turn her head away.

On the shore, he placed her on her feet. Swallowing hard, she pulled her shirt down and swung her ponytail back over her shoulder. "Sorry. And thanks."

He stared at her for a long moment, his expression unreadable. "Be careful. I don't need to haul someone else out of here." At least his voice had lost some of its edge. Brushing past her, he continued down the trail. "Let's see what we can find."

She took a deep breath and followed. Peering through the foliage, she resumed the search for any sign of humans. But not just any humans. Although she didn't know Rachel, her mind conjured up an image of Summer a few years before Lenaia left Mayim. Glowing skin, swollen pregnant belly, and vibrant, fire-cracker hair that flowed with her every movement. She'd been so happy to be a mom. Before Lenaia could put a lock on her mouth, the words popped out. "How is Arielle doing?"

At the stiffening of his shoulders, she knew she should have gone with her original instinct to keep quiet. He answered without turning around. "She's staying with some church friends right now." They walked for a moment in silence before he continued. "She thinks Mom went out of town." He dipped his head, turning just a bit so she could see his guilty glance. "I didn't know what else to say."

She couldn't blame him. Arielle had just lost her dad. Until they knew what had happened to Summer, Zayden wouldn't add to her grief.

A white square on the ground captured Lenaia's attention. She stepped closer. Just a used tissue. She resumed the search. "Rachel is from Mayim also, right?"

"Yes." Zayden ran a hand through his hair. "We were friends in high school, though we haven't talked much lately."

"Does she have a family?"

He hiked his backpack up. "She married an older guy who's a real jerk. They have a two-year-old boy."

Her heart ached for that little boy and for Arielle. They couldn't possibly understand how life was filled with awful things they couldn't control. For that matter, neither could she.

The trail weaved back and forth through sturdy pine trees as it climbed in elevation. Time passed in a silent haze, a silence that seemed to have its own electric charge. Her mind drifted again to the last time they'd searched together. Back then, they'd requested to form their own search party, and despite the somber work, they had still managed to enjoy spending the day together. They'd even had a snowball fight after searching a small ice melt cave near the Nisqually Glacier.

She refocused on the up and down rhythm of her feet. Maybe an innocuous subject would help take their minds off the tension of the search. "How are things in town?"

He turned his head, apparently deciding whether or not to respond. "You know how it is. Nothing much changes in Mayim."

She searched his face, trying to interpret his tone. Did he mean he hadn't changed?

He turned to face forward again. "The newest face around here is probably Griffin and you've met him. He doesn't live in town, but he's there once in a while."

"What do you think of him?"

"Uptight, something to prove kind of guy. He should do okay once he mellows out."

Similar to her assessment, although, she would have added

insecure to the list based on how threatened he was by her presence.

A few more miles passed with the two of them steadily climbing. She kept her mind busy with the search, refusing to think about how Zayden had adjusted his rhythm to match hers to keep her from straining herself in the climb or the familiar warmth of his arms when he'd caught her in the river. Their relationship had died when she'd left and it needed to stay that way.

They crossed through a meadow full of stunning flowers growing in patches where the snow had melted, and then several more meadows like jewels strung in a necklace around the volcano's throat, until they reached the Panhandle Gap, a land bridge which formed a divide between several glaciers. They traversed the snow-covered portion slowly, making sure each foot held before stepping out with the other.

Halfway across, she glanced back. The shimmery blue opening of a small ice cave stood out on this side of the gap. She tapped Zayden on the shoulder. "Should we have a look in there?"

He followed her gaze. Although the cave sat at a little lower elevation, they didn't have to travel downslope much. Taking a wide stance with each step, they crept across the rough ice. She had ice spikes in her pack, but her thick-treaded boots seemed to work fine for this short stretch.

At the cave entrance, he stopped and peered inside. "I won't fit in there."

She came up from behind and shimmied around him. "I can. I'll check it out."

"Don't go far."

She squatted down into a duck walk. A few steps in, she was forced to scoot through on her knees to get to the far end of the cave. Only about ten feet long, the cave had smooth, gray-blue sides and a blackened, concave roof, probably from a fire. On the ground, she found sheets from a newspaper, matches and an icepack.

She dragged the items out and presented them to him. "The newspaper and matches I understand, but an icepack?"

He made a sounded like a snort. "Those aren't from one of the women."

Dark disappointment settled over her. "How do you know?"

"Remember the old coot who lives up here somewhere? We called him Crusty because he almost never bathes. I've seen him use an icepack on his crooked back and also to preserve his food after he cooks it."

"He's still up here?"

Zayden gave her a probing look, his dark eyes focused almost to black pinpoints. "I told you, not much changes around here."

Her left foot started to slip. She shifted backward until she found a better foothold on the ice. "I guess not."

He leaned against the opening of the cave, supporting himself with an outstretched arm, and searched her face. She wanted to pull back but couldn't for fear of losing her footing. He was much too close for comfort.

He leaned closer. "Why did you come back?"

Looking into his eyes was too intense. She focused on his chest. "There are some problems with one of the tiltmeters."

He lifted her chin until she had to look at him. "No, I mean why did *you* come?"

She swallowed. What kind of answer was he looking for? "The USGS asked for me. Besides, Rowan Consulting has only one other volcanologist and she just had a baby."

He twisted his lips to the side. Was he disappointed or relieved? She couldn't tell.

"Makes sense." He pushed off the ice and started to climb the small slope, but then glanced over his shoulder. "We'd better keep looking. Women who go missing don't usually come back on their own."

CHAPTER 5

*L*enaia followed behind Zayden as the trail wound down through the stair-step topography leading to Summerland, an open meadow with a million varicolored wildflowers, like tiny gemstones affixed to the mountain. The beauty of the scene felt at complete odds with the focus of their mission.

After stopping for only a moment to check for signs of people, they descended again into the forest through a series of switchbacks to Fryingpan Creek. They were making good time, but Lenaia's legs burned from the exertion and they hadn't seen any sign of Summer or Rachel.

Lenaia rubbed at her stiff neck. Too much turning her head back and forth to search the ground. As they continued hiking in silence, she couldn't help thinking of the last time she'd hiked with a man—the day she met Travis. He'd rescued her from a group of poachers in the Costa Rican jungle. Then, she'd helped him track the creature he was looking for. Those moments were filled with teasing and light conversation, not this uncomfortable subtext from the past that crackled between her and Zayden.

The trail climbed over one final ridge, then descended as it wound through the river valley, roughly following the road along the east side of the mountain. A few uneventful miles later, they reached the White River Campground. The sun hadn't completely set yet, but the campground was fairly dark, and with the darkness came cooler temperatures.

She climbed on top of a picnic table, hooked the heels of her boots on the wood bench and leaned back on her hands. Her legs ached with the tired, yet satisfying, feeling of having worked for more than ten hours. And yet, they hadn't found a thing.

The river rumbled through enormous white boulders strewn along the riverbed, the remnants of past floods. Summer or Rachel might be out here alone, watching darkness fall again, waiting for help.

She tilted her head and glanced at Zayden. "Do you think we missed them?"

He put his hands back and matched her pose. "We don't even know if they're out here."

"That's not an answer."

He leaned forward, putting his arms on his knees. "I don't know. We did the best we could."

She resisted the urge to put a hand on his back. He'd been through so much in the last few months. She understood what the loss of a loved one could do. "Zayden, I'm so sorry about what happened to Dan."

His jaw stiffened. With a quick nod, he pushed off the table. "Let's move closer to the road. Griffin should be here soon."

She forced her tired legs to follow him through the maze of tent sites, all of them empty.

As they reached the old park ranger's cabin, headlights lit up the night. Griffin's truck came up the road and stopped next to them. He rolled down the passenger side window. "Any luck?"

"No." Zayden threw the icepack on the seat next to Griffin. "The only thing we found was this. Pretty sure it belongs to the crazy old man I've seen around here."

Griffin shoved it onto the dashboard. "Okay."

"Anyone else find anything?" she asked.

Griffin shook his head. "Nope."

The women might still be alive then. Not that they could do anything to help them until morning. Her thoughts returned to the reason she'd come to Washington. "Have you been to the visitor's center to check the tiltmeter on the computer?"

From the corner of her eye, she saw Zayden turn away and head into the trees. "All business," he muttered under his breath like it was a curse word.

She crossed her arms and stared at his retreating form. What was that supposed to mean?

Griffin didn't speak until Zayden had disappeared from sight. "What's his problem?"

"Not sure. So, have you looked at the STAR tiltmeter today?"

Griffin narrowed his eyes at her. "There's something going on between the two of you."

Seriously? He didn't have to be Albert Einstein to figure that out. "Can we focus, please?"

He blinked like he found her attitude surprising. "The STAR station is still malfunctioning, obviously, since we didn't get there to fix it today. I didn't see any new problems."

"Let's hope it stays that way."

"Get in. I'll take you and psycho guy back to the trailhead."

She turned to see Zayden striding toward them. She opened the cab door and let him get in first.

Thirty minutes later, Griffin dropped them off at Zayden's truck. Then, Zayden drove her back to the visitor's center where her rental car was parked. Lenaia retrieved her keys from the truck's cubby, then came around the back of the vehicle.

Zayden stood by the tailgate, staring at her as if waiting for her to say something.

She shifted her feet in the dirt. "I hope we find something on the women soon."

"Then you can get back to work." He pressed his lips together. His way of pouting.

She put a wrestling hold on the sarcastic comment that wanted to break out of her mouth. No way would she apologize to him for working. He still had a job, didn't he? Or maybe not now, while looking for his sister-in-law. "Are you still working for the city?"

He pushed his hands into his front pockets. "I'm the Evacuation Planning Coordinator for Mayim."

"Oh, good. Helping people in a disaster sounds like a great match for you. A much better fit than when you were the auditor."

"I suppose so. I enjoy my position, but it's just a job."

The way he said the word "job" caused a ripple of longing inside her. Her career in Washington State had been wonderful and too brief. Even though Zayden had begged her to stay, she'd had no choice but to go. Leaving and losing their relationship had been just as hard on her. She took a breath to clear away the feeling.

"Well ... I'm sure I'll see you around." She turned to go, but he put a hand on her forearm. She looked down at his touch, and then up into his shadowed eyes.

"You coming here isn't a coincidence. God has a plan."

Shivers ran through her. She pulled back, trying to get some distance to deal with her body's autormatic response. Her heart belonged to Travis, and although she felt a residual attraction to Zayden, it didn't match the intensity of her connection to Travis.

Zayden allowed her to pull away. What plan did he mean exactly? Before she could ask, he jumped into his truck, and took off.

Saturday morning dawned bright with a circle of mist confined to the mountain's peak. But by the time she made it to the western part of the Wonderland trail the rest of the mountain had disappeared into a misty fog. Mt. Rainier often created its own clouds as it forced warm air to travel upslope, but rarely did the clouds filter down to lower elevations. And yet, this afternoon the fog permeated everything like a chilly cocoon.

Maybe she should have brought Griffin with her, but she didn't want to ask him to work on a Saturday. She searched the ground under her feet, trying to get her bearings. Nothing looked familiar. Her mission to check on the STAR tiltmeter, and keep looking for signs of the missing women, might be over before it began. Even with the GPS coordinates, she couldn't get to the monitoring station if she couldn't find the trail because too many steep ridges blocked the way. The trail, if she could find it, would take her along the smaller ridges to the ridgeline that ran between the Tahoma and Puyallup glaciers, the backbone of the mountain.

After spinning in a complete circle again and not spotting any defined path, she headed the only direction she hadn't tried yet —east.

According to Griffin, the equipment malfunction started right in the middle of his core-drilling project on the Puyallup. Pure coincidence or something else? The drilling would have caused a disturbance for sure but not enough to break the tiltmeter. What could cause a mechanical failure in instruments that were designed to withstand extreme weather and ground fluctuations?

Of course, she couldn't rule out a man-made cause. But why would anyone hike over the rough terrain between two glaciers just to mess with some scientific instruments? It didn't make sense.

The mist thickened as she hiked higher in elevation. She climbed another half a mile before common sense turned her around. No use wandering around lost anymore. She might walk right off a cliff. Thankfully, she had her compass. Her four-wheeler, borrowed from the Park Service, would be generally southwest of her position. Without the trail, she'd have more climbing and backtracking to do, but she'd make it back.

Weaving through the trees, she breathed in the refreshing scent of pine and dirt—the smell of Christmas in April. She and Zayden had spent countless hours hiking, camping and fishing in these woods. These slopes were bursting with memories. Their memories. Back then, spending time with him had felt easy, not forced like yesterday. She'd known of his secret fear—bears—the reason he carried a gun everywhere. And he knew how much she hated fishing because she couldn't stand watching the fishes' silvery bodies puffing in and out as they gasped for air.

Once, they'd even camped on a glacier. Two brown tents side-by-side on the white ice. He'd thought her silly to insist on her own tent. Most Christians didn't hold to such outdated ideas, he'd said. But she didn't care what other Christians did. She only wanted to please God. Although Zayden had said he was a Christian when she'd met him, he'd refused to go to church with her. Underneath his confident exterior, she had sensed a deep hurt surrounding him like a shell. A protective barrier between him and God. Only, she didn't know where it came from because he wasn't the type to open up easily.

Her foot caught on something and she tripped. Momentum carried her forward, slamming her into a tree, palms first. She barely snapped her head back in time to avoid smacking her forehead on the trunk.

As she pulled back from the bark, her palms ached more than she would have thought possible from her collision. She rubbed them on her pants, but the ache continued, morphing into a stinging burn.

She rubbed them in the dirt. No relief.

There had to be something in her backpack that could help. She dropped it to the ground, fumbled with the zipper, rummaged around, and finally grabbed baby wipes from an interior pocket. Sliding one across her hand, the burning eased, but only a little bit.

"You should be more careful where you walk." The gravelly voice came from the shrouded mist in front of her.

She took a step backward. "Who's there?"

A hunched-over man walked slowly out of the fog. He wore a dirty, long-sleeved sweatshirt, ripped jeans, and shoes that looked like deck shoes. *Crusty.* At least that's what they had called him years ago.

"Come over here." He pointed to her hands.

The burning had intensified into a blaze so strong that she didn't care what he did to them. She moved closer and stretched her palms out. His rough hand held one of hers tight as he tugged a piece of folded wax paper from the pocket of his holey jeans. With two fingers, he extracted a few pieces of grass from the wax, rolled the clump around until a small amount of liquid came out, then rubbed the liquid on both of her open palms. The burning subsided to a dull ache.

"What is that stuff?"

"The only relief from the effects of stinging nettles. You're welcome." Crusty turned away, heading back into the forest.

She pressed her palms to her chest. "Wait, you put the stinging nettles on the trees?"

He looked over his shoulder. "To protect my home, of course."

"You live here?"

He swung around and looked her up and down for a long time, as if trying to decide if he wanted to stay or go. After a minute, he swept his hand behind and gestured to his left. "I don't invite many people in."

She twisted her lips. So was he inviting her in or dismissing her? "How long have you lived here?"

"Maybe ten years, give or take. I don't have a need to keep track."

Weird, this guy looked like a crazy old hermit, his jeans and sweatshirt had enough dirt for a decade, and yet, he carried himself with an air of authority, despite his hunched back. His voice had a rough cadence to it, like boots walking on gravel. From years of disuse maybe. "Where did you live before you came here?"

Crusty squinted at her. She couldn't tell if he was surprised by all her questions or annoyed. "Same place you did."

The same place. Did he mean Mayim? How did he know she'd lived there? She'd seen him from a distance on a few occasions, but she didn't think he'd seen her.

He tugged at the bottom of a long, greasy strand of hair. "Why are you back?"

She bit her lip. Should she tell him about the problems with the equipment? For all she knew, he might have something to do with it. "I'm helping out because of the government shutdown. I was looking for the STAR tiltmeter, but I can't find it in the fog. Now, I'm trying to get back to the four-wheeler I left on Westside Road."

Crusty moved away and motioned for her to follow. She

moved forward, then stopped. Following an old hermit deeper into the woods probably wasn't a good idea. He glanced back as if he sensed her concern, but he didn't stop. She trailed behind with slow steps. He had no reason to hurt her and he'd just healed her hands.

They walked twenty yards before she saw his house, if it could be called that. A three-walled structure cut into a large, over-hanging slab of andesite lava rock. An old mudflow must have already cut through that rock because no one could have done it by hand. The three exposed walls were stripped pine tree trunks stacked one on top of the other and held together by some kind of mud cement. Crusty pointed at the front door—a heavy tarp. "I pile rocks in front of the door at night, but the spiky trees and a few other security measures keep me safe."

She rubbed her palms, although they barely hurt any longer. "You mean the *poisoned* trees."

"Yes, but it works." He gave her a grin. "If I hadn't come along, you would've gone searching for water to wash your hands off, which takes you away from my house."

So, why was he showing it to her now? Standing next to the house, it looked barely tall enough for her to stand up inside, much less Crusty, who was a few inches taller. "What do you do in the winter? The snow must go over your roof."

"Yep, but I've got no need to go out. All summer, I store up food in my underground stash." He peered at her for a few more seconds before turning his back. "Follow me. You're on Emerald Ridge, by the way."

Well, she knew that much, but Emerald Ridge was huge.

He led her several yards away, over the top of a barren, rocky knob. He stopped to point with a bony finger at an angle. "If you head this direction, the slope is manageable and you'll get back to the trail." He turned his back on her and walked away.

"Nice to meet you," she called to his retreating form.

She heard his quiet response just before he disappeared into the mist. "You too, Lenaia."

The dense trees swallowed her as she worked her way downslope. She should have asked him about the tiltmeter. The secretive man living so close to the STAR monitoring station was suspicious. Although he'd trusted her with the location of his home, she didn't trust him. Then, it hit her like a sickening punch to the gut. Crusty knew more than she'd thought because she'd never given him her name.

AT THE BED AND BREAKFAST, Lenaia was a little ahead of the dinner crowd. A single couple sat at the center table, finishing up their food. She smiled when she recognized Pastor Doug Winslet, the pastor of the church she'd attended when she'd lived in Mayim.

"Lenaia, dear." Marge swept out from the kitchen. "Glad you're back. Sit down while I get you some dinner."

Her stomach rumbled in answer. "Sounds great."

"Grab a seat anywhere." Marge gestured to the center table. "Although I don't recommend sitting next to this old guy."

Lenaia laughed along with the couple sitting at the table. "Good to see you again, Pastor Winslet."

The pastor grabbed her hand in both of his. "You know I only go by Pastor Doug."

"I know." While in Mayim, she'd spent time at their house babysitting their youngest son, Scottie. She turned to his wife and gave her a warm hug. "Carol, how are you?"

"Oh, we're always fine." Before she pulled away, Carol patted Lenaia's cheek. "You're still so lovely."

"Thank you." She shifted uncomfortably, as she always did whenever anyone mentioned her looks. Probably a side effect of trying to be taken seriously in a male-dominated field.

Carol tugged on Lenaia's arm, and she sat next to the woman.

She swept her eyes over their faces. The last five years had embedded new creases and wrinkles in each of them. Maybe life hadn't gone as easy as Carol would have her believe.

"Tell me what you've been doing," Carol said.

"Working mostly."

"You handle the danger in your job so well."

This time, Lenaia blushed at the compliment. "I love it. I've had a great time traveling to volcanoes all over the world."

"Oh, I'd love to travel." Carol glanced at Pastor Doug. "With my traveling companion, of course." Pastor Doug smiled and Carol returned her attention to Lenaia. "Do you have someone in your life, dear?"

"Actually, yes. We've been dating for about a year now." Speaking of Travis, she hadn't called him at all yesterday. He was used to her erratic schedule, but she should give him a call tonight so he wouldn't worry.

Marge returned and placed a bowl of potato soup along with two breadsticks on the table in front of Lenaia. Marge went back for a glass of iced tea and handed it to Lenaia, before heading to the kitchen.

"How are things at the church?" Lenaia asked.

Pastor Doug glanced at his wife. Carol shifted her eyes to the table. The pastor returned his attention back to Lenaia. "There have been some issues with the church, but we're working things out."

Lenaia took a spoonful of soup and blew on it. "What kind of issues?" She savored the creamy, warm liquid. Marge was quite a good cook.

Carol let out a sigh that sounded like she'd held it for years.

Pastor Doug grabbed her hand. "This has been a rough year ... "

His voice trailed off as the volume on the television increased. Another guest stood with the remote in her hand. Obviously, she'd turned the sound up to hear the current interview.

On the screen, a flaxen haired reporter stood by the side of a two-lane road. To her left, a dark-haired man, probably in his thirties, shifted on his feet and clasped his hands in front. Below his image was the name Councilman Morgan Marshall. Lenaia had heard the name, but never met the man. He certainly hadn't been a councilman before she'd left.

Microphone in hand, the reporter delivered her questions with the clipped, practiced words of a professional. "Councilman Marshall, what are your hopes for this evening?"

"I need my sweet Rachel home tonight. I know we can find her if everyone will go out to search."

She couldn't imagine what Mr. Marshall was going through, but searching in the dark was a waste of manpower, especially if Rachel was on the mountain. Not only might a searcher walk right by her and not know it, but the person searching was just as likely to injure themselves.

The camera zoomed in to focus solely on the reporter. "Rachel Marshall, mother of a two-year-old boy, who disappeared late yesterday, is the second woman from Mayim to go missing. Summer Planke, recent widow of Dan Planke, disappeared three days ago, leaving her eight-year-old girl alone. The police have made no comment on the situation, except to say they know of no connection between these disappearances and also no connection to the other missing women from the northern part of Seattle, many of whom have been found dead."

Pushing the soup away, Lenaia excused herself from the pastor and his wife. She dragged leaden feet up the stairs and into her room where she dropped to her knees by the bed. Her thoughts tumbled out in a jumbled mass of prayer. Even if the words couldn't help Summer or Rachel, they calmed her fractured soul a bit.

Not five minutes later, Lenaia was pulled from the edge of the bed by her ringing phone. "Hello?"

"Hi, sweetie." Travis's voice broke with the static of a bad connection. "First things first, I'm sorry about our fight."

She flopped onto the bed, pressing the phone tight to her ear. His deep voice calmed her spirit, but she needed to make sure he understood why she'd gotten mad. In a gentle tone, she asked, "Are you sorry we fought or are you sorry about what you did?"

A rueful chuckle came over the line. "Both, of course. I shouldn't have told Jayna about how you're struggling. I should have kept it between us."

"Thank you." Hopefully, in the future he would honor her need for privacy. Travis might be an open book himself, but it wasn't up to him to disclose the details of her life to everyone. "I have some issues to work out right now. I know that."

"Okay." The resigned tone in his voice gave her pause. He knew of her independent nature and most of the time he seemed okay with it. Now, more than ever, she needed him to give her space to process her emotions, maybe even heal.

"So, do they really need you out there?" he asked. "When are you coming home?"

"You must not be busy enough," she teased. "Jayna can give you more work if you're bored."

"I'm busy, but I miss you. And Trudy and the kids are coming to visit tomorrow. They'll miss you too."

She smiled. Despite the way they'd left things, Travis missed her. She belonged with him and the rest of his fantastic family. From day one, Trudy had treated her like another sister, and her kids were adorable. "I'm sorry I won't see them."

"So tell me about what's keeping you away."

She pulled her legs up to her chest. "One of the monitoring stations on the mountain is on the fritz. They've gotten some crazy readings."

Travis stayed silent for a moment. He was a paleontologist, but he knew enough about volcanology to know that monitoring the swell of the mountain was essential to protecting anyone near the volcano. "What's wrong with the equipment?"

"I don't know. I haven't been able to go up on the mountain to check it out."

"Why not?"

"Today was too cloudy." No need to tell him about her failed hike or Crusty, the weird hermit. It would just cause Travis to worry. "I meant to call you yesterday, but I was wiped out from hiking. I spent the whole day looking for two missing women."

"Missing women? Like a search and rescue?"

"No one really knows what's happened to them."

A short pause came over the line before Travis continued in a softer voice. "Did you find them?"

"No."

"I'm sorry, Lenaia."

"It's fine. We did what we could." A small voice in her head accused her of deceit. It wasn't fine and she'd only blown off the topic so she didn't have to talk about it.

His tone dropped even lower. "This is a lot to deal with on top of everything else, sweetie. At the risk of causing another fight ... "

The pause was his way of asking permission to poke the bear. Might as well get it over with. "Go ahead. Say what you need to."

"Would you be willing to see someone while you're up there?"

She fell back against the headboard and grabbed a pillow, cradling it against her chest. She should have known he wouldn't give this up. He was relentless. A man who had chased a mysterious creature to another country just to get answers. A man who had chased after her with the same determination. She sighed. He cared enough to keep asking. She shouldn't take that for granted. "You just aren't going to let this go, are you?"

"Getting the emotions out can help. Believe me, I know."

He was referring to the counseling he'd gone through when his other sister, Marie, had died. The comparison took the fight right out of her. Of course, he knew what her pain felt like.

"Do you know anyone there you can talk to?"

She opened her mouth to tell him she didn't need to when a

series of images flashed through her mind. The body of her uncle lying in a silk-lined casket, his face pale and shriveled. Nina, a young friend from Costa Rica, her body slumped lifeless where she'd fallen after a blow to the head. Eight-year-old Arielle crying for her daddy who had disappeared into the blinding heat of a lava tube. Lenaia's heart spasmed with escalating guilt and fear as each scene changed. Maybe Travis had a point about seeing a counselor, someone who knew how to help. It might not be her best idea to stuff these feelings deep in her gut and hope they transformed into something less toxic before they bubbled back up. But who could she trust here?

The answer came to her immediately.

CHAPTER 7

*L*enaia forced her feet to carry her over the threshold into Harvest of the Saints Church. Every step was a forceful effort of her will. She might not have been completely honest with Travis about her issues, or even with herself, but at church she couldn't hide. What was the point of pretending with God? He knew where her heart was, which of course was the reason she hadn't been to church in months.

She made her way down the narrow hallway leading to the sanctuary, then stopped short. Pastor Doug stood halfway to the front, his gray dress pants and shirt blending with the dark gray industrial carpet, greeting members on their way in. He caught her eye and smiled. She tried to smile back but was pretty sure it came out crooked. Standing in this church, it felt like no time had passed since she'd lived in Mayim. And yet, she also felt like she'd aged fifteen years in the last five.

She approached the pastor and took his outstretched hand.

"Lenaia, good to see you this morning."

"You too, Pastor."

They stared at each other for a moment. No one came up behind her to force her into the sanctuary, and she couldn't seem to make her legs move. Being in God's house had a way of throwing a sledgehammer into the wall she'd built around her heart.

Eventually, Pastor Doug put a hand on her back and gave her a gentle push. She harnessed the momentum and went with it, finding a seat by herself in the third row.

She took a good look around the sanctuary. Not much had changed. Three steps in front led up to a stage with a podium in the center and music equipment scattered around. An enormous screen displayed the church logo and the title of the sermon, "What If Jesus Came Back Today?"

Her stomach flipped over. If Jesus came back today, he'd see what a miserable job she'd done at protecting the people in her life. Bodies littered her path through the world, and she was powerless to help anyone.

The lights dimmed and the congregation quieted. Pastor Doug came down the aisle on his way to the front. As he passed, he leaned down and whispered in her ear, "Hang around after the service. I'd like to talk to you." Then, he ran up to the podium while flipping the switch for his microphone.

He hadn't given her a chance to say yes or no. Kind of rude for a pastor. But she'd planned on talking to him anyway.

The service passed quickly because she couldn't seem to concentrate. Her mind wandered, jumping from the anatomy of a tiltmeter, to Travis's heart-stopping smile, to the crazy old man on the mountain, and finally to Zayden. The one thing Zayden had done right in their relationship was that he respected her need to work things out alone. He'd always given her space. If only Travis would do the same.

She shook her head again to clear it and refocused on the service. Had she heard anything Pastor Doug had said? Too late now; it was about over.

The pastor finished with a prayer. "Dear Lord, help us to walk in Your ways this week. To see the world with Your eyes.

To heal and protect and serve as You would. In Jesus's name, amen."

To heal and protect like Jesus? She couldn't measure up to that in even the slightest way.

As the congregation filed down the aisle and moved through the lobby in a noisy gaggle, Lenaia stayed in her seat. She stared at the enormous wooden cross mounted on the wall up front. She could never repay what Christ had done for her. He'd brought her close at a time when she had no one else.

After her father's death in a plane crash, her mother had lost all interest in staying alive. She'd slept all the time, and during her few wakeful moments, she refused to talk. Lenaia went through half of her second-grade year without speaking a word to her mother. If the school needed something, Lenaia took care of it. She made dinner every night, mostly for herself, because her mother rarely ate. Even at eight years old, Lenaia instinctively understood if anyone else had known of her mother's condition, she would have lost her mother too. That was when she became good at hiding her feelings, everything except the loneliness. That emotion became a living thing she fought with every day for the sake of the one parent she had left.

Then, a friend at school gave her a Children's Bible. She didn't understand most of it, but every time she read, it felt like someone had wrapped her in a warm hug. When she found the words in Matthew, chapter 5, "Blessed are the poor in spirit, for theirs is the kingdom of heaven. Blessed are they who mourn, for they shall be comforted," the words rang true.

And they came true in her life. When she asked for comfort, Jesus calmed her. He eased her loneliness. She grew to cherish her vast amounts of alone time as time spent with Him.

A year later, she found a real Bible in her dad's old stuff. She started reading it to her mother, stumbling over the big words, while her mother lay in bed staring at the wall. It took some time, but one day, her mother rolled over and wrapped her arms around Lenaia's neck in a hug. The powerful words had brought her mom back, at least for a time.

Lenaia tore her eyes from the cross and bowed her head. Jesus had restored so much in her life. She owed him everything and now she was failing Him. Every time she turned around, someone died and she couldn't do anything about it.

A light touch landed on her shoulder. Pastor Doug leaned down. "There's nobody in the coffee shop. Do you want to go talk there?"

She nodded and they made their way to the small room at the back of the building. Low tables were encircled by cushy chairs and flanked by fashionable end tables. The pastor took a seat in a chair facing the rear windows. She sat across from him and scanned his weathered face. What did he want to talk to her about?

"I'm glad you came to the service."

"Thanks I'm afraid I didn't do well listening today. I've got a lot of things on my mind."

"Things you want to talk about?"

She shrugged. "Not really." It was on the tip of her tongue to ask him if he would be her counselor, but she held back. Maybe Pastor Doug wasn't the same guy she'd known. Maybe he had changed.

"It's nice to have a friendly face here." His eyes focused out the windows. "We've had a few issues at the church recently."

Her face heated in embarrassment. He'd said that last night, but then he hadn't gotten the chance to explain because she'd run off. "What kind of issues?"

"Well, I've always disliked the rift between our church and Christ's Devoted Church."

Lenaia tilted her head. "You mean, the *excitable* ones in the church outside of town, near the river?" Excitable was the nicest word she could think of. The one time she'd visited had been enough. The ushers all wore black suits and earpieces like they were part of the Secret Service, ready to tackle anyone who approached Pastor Marty Smith. For his part, Pastor Marty screamed out from the pulpit in ecstasy every three or four sentences. And then there was the church member who would randomly run in a circle around the congregation to show how Pastor Marty had healed his legs, and another, who had put a beanbag on Lenaia's shoulder to protect her from demons. She'd thrown the beanbag away after the service.

Other than seeing him at the pulpit, Lenaia had only seen Pastor Marty one other time. At a blood drive, where he was protesting the removal of human blood as a desecration to the body. The man seemed to enjoy making a stir.

Pastor Doug smoothed a hand over his mostly bald head. "For goodness sake, we're the only two churches in town. We should be able to get along. So, I invited Pastor Marty to come preach one Sunday."

Lenaia cringed. "What happened?"

"Pastor Marty's sermon offended a lot of people. Carol and I are still dealing with the fallout."

"What did he preach about?"

Pastor Doug scrunched up his face as he answered. "Wealth. He took James, chapter 5, God's warning to rich oppressors, out of context and said God's will is for no one to have money. Therefore, you have to give all your retirement savings to the church or you will be lost to hell."

"Oh, my."

"You can imagine that didn't go over well with my parishioners, many of whom are on fixed retirement incomes. What I was hoping would bring our churches together actually pushed them further apart."

"I can see why." Lenaia tucked a strand of hair behind her ear. "But I'm sure your response has let people see that Harvest of the Saints is a Bible-believing church. Meaning the whole Bible."

"I hope so. It's been a rough year." He rolled his bottom lip over his teeth. "I wanted to bring this up last night, but the broadcast interrupted us. It was for the better because Carol gets overwhelmed with talking about it anyway. However, I believe we need as many people praying for us as possible."

Lenaia leaned closer. "I'll pray for you both. What else is going on?"

"Our youngest son had an accident."

"What happened to Scottie?"

Pastor Doug stared down at the gray carpet. "One night, he was at home while Carol and I were at church. He tripped going down the stairs, fell and broke several vertebrae. The doctor says he'll never walk again, but I don't believe it. He gets more feeling back in his legs every day through physical therapy."

Her shoulders slumped. "I can only imagine what you and Carol have gone through with this."

"The worst part is, I was supposed to be there that night. I had planned to stay home, but then a church member wanted prayer for a medical procedure. I stayed here instead. If I would've been there, I could have gotten him help sooner."

Lenaia saw the depths of regret in his eyes, like looking at her own reflection. Her head knew the deaths surrounding her might not be her responsibility, but her heart wouldn't listen. "How are you and Carol managing?"

"It's not easy, but we've had many people step up to help. I'd be lying if I said I haven't yelled at God several times, but He's using this to grow my faith in how He provides for us. In fact, we were at the bed and breakfast the other evening because Marge has started making extra food for us twice a week. Carol and I get to have dinner out for a few hours, and then we bring dinner back for Scott. It's been a blessing."

To hear him say the word blessing in the middle of his pain caused her heart to skip a beat. This man had a faith as strong as steel. Not like hers, which seemed as crumbly as burnt paper.

Pastor Doug swiped a hand across his face, as if to wipe away the difficult topic. "My turn to change the subject. You sure you don't want to talk about what's got you so distracted?" He peered at her. She felt like he could see right through her skin, straight to the issues clogging up her heart.

At this point, she usually minimized her issues, but Pastor Doug had been so open with her and something in her longed to confide in him. Plus, he'd helped her years ago when she'd wrestled with her relationship with Zayden. Maybe his advice could clear her head this time too. She opened her mouth to tell him about her guilt, but what came out instead surprised her. "My boyfriend, Travis, wants to move our relationship to the next level."

Pastor Doug raised his bushy eyebrows. "What do you mean he wants to take it to the next level?"

Lenaia blushed, catching his assumption. "I mean, he wants to get married and start a family."

"And you're not sure?"

"I don't know. At one time, I thought I was, but I guess ... "

He tapped a finger against his lower lip. "Sounds like you're afraid."

She looked into his warm brown eyes, debating about how much more she wanted to say. "Maybe."

"What are you afraid of?"

"Not being able to do my job."

Pastor Doug nodded as if he understood, but did he? Could a man understand the pressure on a working woman once she had a family waiting for her at home?

"How can I run around the world endangering my life on volcanoes if I've got a husband and kids to think about?" But that wasn't really all of it. Deep inside, she felt a greater struggle. What if she kept losing people? What would happen if she lost Travis?

"Do you still feel called to do your job?"

"I love volcanoes and I want to help people. Same reason why I chose to live in this town five years ago, instead of doing my job from somewhere safer, like Seattle. I wanted to be here to help in case the mountain did something."

He pointed up to the ceiling. "If God is still calling you to do this, He will help you find a way to continue."

Pastor Doug made it sound so simple. Talking to him felt more like working stuff out together, not like he was trying to fix her. He would be the best choice for a counselor. "Well, I sort of promised my boyfriend I'd look into seeing a counselor about this and some other stuff. Would you be willing?"

Pastor Doug smiled. "I would be, if you're willing to give this old guy a break from being perfect."

She couldn't fathom the expectations his congregation would unconsciously put on him to be perfect, to represent God well. People demanded gracious, kind, and infallible pastors. "Absolutely."

He put his hand up for a high-five. That was Pastor Doug, serious one minute, lighthearted the next.

She smacked his hand. "Now, let's talk about something else."

He dropped his hands to his lap, as if he'd never breached pastoral decorum. "So who are you working with up on the mountain?"

"Griffin Wall. Do you know him?"

"I used to know him. Has he really come back?"

"What do you mean? He lived here in Mayim?"

Pastor Doug nodded. "He moved out of the area before you even came to town. I thought he'd never return."

"Why?"

"He was just a boy when I knew him, probably twelve or thirteen. Oh, what he had to endure." Pastor Doug looked up at the ceiling for a moment. When he looked back at her, she saw deep compassion written into the wrinkles around his eyes. "He lost both his parents. His mom died, and then his dad left."

"That's terrible. His dad just left?"

Pastor Doug pursed his lips as if he didn't want to say more.

He gave a heavy sigh before speaking. "I don't think Art could handle his wife's death. Griffin wanted to stay in the area, but no one at their church was willing to adopt him. He ended up being raised by an aunt in Seattle. About six months ago, somebody mentioned to me that he was working for the USGS, but I didn't know he'd come back to this area."

Griffin might have returned, but had he really dealt with the past? Maybe he felt as out of place here as she did. "I guess we're all drawn to the places from our past."

A flicker of hope danced through her chest. Maybe with Pastor Doug's help, she could finally leave some of the pieces of her past in the past.

CHAPTER 8

$\mathcal{L}$enaia followed Griffin up the steep slope of the Puyallup Cleaver, the dividing line between the Puyallup Glacier and the Tahoma Glacier, and the highest ridgeline on this side of the mountain. They had left the tree line hours ago and since then had strained over the steep terrain on the way to St. Andrews Rock and the site of the STAR monitoring station.

In her attempt to find it on Saturday, she hadn't gone quite high enough. Funny how her memory and the fog had made the mountain seem smaller. Now, the clear summit stood out as a hulking, white behemoth against a teal blue sky.

No defined trail existed up here, so they picked their way over the loose rock, the remains of a debris flow from a previous land-slide on the Tahoma. As the elevation rose, the cleaver narrowed to the width of their feet. They kept to the center, away from the steep sides. She huffed in short breaths of the oxygen-poor air.

About the time she thought her lungs might burst, Griffin sat down on a rock outcrop to take a break.

"You okay?" he asked.

She stretched out a smile between gasps. "Yeah, not many

beauties as high as this one. My lungs have to adjust to the altitude every time."

"Not surprising. We're almost to ten thousand feet." He picked up a rock and threw it, sailing it into space for a brief moment before it plunged hundreds of feet down to land on the Tahoma Glacier, a dark blemish on the bright ice. "But no worries. We're also almost there."

She turned to look at him. "So you've worked for the USGS for a couple of years?"

He tilted his head. "Have you been checking up on me?"

"No. It was just a guess. You said you've been here only a few months and I figured this wasn't your first assignment." Usually, small talk wasn't this painful. She tried again. "Do you live around here?"

"I live in Tacoma."

"That's a long commute. Why haven't you gotten a place closer? There are a lot of cute little towns near here, like Orting or Ashford." She deliberately didn't mention Mayim.

His mouth curved upward into an awkward smile. "I'm not really a cute-little-town kind of guy."

"But you're obviously the outdoors type. Are you happy living in the city?"

Griffin picked up another rock and threw it. "In my experience, people in small towns are small-minded. And you can add boring to that. Besides, my territory covers more than Mt. Rainier. Although I'm principally here, I do travel to Mt. Baker and Mt. Hood occasionally."

"I see." She rolled a piece of dark rock around in her palm. That made sense because Mt. Baker was north of Seattle and Mt. Hood was south. Tacoma sat right in the middle.

Griffin jumped to his feet. "Come on. Let's go figure out what's happening with the tiltmeter."

As they continued up the slope, she gazed out at the expansive view. The breathtaking beauty of pure white glacial ice skirted by steel gray lava rock and deep green pine trees. She'd missed this place.

An hour more of climbing and they reached the base of St. Andrews Rock, a jagged remnant of the mountain from centuries ago, when it used to be much larger. The summit had stood hundreds of feet higher before huge eruptions caused landslides which led to the Osceola Lahar—a violent mudflow that traveled all the way to Puget Sound. Somehow, St. Andrews Rock had survived the chaos, an enduring reminder of the mountain's former glory.

They climbed to the flat portion of the massive rock where the scientific equipment jutted out. An angled apparatus—the GPS locater—sat above a metal box, along with four flat, shimmering slats that straddled the box to give the device solar power. Two of the slats were broken in half. Griffin had really torn them up when he'd brought in the drilling equipment for his project.

He wiped away a layer of light snow from the box and pulled the metal cover from the ground. To reduce surface noise, the tiltmeter was buried in a two foot deep borehole. He pushed the cover all the way back on its hinges, letting it rest on the ground. "Ugh." He swept his hands along the rock until he held up a mangled lock. "Somebody cut the padlock."

She dropped to one knee next to the hole, dug her flashlight out of her pack, leaned over, and directed the beam inside. She discovered the problem immediately. A thick ream of cotton was stuffed between the two plates that fed data to the data logger. If the machine registered an increase in elevation, it wouldn't be able to record it with the obstruction.

She pulled out the wad of cotton and stood. "This could be the reason you aren't receiving any data after the anomaly."

"Why would anybody do this?"

"Good question." She placed the cotton in a plastic bag, then stood. "But I don't have an answer."

The thick cover creaked as Griffin swung it closed. "At least they didn't damage it completely."

"No, but we still have the issue of the lava dome. I don't think a bundle of cotton would cause the excess tilt that the tiltmeter registered before it stopped transmitting."

Griffin blinked at her. "You think the data could be real?"

"I'm not ready to rule it out yet." She looked down at the ground beneath her feet. Even to her trained eye, the expansion caused by a lava dome might not be visible because of the nearby glacier. An undulating landscape, like a roller coaster of jagged rocks, led to the glacial ice, disguising the real slope of the land. If there really was a lava dome up here, why would someone want to cover it up? More importantly, who would know the mountain well enough to come up here? "That old guy who lives on the mountain might have seen something."

Griffin shoved the broken padlock in his pack. "We can ask him, but you'll have to lead the way. I've never met him and don't know where he lives."

"I think I can find it again, but before we go ... " Lenaia moved to the base of St. Andrew's Rock, searching for a small, relatively flat ledge. When she found one, she dragged her pack over and unzipped the large compartment, then she pulled out a two-inch camera, secured it to the ledge with a rope, and tilted the lens toward the metal lid.

Pointing with one arm, Griffin shook his head. "That's pretty obvious. Won't they just destroy the camera too?"

"Maybe, but after we activate it, this camera will feed to a satellite. Even if someone breaks it or pulls it off, we should still get a screenshot of them doing it." She zipped up her pack. "Ready to go?"

Griffin nodded and gestured for her to take the lead. They headed down the steep-sided cleaver. After hiking back to the Wonderland Trail, they were once again surrounded by dense forest. She adjusted their course to the southwest toward Emerald Ridge.

A couple of hours later, she veered off the path as she had two days before when she'd stumbled across Crusty's log house. It took almost an hour to find it nestled in a small rise. A great location. Accessible, but hard to spot for the general observer.

"Don't touch the trees," she warned Griffin.

"Why?"

"Trust me. He's got the place booby-trapped."

The tarp that served as a door for the structure flapped in the light breeze. She peered into the small space. No one at home.

"Hello?" Her voice dispersed into the woods surrounding them.

No answer.

She walked around the three visible sides of the structure. No signs of life.

After climbing the thick ridge that served as the fourth wall without seeing anyone, she circled back around to where Griffin waited.

"Find him?"

She shook her head. "Must be out enjoying the beautiful day. I'll see if I can track him down later. Let's get back and get the camera feed up." She tapped the piece of cotton, now in the side pocket of her pack. "If somebody tries this again tonight, I want to see who does it."

ZAYDEN STRODE up to the front door of the plain ranch style house and raised his hand to knock. He stopped, holding his fist in midair. Did he really want to do this? Morgan Marshall was a city councilman and the head of the Planning and Zoning Committee in Mayim. Confronting Morgan could end his career. But if the rumor he'd heard around town held any truth, his career was already in jeopardy.

He knocked twice and waited.

A minute later, the outside lights flipped on and the door opened. Morgan stuck his perfectly styled head out. His dark hair didn't move as if he'd sprayed a hard candy shell over the top of it. He wore an expression halfway between amused and surprised, as if he couldn't quite believe Zayden had paid him a visit. "Mr. Planke. What are you doing here?"

"Can we talk?" Zayden tried to keep his voice neutral.

Morgan tilted his head and gave a smooth grin. "Of course. Would you like to come in?"

"We can just talk out here." Zayden had never been inside Morgan's house and he preferred to keep it that way. His job forced him to get approval from the council for his evacuation planning projects and Morgan had always been the most obstinate council member. Probably because of the unfounded rumors about Morgan's wife, Rachel. One night last year, Zayden had run into Rachel at the library. He listened at one of the back tables as she unloaded about Morgan's persistent withdrawal of affection and his lack of interest in coming to church with her. Typical neglected housewife stuff, nothing dramatic, but someone else must have overheard their conversation because by the end of that week, the rumor was all over town that Rachel was having marital problems and Zayden was helping her with them.

It had all happened before Morgan became a councilman. Morgan had never addressed the rumors with Zayden, but perhaps he'd been biding his time, waiting for an opportunity to make a big statement.

Morgan stepped out to the porch and folded his arms. He was tall, but not quite as tall as Zayden. After a few seconds of looking up, Morgan motioned for them to sit in one of two wooden chairs off to the side. Zayden sank into one gratefully. He'd once again spent the entire day on the mountain looking for Summer and Rachel.

Yellow bulb lights illuminated the sitting area, but Zayden stared out at the night sky, rather than look at Morgan. "I'm sorry about Rachel. How is little Stevie doing?"

"He's with my cousin. We shouldn't discuss Rachel. It's not your place." Morgan's voice was rock-hard.

Okay. Either Morgan wasn't as broken-up about his wife as he liked to show on camera or he didn't feel like sharing his emotions with Zayden. "What happened at the committee meeting today?"

"We made a few flood control decisions, along with a ruling on the zoning of an abandoned building downtown. A productive meeting, all things considered."

"All things considered?" Zayden looked over at him, but Morgan feigned stupidity. Of course, he wouldn't just admit to it. "Did you talk about anything related to evacuation planning?"

"The committee didn't make any decisions today regarding evacuation planning."

That sounded rehearsed. "You didn't answer my question. Was the subject brought up?"

Morgan twisted his mouth into a crooked frown. "You must know it was or you wouldn't be here. Who talked to you?"

"Does it matter?"

"It matters to me. I like to know who I can trust." Morgan tapped his knee. "Was it Cindy? She's always treated you like the son she never had."

"It wasn't her." He had more friends in this town than Morgan knew. "What I want to know is why?"

"Look, it's not personal."

Zayden almost laughed. It was always personal with Morgan. He held his tongue as the man continued.

"Times are tough. Mayim isn't exactly growing. No one wants to move here. Personally, I blame the Discovery Channel. That blasted documentary they did on catastrophic mudflows from Mt.

Rainier scared even me." Morgan turned his eyes to Zayden. "Anyway, our tax base can't support your salary."

"In your humble opinion?"

Morgan put a hand over his heart and pasted on the charismatic smile he used at council meetings. "Yes, in my humble opinion."

Zayden clasped his hands together to keep from clenching his fists. The town also couldn't afford the biannual raises requested by the planning committee for themselves, but that didn't stop them. He took a deep breath. Getting angry wouldn't help the situation. "Evacuation planning is an essential need. If you get rid of all disaster planning, then even the locals won't want to live here. What the Discovery Channel special showed is how prepared the town is and how the council cares enough to protect the people. If you cut my position, you won't even have that."

Morgan shrugged. "Someone on the committee will assume the responsibility."

A hot pulse of anger swept up Zayden's neck. He stood and glared down at Morgan. "So it's decided then?"

Morgan leaned his head back to look up at Zayden. "As I said, nothing has been decided. We gave it a fair discussion at the meeting."

Zayden stepped around Morgan's chair and headed down the steps. At the bottom, he turned back. "Fair? Then why wasn't I invited?"

Without waiting for an answer, he strode to his truck. As he opened the door, he heard Morgan's sarcastic reply. "Because of course you would have acted like a professional."

His hand froze on the door handle. Morgan just had to bring it up. The fight over the automatic emergency paging system hadn't been Zayden's finest moment. He'd lost his temper and screamed at several council members. Why wouldn't they want to give as much disaster warning as possible to the townspeople? Money, it was always about money.

Tonight, though, Zayden got the impression that Morgan held some sort of a grudge. Whether this was about Rachel or the paging system, he wouldn't give Morgan any more ammunition. He got into his truck and slammed the door. He couldn't imagine how Rachel had dealt with Morgan every day. Zayden wouldn't blame her if she'd left Morgan for good, but it seemed unlikely. She would have taken Stevie with her.

CHAPTER 9

$\mathcal{L}$enaia stepped into the narrow front hall of Pastor Doug's house. "Thanks for agreeing to squeeze me in today. I've got an appointment in an hour, but before we get started I'd like to say hi to Scott."

Pastor Doug placed a meaty hand on her shoulder. "I'm sure he would love to see you."

She followed him through the entryway and up the narrow carpeted stairs to the second level.

He sidestepped at the top. "Watch out for the chair."

She swung wide to avoid the mechanical chair lift, then joined him on the landing.

"We're hoping to either build or buy a ranch style house, so Scottie can manage better, but we haven't found the right one yet."

A voice called from the rooms beyond. "Don't call me Scottie, Dad."

Pastor Doug turned to give her a big smile, as if he'd used the name Scottie to get a rise out of his son. He led her down a short hall to a bedroom at the end. The face that greeted her was a surprise. Scott had been a gangly and awkward preteen when she'd left. In the intervening years, he'd turned into a handsome young man. Bright blue eyes and angled face—something she guessed his dad would have, if he wasn't quite so rotund.

"Lenaia, hi?" Scott put down a notepad and laid his pen across it. He looked normal and healthy, except he couldn't get out of bed and walk. He couldn't drive to a movie. He couldn't go for a stroll on the mountain trails. Lying in bed all the time would drive her crazy.

She cleared her throat. "How are you?"

He shrugged. "Okay. What are you doing back here?"

Pastor Doug placed a folding chair beside the bed and motioned for her to sit, then he leaned against the far wall. She took the seat and opened her mouth to respond, but she practically choked on the words. Why would he want to know how her life was going when he was dealing with so much?

"I'm back in the area to work on the mountain. It's just a temporary assignment helping Griffin during the government shutdown."

"Griffin?" Scott raised his eyebrows at his dad.

"Griffin was a few years older than you when he lived here. Remember, he had to move after his mom died."

Scott nodded. "I remember now. I'm surprised he came back after all that." He smoothed the sheets over his legs. "Of course, with the way I am, I may never get a chance to leave."

She noted the sad, faraway look in Scott's eyes. Was he remembering his plan to travel the world and write books? When she'd left, he was working on The Undercover Country series—travel books from the perspective of the poorest people in the country.

When he caught her staring, he quickly changed his expression. "So why does Griffin need help? There shouldn't be anything going on in the park if it's under government shutdown."

Pastor Doug and Lenaia exchanged glances. The problems weren't exactly a secret, but she didn't want word getting all around Mayim. "We're having issues with one of the tiltmeters."

She hesitated to say more, but she could trust Scott and Pastor Doug to keep a confidence. "Somebody sabotaged it."

"Why would they do that?"

"Good question. That's what I have to figure out."

Scott picked up the pen and drew lazy circles along the bottom of the page. "Could it be a prank?"

She thought of the camera. Hopefully, they'd caught something on it last night. She was meeting with Griffin in an hour to find out. "Maybe, but I don't think so. It's not easily accessible."

She scooted the chair closer to the bed to get a look at the page. "What are you writing?"

"I wrote a poem about how God gets our attention."

"And how does He do that?"

Scott's eyebrows sagged. "Usually with a smack upside the head."

She could see why he'd feel that way. "Can I read it?"

"No, it's not ready yet."

"When you're ready, I'd love to read it. I'm glad you're still writing."

"At first, I didn't even want to pick up a pen since I can't write my travel series." He gave a quick glance to his motionless legs, tucked under the covers. "But I've learned to love writing again. Do you write?"

"Oh, no. The only thing I write are research reports, and maybe an occasional scientific paper. If you asked me to do anything creative, I'd stare at the screen until my head imploded." She almost said, *I'm happiest on a mountain,* but stopped herself just before the insensitive words tumbled out. What would she do if God took her ability to explore away from her? A sharp tingle of fear ran down her spine, surprising her. She knew when she'd started to fear what God might do. It was right after her uncle's death.

"Scott, it was great to see you again. I wish I could stay and talk longer, but I have an appointment."

"I hope you can come back soon." He tilted his head and peered at her. "I love visitors. Guess who else comes to see me all the time?"

"Who?"

"Zayden Planke."

She blinked and her mouth dropped open. The Zayden she'd known would never have found time for Scott. When she'd dated him, he was often too busy with work or hunting to see even her.

She took Scott's hand and squeezed it. "I'll try to stop by again before I leave town. Okay?"

"Thanks for coming."

Pastor Doug led her out of the room, through the hallway, and to the study downstairs. "We can talk in here."

She sat in a comfortable chair across from a wooden desk. Instead of sitting on the other side of the desk, Pastor Doug turned the chair next to her and sat.

She scooted her chair around to face him. "Scott seems to be adjusting well."

"He is. Until this happened I had no idea how strong he could be."

"I know I'm not here for long, but if I can do anything to help you or Carol, please let me know."

He gave her a half smile. "Actually, we're doing fine. We're closer now as a family than we've ever been. Probably closer than we would be if this hadn't happened. I'm not sure I can call this a blessing yet, but believe me, Lenaia, God knows what He's doing."

She flinched and looked down, hoping he didn't notice. Did God know what He was doing when He let Uncle Jim die? Her dad's death had hurt, but at least she knew they'd see each other in heaven. But as for her uncle, no one, except for God, knew.

"What would you like to talk about today?" Pastor Doug leaned forward in the leather chair, pushing against the fluffy cushions. His face was concerned and kind, so why did she feel like running out of the room?

She let out a strained laugh. "I don't really want to talk about anything."

"I know. You're here because your boyfriend asked you to come. I think it's noble of you to try to ease his mind." Pastor Doug leaned back in the chair. "Let's start with something easy. What's your boyfriend's name?"

"Travis Perego."

"Why do you think Travis wants you to talk with someone?"

Lenaia shifted, her jeans squeaking along the leather. "I'm not sure exactly." What was the point of a counselor anyway? Reliving the trauma wouldn't change anything.

"Why *don't* you want to be here?"

"Because you're going to want me to talk about painful things. Like what happened in Hawaii when Dan fell into ... " She couldn't say *lava tube* out loud, even though the word jumped around in her head all the time, along with the image of the barren land-scape where a man should have stood. What had Dan felt when he dropped in? Did he feel pain before he died?

Pastor Doug met her gaze with squinted brown eyes. "And what if I didn't force you to talk?"

"Huh?"

"I want to help you, so I'll make a deal with you. I don't know what happened in Hawaii and you don't have to tell me. Hawaii is yours. You went through the painful experience; you know the raw edges flanking the wound. I won't make you talk about it. When you feel like you're ready, then *you* bring it up, but I won't. Deal?"

This probably wasn't what Travis had in mind when he'd asked her to see a counselor, but it sounded good to her. "Deal. But there's a catch, right?"

Pastor Doug lifted his hands in the air, palms to the ceiling. "I'm here for you no matter what you talk about, even if you talk about your favorite pair of socks. As long as you come, we'll talk about what you want to talk about."

She glanced around at the myriad of civic awards on the wall. Was this how Pastor Doug had won them all—one person at a time with unfathomable patience? The awards hung right next to the most impressionistic paintings she'd ever seen.

Pastor Doug pointed at the awards. "Those I didn't hang. Carol likes to put them up." He swept his arm to the paintings. "I did hang those. Do you like them?"

The artist had swirled and swooshed the paint in so many directions that the intended shape was almost obscured. Almost. "I kind of like them. The colors are nice, but I wish the image was sharper."

"I'm not surprised. Given that you're a scientist, you enjoy using the logical, concrete part of your brain. But I chose these because I think they represent life. We have a fuzzy image of what our life is supposed to be like, but then God comes along and swirls everything around to make something more beautiful than our original idea."

Something more beautiful? God hadn't done that in her life. The pastor was right about one thing, though—she couldn't recognize the image of what she'd thought her life would be.

"Is there something else you want to talk about? Besides my paintings, I mean."

She grimaced. "Does it have to be painful for this counseling thing to work?"

He laughed and for a moment he looked like he might give her a hug. Instead, he leaned forward in the chair again. "No. But, as a pastor, that is my specialty."

She captured her hair, tugged it over her shoulder and ran her fingers through it, pulling out the knots. Travis wanted her to talk about Uncle Jim. After a year, she ought to be able to at least discuss the facts logically. "My uncle died in Costa Rica last year."

Wrinkles furrowed trenches between Pastor Doug's brows and cocooned his eyes. "Do you want to tell me what happened?"

No, she didn't. Not the whole story, anyway. Her name was

mostly kept out of it, but Uncle Jim's name had been all over the news, along with Travis because he exposed the truth about the mysterious creature Uncle Jim had created. "Someone shot him, and I couldn't save him."

"You were there?"

"Sort of. I was out of it, mostly unconscious."

The pastor tilted his head. "You weren't really in a position to help him, but you feel responsible for your uncle's death?"

She looked down at her feet, pretending to examine the laces on her hiking boots. Although it wasn't rational, guilt welled up inside her. She tried to push it away, and yet, the guilt continued to bubble up like gas rising from a deep well. She should have done more to save him from being shot, and more importantly, she should have talked to him more often about Jesus. While she'd still had time. "I guess I thought I'd have more of a chance to help him."

"Help him how?"

She opened her mouth and shut it. She'd never tried to put into words the heartbreak of her uncle's death and his rejection of Jesus. When she had first accepted Jesus, she told Uncle Jim all about it. He laughed at her then and every time she brought it up for months. Finally, she gave up trying to convince him, assuming her actions alone would speak for her faith. Until he died, and the opportunities were gone. Would Pastor Doug understand the guilt or would he tell her what a weak Christian she'd been? "I should have talked more about Jesus. I could have made him understand. He thought Jesus was a crutch for me—my way of coping with my father's death. He wouldn't even consider the possibility Jesus might be real."

"Why not?"

"He used to say, 'How can I respect a god who can't force me to bow down to him?' I told him that God *could* make him bow down, but He never *would* because forced love is no love at all."

"What did your uncle say to that?"

"He said, even if my god exists, then love makes Him weak."

Pastor Doug nodded. "Many men equate love, and especially mercy, with weakness." He rested his hands in his lap. "Do you think your uncle loved you?"

She lifted her head. "In his own way, I think so, but probably because I was the only person who ever tried to understand him." She swept her hair back over her shoulder. "Then again, he tried to control me most of the time."

"Maybe he tried to control you because he felt threatened by the part of you he didn't understand. The part that loves Jesus."

She shrugged. "He did try to get me to turn my back on Jesus. It was a game to him. Once, he even tried to get me to gamble away my faith." At Pastor Doug's confused look, she elaborated. "He said if Jesus existed and loved me, then He could turn up a number six on the dice if I asked Him to. Uncle Jim dared me to try it, but I refused."

"How did he handle your refusal?"

"He called me a coward." She sighed. "Does that mean he didn't love me after all?"

Pastor Doug ran a hand over his shiny dome. "Not necessarily. Like many of us, your uncle didn't give much thought to love. Most of us are just trying to get our own needs met. Your uncle wanted your devotion all to himself. That's a kind of love, although not a pure love."

"I suppose." She pulled at the hem of her shirt. It didn't matter whether Uncle Jim had loved her or not; he was her uncle and she'd failed him.

"Do you think God loved your uncle?"

The question surprised her. She pondered it for a moment. "He must have, because God is more loving than me and, despite his nature, *I* still loved my uncle."

"So, if God loved your uncle, He would do all He could to reach him."

She bit her lip and blinked back moisture in her eyes. "What if it wasn't enough?"

"Then, you have to respect your uncle's choice."

Lenaia opened her mouth to say something, but nothing came out. Pastor Doug had a way of cutting straight to her heart. Was she trying to take away her uncle's free will, even after death? Was that why she couldn't let it go?

"None of us knows the moment of our death. That's God's domain. All we can do is prepare ourselves and others. You obviously had influence over your uncle, but you couldn't make his decision for him."

A tide of anger swelled in Lenaia's chest, threatening to choke her. The words "God's domain" replayed in her head. Why would God take her uncle when he wasn't ready to go? If she would have had more time, she could have convinced him.

Confusion swirled through her head. She was mad at God, mad at herself—just mad all around. Talking about this was a mistake. She stood and moved to the window, staring out at the postcard perfect view of the Nisqually River framed by tall pine trees. Beautiful and unrestrained, the water churned by on a desperate race to the ocean. She felt too much of that chaotic energy in her life.

"God won't force anyone to come to Him." Pastor Doug spoke quietly but with strength. "If you try to take responsibility for your uncle's decision, then your love for him was all about control as well."

She pushed away from the window to check her watch. It was time for her to go meet Griffin. She grabbed her backpack from under the chair and strode to the door. At the threshold, she stopped and turned back. Pastor Doug might think her a weak Christian, but so what? "You're a hundred percent right. I can't control anything. God's going to do what He wants anyway."

LENAIA PULLED open the door of the visitor's center. The interior air quality had moved from stuffy to stale. At least, Griffin had taken to leaving it unlocked when he was inside so she could come in without having to call him. She let the door swing shut behind her and climbed the stairs two at a time. At the end of the hallway, she opened the door to the office. Griffin stood hovering over his computer in the corner.

"You look anxious for only ten o'clock in the morning."

He glanced at her, then returned his eyes to the screen. "I've got something you need to see."

She dropped her backpack at the door and went to stand behind him, peering over his shoulder.

He clicked on the screen. "This is the footage from the camera last night."

A pixelated black and white image appeared on the screen. She recognized the broken GPS equipment and the metal protective box for the tiltmeter, rendered in the greenish gray haze of infrared.

"The footage isn't the highest quality." He swept a hand toward the screen and stepped back.

The image stayed static for a moment. Then, a sliver of movement flashed in the lower right corner. In the distance, a dark figure bobbed up and down, making a slow trek up the rocky pass between the glaciers. The beam of a flashlight played over the snow, making a bright zigzag pattern. She held her breath as the figure came closer.

A few minutes later, the person came into focus. She let out her breath in a disappointed rush. The face was obscured by a ski mask.

At the box, the figure stopped and bent over to open the lid, then the person shrugged a pack off their back and pulled out a tool. At first, Lenaia couldn't see what, but then she recognized a pair of wire cutters glinting green in the infrared.

With the cutters in one hand, the figure leaned into the hole.

She watched as the person's arms shifted around. Although she couldn't see it, she assumed the person was cutting the wires that held in place the leveling portion of the device. Now, the tiltmeter would register nothing, permanently.

The figure finished working and put the wire cutters back in the pack. She watched the flashlight beam fade away as Griffin stepped around to close the image file.

She took a deep breath and released it as a groan. The tiltmeter was useless now. If Mt. Rainier had a lava dome, they'd never know it. How was she supposed to assess the threat to the town? She kicked one of the legs supporting the desk. "Who would do this?"

Griffin shook his head and gave a shrug. "Maybe that old guy? What did you call him?"

"Crusty." He lived near the equipment. It wasn't that much of a stretch from sabotaging trees to sabotaging equipment. He was as good a suspect as any. She tapped her foot. "But how would he know about the camera?"

"You're assuming this person knew because he was wearing a ski mask. Last night, the temperature got down near freezing up there. On the glaciers, the wind can whip up rocks and snow together. This person might have been wearing it for protection."

"That's possible. Still, did you tell anyone else about the camera?"

"After we came down I told Randy." Griffin scratched his chin. "Oh, and I told Zayden. I ran into him on the way out yesterday and he grilled me about why you were here. What's that guy's deal with you anyway? I can't figure out if he can't stand you or he's in love with you."

Heat rose in her face. Although, it wasn't Griffin's business, she didn't have anything to hide. "We used to date. When I left town, it was hard on us both."

Griffin crossed his arms and leaned on the desk. "So why'd you leave then?"

She turned her back on him and walked to the other end of the room. If she told him, he'd probably ridicule her, but she wouldn't be ashamed of her beliefs. "A few years into my geology career, I started asking questions." She turned around and leaned against the wall. "Questions with hard answers. Like where did everything come from?" Griffin raised an eyebrow. When he remained silent, she continued. "I started investigating the evidence for creation. I found more evidence for creation than for evolution. When it all came down to it, I had to take a stand. I chose God."

He snorted. "Let me guess, your boss realized you'd gone off the deep end and fired you."

"Yes, Sherry petitioned my boss to have me fired. I could have stayed in Mayim if I'd taken a different job." Lenaia shook her head. "I couldn't give up volcanology. Zayden thinks I left him, but he never offered to come with me. We both wanted our own lives at a time when they didn't intersect anymore."

"I gather Zayden didn't share your unique geological philosophy."

"No, in fact, he thought I was crazy too." Zayden had told her he believed in God, although he never put any weight behind the statement. He wouldn't go to church with her, preferring to hunt on Sundays, even in the winter. The longer she'd stayed with him the further away from God she'd felt.

Griffin looked her over slowly from head to toe. "And you still believe that stuff?"

"Of course I do."

He gave her a twisted grin. "Then I just lost a lot of respect for you."

She narrowed her eyes. "You're not the first." Good thing she didn't live her life based on the respect of others.

"Seriously." He pushed off the desk and took a step toward her. "You believe some supernatural creature created the earth in six days?"

She pushed off the wall and met him in the middle of the

room. "Is that any crazier than believing everything came out of nothing?"

Griffin opened his mouth to say something else, but the phone on Randy's desk rang out a shrill tone. Griffin twisted around to grab it. "Hello?"

She crossed the room and bent down to grab her pack. She wasn't going to debate further. Let Griffin think what he wanted about her. She swung the pack onto her shoulder.

At the door, she turned and gave him a dismissive wave, but he pointed at her while shaking his head. He crooked his finger, motioning for her to come back.

"When?" He pressed the phone tighter to his ear. "Okay, I'll organize it for this afternoon."

He hung up and met her curious gaze. His hazel eyes had turned a darker shade of green.

"What?"

He wet his lower lip before answering "Searchers found something of Rachel's on the mountain."

CHAPTER 10

*L*enaia trudged through the trees on the southeast side of the mountain, following behind Park Ranger Randy Turnbuckle. The searchers had found a shoe that Morgan Marshall confirmed as belonging to Rachel. The hunt for her was again in full force, but now on this side of the mountain.

As they walked, Randy had given her more information on the circumstances of Rachel's disappearance. Morgan said he had gone out to run an errand at about nine o'clock that evening. When he returned, the front door stood open, a window screen had a slice through it, and his wife was nowhere to be found. Other than the window screen, there was no sign of foul play.

Lenaia still held out hope that Rachel might be alive, but her optimism dampened with every passing hour. And what about Summer? Would they find her if they found Rachel?

Randy moved quickly through the trees in front of her, his ear-length, graying hair blowing in the breeze. He'd probably hiked on this mountain every day for the last twenty years. The sun and wind had left his face weathered, but his body in better physical shape than hers.

The trail leveled out into a relatively flat area. By unspoken agreement, they wandered on and off the trail in opposite directions, weaving through the trees, searching for any evidence of Rachel.

As the slope increased, along with the rocks, she came back to the trail and fell in line behind Randy again. Even though they were searching on the other side of the mountain from the tiltmeter, her geologic mind was still analyzing the lay of the land. "Did Griffin tell you about the possible lava dome?"

Randy stopped and spun around to look at her. "No. Is a lava dome as bad as it sounds?"

"Yes. It's a collection of magma in one area that pushes up the rock. Rainier doesn't usually get them because the lava here has less silica." She waved her hand at his confused look. "Never mind. What I mean is the lava here is more fluid, so lava thickening and building up into a dome is rare. But don't panic yet. We haven't been able to confirm it. I was just curious if he'd said anything to you."

Randy started walking again. "Nope. And I'm not surprised. Griffin barely talks to anyone around here."

"But he told you about the camera and the sabotage."

"Yeah. He was chatty yesterday."

She kicked at a thick bush to make sure nothing was hidden beneath it. "Any idea who might be behind the sabotage?"

Randy paused for a second, then resumed walking. "Not a clue. The whole thing is confusing. I can't figure out the why."

She dodged a tree. "Me, neither. Except it seems strange that someone sabotaged the one tiltmeter that might be over a lava dome."

Randy turned around again, and she almost ran into him. "The lava dome is under the STAR station?"

She took a step back and nodded. "Weird, right? Maybe it's a coincidence because like you said, I can't figure out why."

Randy twisted his lips. "Is the lava dome likely to blow?"

She smiled at the casual way he asked. Park rangers in volcanic areas accepted the same risks as geologists, maybe even more so. Randy knew any normal day in the park could be his last. "Probably not anytime soon. But it's hard to tell without good readings from the monitoring station."

As the slope leveled out once more, she veered off the path to the right. Her arm brushed back a tree branch and her feet froze instinctively. Not from what she saw, but from what she smelled. Mixed with the familiar sharp scent of pine, she caught an underlying current of flowers. Roses, maybe? She turned her head and sniffed deeply. It was faint, but definitely perfume.

"Hey, I'm going to check something out. I'll be right back."

"Don't go far."

She ducked under the branches of one pine tree and skirted through another, drawn to a small dot of color. As she got closer, the dot grew into a stream of pink fabric. A glittery salmon-colored scarf was caught in the needles of a tree. She picked up the lightweight material and brought it to her nose. Clean, with the strong scent of roses. A chill laced cold fingers of dread up her neck. This couldn't have been out here for long.

"Randy." She tried to keep her voice steady. "Over here."

A minute later, he came through the trees. With wide eyes, he stared at the fabric draped across Lenaia's arm.

"Do you think it's hers?" she asked.

"I don't know her well enough to know her clothing, but I'd say it's likely. Rachel always dressed nice, even though she stayed at home. Let's look around some more." He held up one finger to emphasize his next words. "Stay within shouting distance."

She nodded, and they fanned out in opposite directions. She scanned the blanket of fallen needles strewn along the forest floor. Varying shades of green and brown. Nothing more. After about a hundred yards, she turned around to head back.

"Here," Randy's gruff voice called from off to her right.

She rushed through the trees in a straight line to him. After pushing a thick, spiky branch aside, she stumbled into a small, circular clearing. Randy knelt on the other side of the clearing, near the base of a tall white pine.

A young woman's body lay in front of him.

Her matching salmon-colored dress shirt was torn and her jeans had mud smears up both legs. Arms flung straight over her head, she could have been praising God in church. Only she wasn't in church and would never be in church again. But why was she up here? No one would go hiking in those clothes without a coat at this time of year.

Lenaia covered her mouth with her hand, pushing down a wave of nausea. The pictures of Rachel on the news hadn't done her justice. With her chestnut hair sweeping the leafy ground and her pale flawless skin, even in death she looked like an angel.

Lenaia moved her hand long enough to speak two words. "It's her."

Randy nodded, his gaze still fixed on the body. "Don't touch anything." But then, against his own advice, he leaned over Rachel with his hand outstretched. "What's this?"

A piece of white paper stuck out from the top of Rachel's short, stylish boots. Apparently thinking better of it, Randy reached into his pocket, pulled out a thick glove, and slipped it on before extracting the paper. Folded in half, it was a sparse hand-written note. After reading it, he handed it to her since she was already wearing gloves.

The earth will punish them. NUM 16.

The note trembled in her hands as she glanced from it to the dead woman's body. It didn't make any sense to her.

As Randy replaced the note, Lenaia pressed her eyes closed, trying to block out Rachel's delicate features. Her facial muscles slack. Her eyes open, yet gazing at nothing. This beautiful woman's life was stolen, her child would grow up without her, probably wouldn't remember her, and for what? As some sort of punishment?

The nausea roiled through her stomach, and she turned away

so that she could open her eyes. Too much death. If not for her pale skin, Rachel could have been Nina, the young girl Lenaia couldn't save in Costa Rica. *Why, Lord? You sent Travis to the jungle to save me, but there are so many people you haven't let me save.* It was the same problem every time—she couldn't understand the why.

LENAIA PARKED her car in front of the Mayim library in the long row of surprisingly crowded downtown parking. She needed to access the USGS database to look up the tiltmeter readings at the unaffected monitoring station, a task that was hard to accomplish on her phone, and even harder to do at the bed and breakfast which didn't have Wi-Fi. She could have gone back to the visitor's center to use the office computers, but after finding Rachel Marshall's body, she didn't feel like staying on the mountain.

As she got out of the car and stepped onto the sidewalk, a gathering crowd caught her attention. The group of approximately thirty people stood in front of the sheriff's office two doors down. Curious, she walked closer to stand on the outskirts of the throng.

Peeking between several people, she saw Pastor Marty in the center of the crowd talking to a young reporter. His arms gestured in large arcs while he spoke. Nearby, a two-person camera crew filmed from a tripod while a reporter stood ready with a microphone.

Pastor Marty threw back his head and gazed at the sky. "God has poured out His wrath on Mayim."

The reporter turned the microphone to her mouth. "Let me get this straight. You believe the death of Rachel Marshall is the wrath of God."

Pastor Marty lowered his head to the waiting microphone and stared into the camera lens. "Deuteronomy 29 says disaster and wrath will come upon those who go their own way into sin. This town is not safe until it deals with its secret sins." He swung his arms in the air. "More people will die if we ignore the warnings of God."

Lenaia turned to go. No sense hanging around to give this guy the attention he sought. Pastor Doug had more patience than she did with people like Pastor Marty.

As she swung around, she bounced off something solid at eye level.

"Sorry." She backed away a step, then looked up.

"You should be more careful." Zayden's tone was teasing, and somehow she found that more disconcerting than his anger.

She blushed and moved to go around him.

He touched her arm to keep her from leaving. "Actually, I'd like to talk to you. Do you have a minute?"

"I guess so."

He moved to a side door of the sheriff's office. She followed, grateful for the shelter of the doorway that would block out most of Pastor Marty's ramblings.

"I heard you found Rachel." Zayden's brown eyes darkened with emotion.

She pursed her lips. How well had he known Rachel? Probably not a question she should ask right now. "Actually, Randy found her, but I was with him."

He tugged on his ear. "Look, you know I'm not good at being politically correct, so I'll just get to the point. I think you should go home."

She blinked. "What?"

"It's not safe here." He looked over his shoulder as if someone might be listening. "Women are dying, from Seattle and here, and no one seems to know if the deaths are connected." He returned his eyes to hers. "You're not safe here, Lenaia."

His gaze and the way he said her name made her heart beat faster. This was the intensity she remembered from long ago. The reason she'd fallen for him in the first place. But for all his fervor now, in ten minutes, he could swing just the opposite and be as cold as ice.

She took a breath to compose herself. "Zayden, I appreciate the concern, but I can't leave. Something is going on here ... "

He grabbed her arm. "I don't want you to end up like Rachel."

Her eyes widened. Since when did Zayden worry about her safety? Her thoughts flew to Travis. He'd be saying the same thing if she would have told him about the situation. "I deal with the risk of death every day. I don't give up because something is dangerous. You of all people should know that."

"I do. That's why I'm trying to talk some sense into you. The risk you're used to has doubled, at least." He opened his mouth and held it there for a few seconds, as if he had to push out what he wanted to say next. "Go home, Lenaia. Any problems here can survive until the other geologists come back after the shutdown."

She tugged her arm free of his grasp. Zayden had no right to tell her what to do. She focused on his eyes while speaking each word carefully. "I'm not leaving until my job is done."

He shook his head, his jaw firm. "What about God? What if He sent me to tell you to go home?"

She clenched her teeth. How dare he use God against her? "Since when do you speak for God?" As soon as she said the words, she regretted them. Zayden hadn't gone to church when they'd dated, but he didn't deserve for her to throw it in his face. She swept her hand over her forehead, pushing away stray hairs. "Look, you know how I feel."

"I know." Zayden brought his hand to her cheek.

She pulled away, backing up to the other side of the doorway. Zayden had gotten the wrong idea about the tiny spark left between them. She couldn't help her physical reaction, but she wasn't going down that road again. She loved Travis.

Zayden dropped his hand to his side. "A lot has changed since you left. I've grown closer to God. I'm going to church. I know none of that is a reason for you to listen to me, but I want to protect you."

Zayden going to church, for real? Maybe some things around here did change. She opened her mouth to tell him once again that she wouldn't leave town, but the reporter's voice kept her silent. The woman had found a new interview subject very close to where they stood. The bright camera light blinded Lenaia, stalling her attempt at escaping the camera shot.

The reporter's blond locks swished around her shoulders as she talked. "I'm standing in front of the Pierce County Sheriff's office in the little town of Mayim with Deputy Alan Smith." Her tone held a note of professionalism mixed with the sweet cadence of the girl next door. "Off to my left—" The cameraman panned toward the mountain. "—you can see the massive form of Mt. Rainier. Today, this serene paradise bore witness to the final moments of a local woman. Rachel Marshall's strangled body was found a few hours ago on the southeast flank."

Lenaia closed her eyes as if that would stop the words from gathering in her head. To hear how Rachel died brought back the horrific image of her body.

The reporter wet her lips before continuing. "This is the first murder of a resident of Mayim since the town's inception in 1885. Isn't that correct, Deputy?"

"Yes, ma'am." The deputy shifted on his feet like he'd rather be fed to hungry lions than talk to her.

The reporter pressed on. "What are the police doing to find her killer?"

"We're currently interviewing known acquaintances—"

"It was him." A voice from the crowd rose above the deputy's.

Lenaia turned to see Morgan Marshall moving toward them.

"He killed her." Morgan came closer, sidestepping the crowd. Stopping five feet from them, he stuck out his finger, his hand shaking, and pointed right at Zayden.

Zayden stared at the man with shock frozen on his face.

The reporter turned to assess the commotion, then she turned back to the camera. "Thank you, Deputy, for your insights." Tilting her head, she motioned for the cameraman to follow, then took off in their direction. Her cameraman struggled to keep up as she expertly cut in front of Morgan and stuck the microphone in his face, but before he said anything, she pulled it back to her own, addressing the camera. "Ladies and gentlemen, this is Morgan Marshall, husband of Rachel Marshall, the woman found on the mountain today." Turning back to him, she said, "Mr. Marshall, what do you want to say?"

She placed the microphone near his mouth. "Zayden Planke killed my Rachel."

The reporter nodded as if she completely agreed with him. "Why do you think so?"

Morgan's eyes sought the camera. "Because he's punishing me. He's about to be fired. And he killed her to hurt me."

Zayden stared down at the ground, his face shadowed, and his posture unreadable. Was he about to be fired? Why hadn't he told her?

"Is this true?" The reporter tried to get the microphone into Zayden's face, but he backed away.

"I'm the head of the Planning and Zoning Commission." Morgan followed after the reporter. She quickly moved the microphone back to him. "A vote is scheduled for tomorrow to decide whether to keep or remove the position of Evacuation Planning Coordinator. His job." Morgan pointed at Zayden again. "I never thought you would hurt her. Why not me, instead?"

Morgan's eyes scrunched up and he buried his face in his hands. Mournful sobs, one after the other, drew all attention to him. Zayden turned and walked through the crowd without looking back. She knew he wasn't the type to defend himself. Even so, he could have at least denied it.

She thought about going after him. Surely, he hadn't hurt Rachel, especially since he'd been going to church recently, and he'd have no reason to write the cryptic note. But even so, he hadn't confided in her about his job. What other secrets might he be keeping?

Lowering her head, she slipped into the library. Even if Zayden was being falsely accused, she couldn't do anything to help him.

CHAPTER 11

Once Zayden realized he was alone on the wooded trail, he picked up his pace to a jog. This wasn't a searching trip. He needed to burn off some adrenaline. The path wound through tall elms and white pine trees, roughly following the Puyallup River.

So much for the peace and quiet of small-town life. But in truth, Mayim hadn't felt like home since Lenaia had left. Seeing her again, touching her, had brought up memories he'd worked hard to bury. Like the memory of the day she'd left. In desperation, he'd gotten down on one knee and promised to marry her if she stayed, even though he didn't have a ring. She cried, as she said no, reiterating that she had to go.

He could have, probably should have, followed her then, but he'd gotten caught up in his own aspirations. Why had he asked her to stay, to sacrifice her dreams, when he hadn't been willing to do the same? He'd given up their relationship for a future in this small town. And now that town had turned against him. Would everyone think he was a murderer now?

He pushed his legs harder, maneuvering to avoid ruts along the trail. Could he leave this time and give up his dream of a small piece of paradise? This time, he might not have a choice. But they couldn't make him leave until he found Summer. He owed it to Arielle.

The path curved and the trees thinned out. Water from the river swirled by in eddies on a journey going in the opposite direction. The rhythmic gurgling soothed him as only the flow of water could do.

Ahead, the path turned again, as it followed a bend in the river. He sped up to a sprint and rounded the curve at top speed. As he came out of it, he dodged to his left to avoid something big and yellow blocking half of the trail.

He circled around and stopped. A dull yellow excavator sat partially on the trail and partially on the levee near the river. The rusted metal tracks had worn grooves into the soft sediment.

Who had driven this thing out here? He didn't know of any county work being done on the levee. Besides, the excavator looked almost pristine. The county didn't keep equipment nice for long.

The bucket sat near the levee. He leaned over to look at the water. It flowed in a circle below his feet, creating a small whirlpool. The water was caught in an indentation in the bank. He leaned over farther to get a better look. Chunks of dirt had been carved out underneath the levee in a wide semicircle. Trenches in the freshly exposed dirt matched up with the teeth in the bucket of the excavator.

He pulled out his phone and dialed Griffin's cell phone.

When Griffin answered, he sounded out of breath like he'd also gone running. "Zayden, what do you need?"

"I need Lenaia Talavera's cell number."

Griffin took a long breath. "What for?"

"I found something out by the river and I want her to see it."

"Look, if you want to ask her out, just say so." Griffin rattled off the numbers.

"It's not like that," he muttered as he hung up the phone.

Zayden dialed, and Lenaia answered on the third ring, her voice quiet. "Hello?"

"Lenaia, it's Zayden. Is this a bad time?"

"No, I'm at the library. Are you okay?"

She meant, was he okay after the incident this afternoon, but he didn't intend to talk about it. "I'm fine. I've got something you need to see. It might be another act of sabotage."

"Where?"

"I'm on the trail near the Puyallup River. Park at the trailhead where we saw the reckless moose that one time. I'll meet you there." She would know what he meant. The moose they found that day had gotten its antlers stuck in a briar bush. Lenaia insisted they couldn't leave it to starve. He'd gotten kicked twice trying to pull the moose out by the hind quarters. And then, once it was free, they ran for their lives to keep from getting bucked. It was one of his best memories.

Silence stretched over the line. Had she forgotten the place or did she not want to meet him? Finally, she answered, "Fifteen minutes."

"Okay."

He ran back to the trailhead in ten. Her car was just pulling in. She got out and headed toward him. Her dark hair had been set free from its usual ponytail and swayed with the rhythm of her steps. He looked away to get control of the tangled ball of emotions knotting up his chest every time he saw her.

"What do you mean another act of sabotage?"

He met her gaze. Her dark eyes were full of concern. "Let me show you." He turned and walked down the trail.

A few minutes later, she pointed at a large bush tucked behind some trees. "We found the moose there, didn't we?"

So, she did remember. He nodded with a smile. "I wish we'd have gotten a picture of it."

"I was just glad we didn't have to go to the hospital. One of its hooves came within an inch of your nose."

"I've always wondered what he chased to get him stuck so far into the bush. Whatever it was, he must have been crazed to get to it."

They walked in silence for a few more minutes. He tried not to glance at her, but he felt her looking at him. Was she thinking about Morgan's accusation? Wondering if she was safe alone here with him?

"We're close," he said.

They rounded the last turn in the path. He watched her eyes go wide when she saw the excavator. She walked up and circled around it. "What's this doing here?"

He leaned over her shoulder and pointed to the edge of the bank. "Digging out the levee, it seems."

She bent at the waist to see. "Why?"

Zayden folded his arms across his chest. "I think someone is trying to weaken the levee protecting the town."

"But we're over a mile from town."

"The levee is one continuous structure which runs from here, through town and a quarter mile beyond. Compromise it here and the town will have real problems in a flood. At least, there isn't much damage done, yet."

She furrowed her brow. He resisted the urge to smooth a hand over her forehead and make the lines disappear. "The county could be doing some maintenance on it."

"I can check with the sheriff to make sure," he said. "But I should have received a notification. The county engineers are required to notify me whenever the county does anything to the levees around Mayim."

Lenaia rested a hand on the side of the excavator. "Okay, let's assume for argument's sake the county isn't doing this and someone else is. Why would they want to weaken the town's flood protection?"

He rubbed his chin. If the town flooded during the next set of rains, who would benefit? One name came to mind, but he couldn't believe the man would do it.

Lenaia gave him a sideways glance. "What are you thinking?"

"If Mayim flooded, it would cause problems for the town—especially for the crazy church and the homes near the river—but it would also cast doubt on me."

"How so?"

"Part of my job is to work with the county engineers to have proper flood protection in place, which includes the levee. If no one knew the levee had been sabotaged, then it could seem like the levee that I helped put in place didn't protect the town."

He watched understanding sweep over her face. "And Morgan Marshall wants you gone. But he said you were about to be fired anyway. Why would he need to do this?"

"Today, he was boasting, but he knows I have several supporters on the committee. He can't be sure how the vote will go tomorrow."

"But doing this to get rid of you seems kind of extreme."

"Maybe, but his house would be in the path of the flooding. At least, his in-town home. He's got another one, at his vineyard, near the north flank of the mountain."

"On second thought, maybe he wants the insurance money from his house." She tilted her head. "Why does Morgan want you gone anyway?"

"He says it's to save the town money."

"I know, but he seems to have made this personal. Why?"

Zayden felt his face flush in anger. "I don't know if it's true, but a friend told me Rachel had written about me in a flattering way in her diary."

"Did you have a relationship with her?"

He narrowed his eyes. How could she think so low of him? "Of course not. We were friends and she was married. Very sweet, but very married."

Lenaia glanced at the excavator again. She moved to the cab, running her hands along it, then pulled open the door and climbed into the driver's seat. He leaned against the door.

"No keys." She pointed to the front left corner of the dashboard. "Maybe we can track this serial number." She tugged her phone from her back pocket and typed the number in to her notes. After she finished, she jumped back down and walked over to him. "I'll talk with the sheriff and ask him to track this down."

"Let me know what you find out." The levee was his responsibility, but since the two acts of sabotage might be connected, he'd let her take the lead on this.

"Of course. So what were you doing out here?" Her voice held a hint of accusation.

"Running." She looked down at his jeans and then up at his polo shirt.

"You're not exactly wearing running clothes."

He opened his mouth, a sarcastic retort on his lips. The look in her eyes stilled his tongue. Beneath their amber surface, he saw trepidation. "I came here to blow off some steam."

She closed the distance between them. The apple scent of her shampoo drifted up from her hair. "For the record, I don't think you hurt Rachel. If I can do anything to help, please tell me."

If she could help? She could help by staying in Mayim this time. He took a step back. *Whoa.* He had no right going down that road. An hour ago, he'd begged her to leave for her own safety.

She brushed past him and started back down the trail. He watched her go, longing to go with her, but knowing he still needed to clear his head. He had no idea what might have changed in her life in the last five years. She looked and moved like the Lenaia he'd known, but deep in her eyes he sensed turbulence. She'd changed in ways he probably didn't understand.

~

Travis Perego stored the last piece of cleaned Pachycephalosaurus bone in the box that it had come in. He'd finished his microfossil work and, although cleaning bone wasn't the most glamorous job, he liked to help out so he could at least touch dinosaurs every day. Maybe he'd find his way back to teaching and research someday. In the past few months, he'd sent his resume to several Christian colleges, with no luck. His credentials most likely weren't the problem. The schools just didn't have any openings. With a heavy sigh, he reminded himself to pray and follow God's leading.

After hefting the specimen box onto one of the high shelves, he put his instruments away and washed his hands. He retrieved his cell phone from the counter and checked for any missed calls. None. Lenaia hadn't called in a couple of days. Not unusual for her, but still he worried.

He dialed her number and the phone rang three times before she picked up. "Hello."

"Hello, sweetie."

"Travis, hi." A loud yawn came through the speaker. "Forgive me. I'm tired."

He fumbled with the key to the front doors of the paleontology building. "Are you okay? It's barely eight o'clock out there."

"I'm fine. Just had a couple of draining days. What are you doing?"

He locked the building and headed across campus to his car. "I've finished up in the lab for the night and I'm headed home."

"It's ten o'clock there. Why are you working so late?"

He paused for a minute to stare out at the moonlit river. "I've adjusted my schedule a little. I feel more comfortable on campus after hours. That way, I don't run into my old colleagues." The ones who still laughed behind his back about his creationist beliefs and called him "Dino Detective" for exposing the dinosaur hoax last year.

"I understand."

A young couple sat on a bench, their bodies entwined as they kissed. He turned away, loneliness rushing over him. "With you gone, I don't have anything else to do, other than work. I miss you. Any chance you'll be done out there soon?"

"I don't think so. Some weird stuff is going on."

He continued down the path toward the parking lot. "Weird?"

"Somebody has sabotaged the tiltmeter twice, and I just discovered someone else, or maybe the same person, has dug out part of the levee close to town."

"So, possibly three acts of sabotage." He ran a hand through his hair. "I don't get it. Why would anyone do those things?"

"That's the part I can't understand. The tiltmeter and the levee incidents together seem like too much of a coincidence, but I don't know how they might be connected."

"Do you have any suspects?"

"I'm not sure. But you know what? I could look through the crazy file at CVO."

Travis climbed into his car. "What's CVO?"

"Cascades Volcano Observatory in Vancouver. Griffin said they have a skeleton crew right now because of the shutdown. If I call, they'll probably ignore the phone, but maybe if I show up I can get somebody to help me."

"Sounds great. I'm excited about anything that will get you home sooner."

Her laughter bubbled out of the phone, but it sounded forced. If only she was here, then he could put his arms around her and get a feel for how she was handling things.

"I miss you, too." Her voice held a sad note.

He tapped his thumb against the steering wheel. "Which is not quite the same thing as wanting to come home."

The line went quiet for a minute. When she spoke, he heard the weariness in her words. "At home, I think too much."

"About?"

Silence stretched over the line like a taut rubber band. He held his breath, hoping she'd break out of her shell and confide in him like she used to. She didn't speak for a long time. He opened his mouth to ask if she was still there when she finally whispered the words, "I think about how I can't seem to make a difference anymore."

It was what he'd expected her to say. She carried the weight of death on her shoulders and wouldn't let the burden go for anything. "You make a difference to me." His heart clenched. If only it would be enough.

"I'm glad you can still say that after I've been away so long. I do miss you when I'm gone. I just need some time to work through stuff."

"Sounds like you're avoiding stuff." As soon as the words came out, he desperately wanted to reel them back in. He had pushed her too hard—again.

"It just takes me longer to work through things." A muffled thump sounded in the background. "I'm sorry, somebody's at the door. I'll call you in a day or two."

"Okay." As she hung up, he let his forehead fall against the steering wheel. No goodbye. No promise to come home soon. "Yeah, sure, I'll just sit here and wait," he said to the empty car.

"I'M COMING." Lenaia hung up the phone and dragged herself off the bed. The weight of the last few days had worked its way into her muscles. She opened the door, then blinked in surprise.

Zayden leaned against the doorjamb, his head tilted, with a lock of dark hair brushing across his forehead. His onyx eyes swept over her, lingering on her legs, bare below the shorts she usually wore to bed. Shifting under the scrutiny, she took a step back. "What are you doing here?"

He swung his gaze up to meet hers. "Can we talk?"

She stepped back and pulled the door open as he walked into the room. "Sure."

Leaving the door ajar, she crossed to the four-post bed and sat stiffly on the corner.

He grabbed the chair from under the little desk, turned it around and sat backward, staring down at the pale peach carpet. "What did you want to talk about?"

Zayden leaned against the chair and picked at a loose thread on his jeans. "Did you find out anything about the excavator?"

"Not yet." She looked sideways at him. He could have asked her that tomorrow or just sent her a text. "What did you really come here to talk about?"

"Us."

Her mouth dropped open. Since she'd been back, he'd waffled between curious side glances and angry glares, even trying to get her to leave town. Not exactly indications that he was thinking about their previous relationship. "Zayden, there is no us anymore."

"Of course not." He fixed his eyes on hers. "But there used to be."

She looked down. He moved his head to capture her gaze again. She tried to stamp out the treacherous part of her that melted under his smoldering gaze. "I have a serious boyfriend."

"I know. For about a year, right?"

She stood and moved farther away to the head of the bed before sitting again. "How did you know that?"

"Pastor Doug told me. He and I have become friends in the last few years. Ever since I started going to church. I asked him how you were doing."

She still couldn't wrap her head around Zayden going to church. What else about him had changed?

He scooted the chair closer to the bed. "I also know you're having trouble committing to the relationship long-term."

She crossed her arms in front of her chest. "I can't believe he told you that."

"He didn't. I can see it in your eyes, a trapped, panicked look." He tapped the ring finger of his left hand. "And also in your bare finger."

She uncrossed her arms and pushed a strand of hair behind one ear. Leaning against the post on the bed, she worked to absorb this new image of Zayden. He and Pastor Doug were friends. He noticed things about her. Gone was the aloof, self-absorbed man she'd said goodbye to five years ago. But he was wrong. She didn't feel trapped with Travis. Not really. Sometimes she just needed some space.

"When you left, I thought for sure you'd come back. I mean before now." He let out a heavy sigh. "It never occurred to me that you'd be fine without me."

"I couldn't stay."

"You chose your job and your faith over us." He pushed off the chair, took one step, and then sat beside her on the bed. "I'm here to tell you that you made the right choice."

She clasped her hands on her lap and looked down. Ancient guilt burned a hole in her stomach. "I remember feeling selfish, leaving you for my job."

"And I convinced myself that you were selfish. That you only cared about your career. But I've realized, just today actually, how selfish I was to ask you to give it up."

"One of us would have had to."

He twisted his body to lean closer. "It could have been me."

She shook her head and glanced up. "It wouldn't have made a difference."

"I know. Back then, we were too far apart spiritually." He lifted his hand and placed his palm on her cheek. Electric tingles involuntarily raced down her spine. "But now?"

She opened her mouth, but nothing came out. Shifting a few

inches away, she cleared her throat and tried again. "I told you. I have a boyfriend."

"But no ring." He returned his hand to his lap. "I'm sorry. That sounds terrible, like I'm trying to steal you away. Although I guess I am, but I can't let you leave again without knowing how I feel. I'm ready to leave here with you, Lenaia. And not because I'm about to be fired. The feelings I have for you haven't changed in five years. I want us to be together."

She scooted away until she ran into the headboard. How many times had she wished Zayden would fully commit to Christ so they could fully commit to each other? Five years ago, it would have changed everything. But now, her heart wasn't free. She loved Travis. And even though she wasn't ready to get married yet, one day she would be, right?

Swallowing hard, she focused on his gray T-shirt. "Zayden, I won't try to deny the attraction between us. It's always been there, but I also can't do anything about it." She pictured the dimple in Travis's cheek winking at her when she delivered a humorous line of sarcasm or when she played with his nieces and nephews, and especially when he wanted to sneak a kiss. "I love Travis."

"I'm not asking you to do anything. I only want to tell you how I feel." He gently touched her arm. "Please, think about how you feel. You have a choice, Lenaia."

A choice? As if she wasn't drifting along, trying in vain to make sense of her life already. She didn't have any choices. None of them did. Stuff just happened, and she could only react. Every time she thought she was getting her life under control, the truth smacked her across the face. People followed their own agenda and so did God. But unlike Zayden's impromptu confession, God usually left her out of the loop.

CHAPTER 12

"*D*id you switch those two paintings?" Lenaia pointed to a wild picture of what looked like a dog and a color-blocked painting that didn't look like anything she could identify.

Pastor Doug placed a glass of water for her and a cup of coffee for him on the small table between them, then he sat and followed her gaze. "As a matter of fact, I moved them around last night. Interesting that you would notice."

"Not really. It's my job to notice things. Sort of necessary for a volcanologist, or at least one who wants to stay alive." Now that she thought about it, as a pastor, he was probably trained to pick up on details as well, except he tuned into people's faces or their demeanor.

He smiled at her. "Thanks for coming back today."

She shrugged and fidgeted with her water glass.

He took a sip of his coffee. "Did you come back just to make your boyfriend happy again?"

"Not exactly."

"Why, then?"

"I'm not completely sure, but I said I'd come and I don't like to quit."

He cocked his head and winked at her. "I always thought you were stubborn."

A bubble of laughter escaped her lips. The word stubborn probably wasn't strong enough.

"Is it so hard to come here and talk to me?"

She pushed down the image of her running out of the office last time and tried to focus. "You're actually pretty easy to talk to, but that doesn't mean this is easy."

"I understand. After twenty years of being a pastor, I've yet to find someone who doesn't squirm during a counseling session."

"I'll bet you've heard some pretty crazy stuff."

"Hmm. Just like I'll bet you've *seen* some pretty crazy stuff out on your volcanoes."

"Yes." Lenaia put down her water glass, instead picking up her cross key chain and playing with the beads dangling off the end. He was probing but staying true to his promise not to bring up Hawaii. Did she want to talk about it?

Usually, she would dump her feelings from a tragedy into a separate locked box and they would stay there until the sharp stab of sorrow and shame dulled. But maybe if she let a little bit out of the box, it would ease some of the pressure. Could she open a corner of the lid and let Pastor Doug peek in? But if she did, she might not be able to wrestle the lid back on.

Pastor Doug stared at her with open eyes, patiently waiting for her to decide what they would discuss. A few more seconds slipped away.

She dropped her hands into her lap. "The whole situation on Kilauea shouldn't have happened. They shouldn't have been anywhere near where the lava tubes ran."

Pastor Doug waited patiently for her to go on.

Lenaia looked up at the ceiling. "I keep going back and forth. I don't know whether God put me there to help the girl or if it's my fault they were there in the first place."

"What do you mean?"

"They knew me. I assume they came out to see me. Even though I was in the restricted area, they probably thought it was safe because I was there."

The phone on the desk buzzed, but Pastor Doug ignored it. "So you're trying to determine if it's your fault or God's?"

Lenaia focused on his wide eyes filled with sympathy. "I guess so."

He twisted his lips together before answering. "Does it have to be one or the other?"

She didn't know what to say to that.

"Dan's death, your uncle's death—both events violated your sense of justice." Pastor Doug put his coffee down and leaned forward to place both hands on his knees. "I don't blame you. We can't understand why some things happen here on earth. I know that sounds like a line of drivel that I pull out whenever someone gets angry at God—and I know you're angry—but it's true. Trying to understand will drive you crazy."

He could say that again, about fifty times over. She'd examined each event from every angle possible and couldn't make sense of it. Objectively, she could analyze senseless tragedy as random. But if everybody had an equal chance of experiencing it, why had she seen so much already?

Pastor Doug tapped her leg to get her attention. "I want you to think about one question. Does God owe you an explanation?"

Lenaia wrestled with that for a minute. The Bible said God was just. He would judge fairly. But where was the justice in burning to death in a river of lava? Or in being shot and dying alone? "I don't know if He owes me an explanation, but I want one."

"And if He gave you one, would it be enough?"

"Enough for what?"

Pastor Doug circled a finger and pointed it to the ceiling. "Enough for you to trust Him again."

Lenaia shifted in the chair. How much of her faith depended on what God did down here on earth? On the way He met *her* expectations? She blew a stray hair out of her face, unsure of why she was suddenly angry.

Pastor Doug leaned back in the chair and took on a posture of reflective listening. At least, he didn't push further.

The anger dissipated as she slammed the lid closed on her tragedy box. She couldn't talk anymore. "You've given me a lot to think about. I'm not sure if it helped to talk, but I'll consider what you said." As she stood, she remembered the other thing she wanted to ask him about—the note. She should probably leave the investigating to the sheriff, but curiosity always got the better of her. Pastor Doug knew everyone in town. If the strange phrase meant something to someone, he should know. "When we found Rachel, she had a note on her body, but it was cryptic."

She wrote it word for word on a pad from the desk.

The earth will punish them. NUM 16.

"Do you have any idea what this might mean? I wondered if the last three could be initials of someone in town, but I don't know about the numbers."

Pastor Doug tapped a finger on his lip as he read over the lines. "Maybe. Give me a second."

To her surprise, he grabbed a Bible and began thumbing through it. Was he going to pray over the answer?

A few minutes later, he snapped his fingers and pointed to the page. "Yep. The book of Numbers, chapter 16. It's the account of a group of Israelites who rose up to oppose Moses. To punish them, God opened the earth and swallowed them whole along with everything that had belonged to them."

"Weird. Rachel was laid on the ground but not buried."

Pastor Doug shrugged. "I can't think of anything else that it might refer to." He picked up the coffee cup and drained the last of it. "Would you like to meet again?"

She grabbed her backpack. "I'll be busy on the mountain tomorrow."

"Would it be all right if I call you later in the day tomorrow? Just to see how you're doing."

Lenaia paused by the door to answer. "That's fine, but you know how cell service is on the mountain. If I don't answer, then I'll try to get back to you when I can." She wasn't meaning to be dismissive, but her job once again gave her the perfect opportunity to avoid the issue. Her first priority had to be finding out who had sabotaged the tiltmeter, not dealing with her prickly emotions.

LENAIA SET the cruise control and let her mind zone out for the three-hour drive back to Mayim. As soon as she'd left Pastor Doug's house, she'd driven to Vancouver to spend the day at the Cascades Volcano Observatory office going through the crazy files. After four hours of combing through incident reports from the last year with her old boss, Sherry, Lenaia had four credible leads to bring to the sheriff.

Despite the success of the day, Lenaia had a hard time shaking off her anxiety. A sabotaged tiltmeter, a dug out levee, a phantom lava dome. None of it fit together. Like she was working on one of those puzzles with the holographic pieces. Every time she tried to fit in a piece, the angle changed and she couldn't make sense of it.

At least she had put some distance between her and Zayden for today. His confession had her heart reeling like ash blowing in the wind. She'd loved him once, but she wasn't anywhere close to the same girl who'd lived here before. Now she loved Travis. And the two men couldn't be more different from each other. Travis was warm and open, and a science nerd trapped in a perfume model's body, while Zayden was intense, his dark good looks hinting at depth and danger. She couldn't even compare the two.

And any comparison wouldn't be fair to Travis. He was her boyfriend.

Confusion sank deeper into her heart. She had no one she could go to for advice on men. Her mother hadn't participated much in Lenaia's life even before the suicide attempt that left her mother near catatonic.

Pastor Doug would tell her to pray and trust in God's plan. But often, she couldn't see any plan. Although she'd always naturally trusted God with her own life—there was no way she could work on volcanoes all day if she didn't—trusting Him was harder when it affected other people. Not only those she couldn't save, but also those she had to choose between.

By the time she reached the Wildflower Bed and Breakfast, it was way past dinnertime. She went inside to scrounge for leftovers and found a mini chicken pot pie in the fridge with her name on it. Marge was the best.

As she ate, weariness enveloped her. For tonight, all she wanted was a soft bed and a quick talk with Travis.

She put her plate in the dishwasher and ducked into the cozy front sitting room dotted with antique dolls and doilies. She lounged on a chaise and dialed the number.

"Hello?"

The sound of Travis's rich baritone eased some of her tension. A sudden urge to be wrapped in his strong arms hit her hard. She could almost smell the sea breeze scent of his cologne across the miles. But she shook off the sudden longing. It was her own fault they were so far apart. "Hi, sweetie. What are you up to?"

"Analyzing more microfossils. How about you?"

She slipped off her shoes and curled her feet underneath her legs. "I just made it back after a long day of looking for suspects."

"Any luck?"

"A few possibilities. Let's talk about something else if you don't mind. Something lighthearted."

"Okay, well I had an interesting thing happen today."

"What?"

"The professor who took my old teaching position, Dr. Oftman, had a funeral to attend and asked me to fill in for him. While I was giving a lecture on the extinction theories postulated for the dinosaurs, one of the students raised his hand and gave me his own theory involving aliens and atomic bombs."

She wrinkled her nose. "Was he serious?"

"Yep, he claims there's proof aliens visited past human cultures, so who can say if they visited the dinosaurs, too."

"Okay, that's weird enough, but what's with the atomic bombs?"

"Apparently, the aliens used bombs as a way of cleansing the earth of the dinosaurs to clear the way for humans."

She laughed. "Atomic radiation as a cleansing strategy. I've never heard that one before. What did you say?"

"I told him I liked his out-of-the-box thinking and to write me a paper giving his evidence."

She shook her head. "That's one of the reasons I love you. You never squelch ideas—even crazy ones." She could always count on Travis to listen with an open mind. Problem was, she didn't always open up.

When Travis spoke again, she heard hesitation in his voice. "And another interesting thing happened at the end of class. A female student stayed after to talk to me. She said she recognized me from the media coverage last year."

"Was she hitting on you?" Lenaia had gotten used to the way women reacted to Travis, like he was the shiniest gum ball in the machine. She didn't let it bother her because he never paid attention to them. Usually, he had no idea when a woman had more than his professional opinion in mind.

"Of course not. She just asked if I was teaching full-time now. Her father runs the science department at Bristol Christian College. When I told her I was only filling in, she said I should call her father if I wanted to teach again."

"Really? Are you going to call?"

"I'd like to. What do you think about it?"

She leaned her head back against the chaise. Would this mean a move for him? If so, they'd face the same dilemma she had years ago with Zayden. "Where is Bristol College?"

"Indianapolis."

"You want to leave North Carolina?"

"Not really, but I do want to teach. Filling in for Dr. Oftman today reminded me how much I miss it."

She took a slow breath. She wanted to support him, to encourage his dreams, but Indianapolis? She'd never considered herself a Midwest kind of woman. When she responded, she tried to keep the uncertainty out of her voice. "You should call."

"You think so?"

She mustered up as much enthusiasm as she could. "Definitely."

"They may not need anyone right now, but it could be a foot in the door."

"You have to try or you'll regret it." And she wouldn't be the reason Travis didn't pursue his dreams. So much for their light-hearted conversation. "Hey, sweetie, I'm exhausted. Will you call me tomorrow to let me know how the phone call goes?"

"Of course. Sleep well, gorgeous."

"I will. You, too." Her heart dropped a beat as she thought of him sleeping alone in his house. Would they share a bed someday or would circumstances pull them apart? He hadn't said he missed her this time, although she knew he did. She missed him too, wanted his arms around her, but more than that, she missed the way they had been when they'd first met. Carefree and full of the joy of just being with each other. The joy she'd felt before the weight of needless death began crushing her heart.

In the past year, Travis hadn't changed. He'd remained rock-solid. The future of their relationship depended on her.

CHAPTER 13

$\mathcal{A}$s Lenaia entered the stuffy interior of the visitor's center, her backpack sang out her ringtone, "My Lighthouse." She dropped the pack to the ground and dug out her cell phone. "Hello?"

"Lenaia, it's Pastor Doug."

"Hi. How are you?" Her voice sounded anxious to her ears. She'd said he could call, but mixing her emotional issues with work felt inappropriate. And she didn't have a clue if she should treat him like a pastor or like a counselor.

"I had a few moments and wanted to see how you're doing."

How was she doing? She had a saboteur to catch, an ex-boyfriend who wanted her back, and a killer in the area. "Um, things are still complicated."

"Can you explain or would you rather not?"

Really, she didn't want to discuss this now. Pastor Doug couldn't help with any of those things anyway. The silence dragged on as she floundered for something to say while she walked to the stairs. "I guess talking about my uncle hit me harder than I thought it would."

"I can see why you'd feel that way, but actually, a reaction like that means you should get some of those feelings out. You know, before they boil over and make a mess."

"Now you sound like my boss." And Travis, too.

"Do you think God wants you to just suck it up and carry on?"

That stopped her in her tracks, with one foot on the first stair to the upper level. It was *exactly* what she thought God wanted. The good Christian soldier who could label everything God's will and never falter, never question, never want to throw the Bible across the room.

"Have you thought more about your uncle since we met?"

She gave a slow nod, even though Pastor Doug couldn't see her over the phone. "I keep coming back to one question. Why?" As she said the word, it resonated on a deep level, vibrating within her soul until a jagged fragment of regret shook loose. When Uncle Jim was shot, she was unconscious. God made sure she couldn't do anything about it. Why would He keep her from helping?

"Protecting your uncle sounds like God's responsibility to me. It wasn't your job to save him." A moment of silence came over the line before Pastor Doug followed up with, "And it wasn't your job to make him believe."

A burning spike of anger seared through Lenaia's abdomen as she remembered Pastor Doug's words from the last time they'd met. *Does God owe you an explanation?* It seemed she would stay stuck on this forever. "So there isn't any why?" Somehow that made things worse. If there wasn't a why then God wasn't in control of this crazy universe.

"If you mean is there any more you could have done, the answer is no."

"I mean, why didn't God let me help him? The Bible says it's God's will that everyone believe in Him. It also says if we pray for anything according to His will, then He grants it. Of all the people in my life, I prayed for Uncle Jim the most. He didn't have anyone except me. Why didn't I get more time with him?"

"I wish I could answer the why for you. Truth is, God put us here to participate in His plan, but it's still *His* plan, Lenaia."

"Then, I guess I've got some issues with the plan." She took the stairs two at a time. This wasn't getting her anywhere. "I'm sorry. I've got to get back to work."

"I understand. I'm glad we could talk. I'll pray for you, Lenaia."

Why bother? The blasphemous thought shocked her. Her heart was drifting on an ocean of doubt, far away from the only land in site, but she didn't have the desire or energy to make it back to shore.

Flipping her arm back, she slipped the phone into the mesh side pocket of her pack and finished climbing the stairs. At the top, she took a steadying breath and headed for the office.

Huddled over his computer in the back, Griffin almost ignored her. When he finally looked up, his face was drawn and tired. Or maybe his eyes were squinted from too much screen time.

"For somebody who's working for free, you're here all the time." She said it with a smile, but she wanted an answer. Either Griffin was the most dedicated employee on the planet or he had something else going on.

He stood and stretched from side to side. "I'm working on a report, plus I've spent all morning fielding calls about the earthquakes we had last night."

She'd spent all morning interviewing suspects on her crazy list because the sheriff didn't have the time, but she wouldn't try to keep score with Griffin. "We had earthquakes?"

His mouth turned into a thin line. "According to the seismic station on the northwest side we did. Only a 3.1 on the Richter scale. If you were sleeping, you'd probably miss it, but I guess some people around here have insomnia."

"Centered under the mountain?"

"Of course. You know what it's like. Mountains get little earthquakes all the time and the locals freak out. They call, and then I have to explain about how the mountain shifts and it doesn't mean an eruption is imminent."

Except they didn't know that for sure. "What report are you working on?"

He put his hands up in mock surrender. "You caught me. I'm still analyzing the data sent from the STAR tiltmeter before it went down."

"Great. If it turns out there's a lava dome, we will need the information. But why haven't you told Sherry you're working on that?"

He stared at her, a faint challenge in his eyes. "How do you know I haven't?"

"I visited CVO yesterday."

His bravado deflated. "I wanted to be the first to work out the specifics of the lava dome, if there is one. It's hard as a young geologist to make a name for yourself."

That would explain why he worked at the computer all the time and his guarded manner. Then again, maybe he was guarded because of his past. She'd also probably hide out in the office if everyone in town knew the most painful events in her life. Perhaps she and Griffin had more in common than she thought.

At least, he hadn't gotten defensive and angry with her. "Look, I don't want any part in the discovery of a lava dome. I'm here to figure out what's happening to the equipment. That's my only goal."

His eyes went wide. "I appreciate that."

"No problem." She leaned against the desk. "Did you get a chance to see if the tiltmeter is salvageable?"

"Yeah. It's not. I'll order another one today."

"Any clues left by whoever sabotaged it?"

He gave a heavy sigh. "Nope. They didn't leave anything behind except a broken machine."

"Too bad." She tapped a finger on her lip, then remembered the other thought she'd had last night before bed. "Can you check on the lahar sensors along the Puyallup Valley for me?"

"Sure, but why?" Griffin moved back to the computer. Still standing, he punched in his password.

"Zayden thinks there might be a problem with the levee and I want to make sure nothing is wrong with the flood warning system."

"If there was, it would be the county who'd know. I'll check their website." He typed on the keyboard, his eyes scanning the screen. After a few minutes, he shook his head and looked up at her. "No reports of problems."

She breathed a sigh of relief. "Thanks. At least, I don't have to worry about that right now."

Griffin logged out and leaned a hip against his desk. He slipped his hands in his pockets. "You shouldn't have to worry about anything else. I can take everything we've discovered to the sheriff, and then you can head home."

"I've already spoken to the sheriff."

Griffin's posture went rigid. "Why would you do that without me? This is my mountain."

She resisted the urge to shake her head. Could Griffin be any more arrogant? He didn't own the mountain. "I needed to talk to him about the excavator, so I filled him in on the suspects I found for the sabotage."

Griffin took his hands out of his pockets and crossed his arms while continuing to stare at her through narrowed eyes. "What did he say?"

"That he's still buried in a murder investigation. He said nobody has died because of the sabotage and if we can't prove imminent danger, then we're last on his list." He'd also told her the excavator Zayden had found was stolen, but Griffin didn't need to worry about that. She straightened to her full height, just a few inches shorter than him. "Why does this bother you so much?"

He dropped his arms. "Sorry. I already feel like Sherry doesn't trust me to do my job because she brought you in, and now you're taking over everything and I won't get a chance to prove her wrong."

She let her shoulders relax. Maybe she should ease up on him. His ambition reminded her of herself five years ago. "Look, I'm not here to make you look bad, but I need to do my job. Let's work together, okay?"

He nodded.

"The sheriff also said since the park is government property and the equipment is too, the feds may want to handle the investigation. He told me to bring him proof of the damage and he'll contact them."

Griffin met her gaze, his hazel eyes steely and determined. Maybe he finally understood this wasn't about him. "Okay, I can send the sheriff a copy of the camera footage. I won't be able to get the broken tiltmeter down off the mountain without a helicopter, though."

"Fine." She held up the four suspicious reports. "Since the sheriff is too busy, I've been checking into these complaints from CVO." She grabbed a red pen from his desk and put a check mark on two of the pages. "These, I think I've ruled out." One was a man who had moved out of the area last year and the other was a woman who still lived in Orting and hated the government because her administrative job at the USGS was downsized. Neither of them had any intimate knowledge of the mountain or even any idea of what a tiltmeter did. Only two suspects remained, Morgan Marshall—the grieving husband and the man who had accused Zayden of murder—and an old man with wild, unkempt hair who lived on the mountain. The report said the mountain man ranted about institutions in general, religious, government, and even private companies, as the work of the Devil. She believed in the Devil, but wasn't so sure she wanted to be the one to judge who was in his employ. "This one." She held up the sheet for the old man on the mountain. "The report doesn't mention a name, but I figure it has to be Crusty."

"Do you think he might be involved?"

"I don't know. He acts strange, but he is a hermit. Not exactly a normal lifestyle. I'll visit him today." She flipped over to the last report. "Then, I've got one more person to visit tomorrow. For this one, I need you to come with me."

"Sure. Why?"

She waited a beat until he met her gaze, wanting to gauge his reaction. "Because the report mentions you specifically."

Griffin didn't even blink. "It must be Morgan. We've had our issues."

Really? Because you're always such a sweet guy to deal with. The sarcastic words were on the edge of her tongue, but she pulled them back in the nick of time. "Tomorrow we'll go talk to him and see if his issues might have led to sabotage."

LENAIA WEAVED through tall pine trees on Emerald Ridge, treading on the soft carpet of needles that rotted on the ground. The cool mountain air helped to clear her head. As a volcanologist, she had plenty of experience with analyzing situations and determining the root cause of a problem, but that usually involved a mountain, not people. Interviewing suspects was completely outside her comfort zone.

Over the crest of a hill, she spied the massive rock that made up the back side of Crusty's house. She circled around the stacked wood walls to the tarp at the front door. "Hello?"

No movement and no answer. She stepped closer. "Anyone in there?"

The silence was broken solely by the chatter of birds.

She pushed open the corner of the tarp. The space was mostly empty. A long table sat along one wall, a bench that looked like it doubled as a bed rested against the other, and a circular hook stuck out of a square cutout at the far end of the floor. For food storage maybe?

"Hello, Lenaia."

She spun around to see Crusty standing a few feet away with a load of sticks in his arms.

She let the tarp flap close. "I was looking for you."

"Why?"

The weathered face, threadbare jeans and dirty, gray sweatshirt gave him a beaten-down look, but his sharp hazel eyes said otherwise. Could he have put on a dark hooded coat to sabotage the tiltmeter? Did he even own a coat? "I need to talk to you about the STAR tiltmeter."

"Yes, you were looking for it the last time you came through here." He pointed to the north. "Haven't you found it yet? It's over there."

His words hinted at sarcasm, but she couldn't discern his tone. She studied his face. "Someone tampered with it."

He wrinkled his nose, then moved to the side of the house and dropped the load of firewood. "Who would do that?"

"That's what I'm trying to figure out."

Crusty came back to face her. He was a few inches taller than her but much too skinny to overpower her. "And you think *I* had something to do with this?"

She'd better put him at ease before she tried to probe into what he'd done or what he might know. "I'll be honest. I'm not ruling anything out at this point, but I didn't come up here to accuse you. I came to see if you've seen or heard anything suspicious."

He backed up a few steps before walking around in a circle. It reminded her of Travis's pacing, but Crusty's tight circles were nauseating. He kept his head down, speaking to the ground. "A couple of nights ago, I couldn't sleep. I was getting some fresh air on the ridge when I saw a light in the distance. Whoever it was went down the cleaver to the Wonderland Trail."

"To the southwest? Or did they come around Emerald Ridge and go directly south?"

"The southwest."

She tapped her finger on her chin. "Isn't one of the campgrounds down there?"

He stopped pacing and stared at her. "The South Puyallup Campground."

If it was the saboteur, maybe they'd left a vehicle at the campground. She focused on his eyes. "Do you have any idea who might do this?"

He bent his head again and shifted the pine needle carpet with his foot. "Could have been anyone. I couldn't see in the dark."

"So, you haven't seen anyone else up there in the daylight?"

"Just the usual park personnel and you."

Why wouldn't he look at her? And only a well-educated person would use a word like personnel. What had Crusty done before becoming a hermit?

He cleared one circle of pine needles, then started another with his other foot. His nervous behavior said he knew more, but didn't want to tell her. "By the way, you know my name, but I don't know yours."

His gaze flew up to hers. The corner of his mouth twitched. "You can call me Wally."

"Is that your real name?"

He smiled, revealing surprisingly white teeth. "Sort of."

She didn't smile back. "How did you know *my* name?"

He shrugged. "When you worked here before, I asked some of the park rangers."

"Why?"

"This is my home. I like to know who is walking through it."

She crossed her arms over her chest. "Why did you come to live up here, Wally?"

"Let's just say, I didn't trust myself to be around other people anymore."

She shuddered and took a step backward. "Meaning you hurt someone?"

Wally turned his body away from her until she could only see his profile. "More like I couldn't help someone."

His words, an echo of her own, sent a shiver of fear through her. She waited to see if he'd explain more.

As she watched, his expression changed from a painful longing to a forced detachment. He angled his body back toward her. "Too many times, people think leaving something in the past means you forget. I wish it were true. I want to forget."

"Forget what?"

Wally stooped to pick up the fire wood.

The thought of what he might have done concerned her. Apparently, it was bad enough that he wouldn't discuss it. Maybe the sheriff would know. "Thanks for the information. If you notice anything else happening out here, come find me."

She began the hike down the ridge toward the trail. Crusty— Wally hadn't told her everything he knew. She was certain of it. And yet, that didn't mean he had anything to do with the sabotage. He didn't seem aggressive. Even so, she couldn't ignore his proximity to the monitoring station.

She remembered the poisoned trees. Could he be passive-aggressive? Maybe he preferred to use sabotage rather than confront a problem. Wally definitely needed to stay on the suspect list.

LENAIA LEFT her backpack by the door and walked into the dining room of the bed and breakfast. A solitary couple was finishing their meal. The place seemed too quiet. Marge was usually hustling around filling drinks and chatting.

She walked through the dining room and into the kitchen. Pastor Doug stood at the sink, elbow deep in suds, cleaning a large pan.

"Pastor, what are you doing here?"

He flipped off the faucet. "Marge had a little accident."

"Oh, no. What happened?"

"She tripped over the vacuum cleaner cord and fell." Lenaia gasped, but he put a hand up. "She's fine, but she hurt her back and fractured her tibia. They're keeping her at the county hospital for tonight. She lay on the floor for a few hours because of her back before anyone found her, so I think they want to make sure she doesn't have any blood clots."

"Do you think she'd mind if I went to see her?"

"I'm sure she'd love to see you."

Lenaia glanced down at the stack of dirty dinner plates. "Do you need help here before I go?"

"No, Carol made dinner and afterward I sent her home to check on Scott. I'll clean up. You go."

"Thanks." Lenaia ran out to her car. The hour drive to the nearest hospital seemed to drag on. Her heart pinched as she imagined Marge laying on the floor by herself, praying someone would find her, while everyone else went about their day of traveling and sightseeing.

At the hospital, Lenaia found a parking spot and went inside where the smell of alcohol and antibiotic cleaner overwhelmed her nose. A quick question at the information desk, and a volunteer directed her toward Marge's room.

The door stood open a few feet. She knocked and walked in. "Marge?"

She was surprised to see Marge sitting up, alert and looking as if nothing had happened. "Lenaia, how nice of you to come see me."

"I wanted to make sure you were okay." A shadow in the corner caused Lenaia to turn to her right. Marge wasn't alone. "Randy?"

Randy smiled at what must have been confusion written all over Lenaia's face. "We've been keeping our relationship quiet, for privacy. We haven't been dating long and the rumor mill is always looking for new victims."

Lenaia smiled back at him. From what she knew of Randy, the two would make an interesting couple, like Martha Stewart meets Survivor Man. She could understand why they wouldn't want the whole town judging them. Lenaia wagged a finger at him. "I hope you're not dating her just for her cooking."

Randy chuckled as he moved to Marge's bedside. "No, but her sweet potato pie definitely sweetens the deal."

Lenaia stepped to the other side and patted Marge's arm. "For the record, I think you two make a good couple."

"I appreciate that."

"How are you feeling?"

Marge pulled the blanket off her left side to reveal a white cast. "I'll have to learn how to get around on crutches, but I'm fine."

"How are you going to run the bed and breakfast on crutches?"

"I can still cook, but I'll probably have to hire a maid for a while."

She grabbed Marge's hand. "I'm so sorry I wasn't there."

"Oh, honey. This isn't your fault. No harm done." She grimaced. "Okay, a broken leg is a little harm, but I'm fine."

"Actually, I'm glad you came." Randy took a step toward her. "I'd like to talk shop if you have a minute."

Marge shook her head. "A small-town man with a big-city work ethic. Go ahead; go to the waiting room to talk." She picked up a paperback novel from the tray next to her. "I'll get some reading done."

Lenaia and Randy walked down the hall to the nearest waiting room. Two other people sat in one corner, so Randy moved to the opposite corner and sat. Lenaia sat next to him, stiff in the high-backed chair.

"I wanted to talk to you about the sabotage." Randy kept his voice low. "Have you found any leads?"

"A few." She tilted her head and squinted at him. "Why? Have you found something?"

Randy shifted his eyes to the others in the room, and then back to her. "Maybe, but I'm not sure."

"If you know something, you've got to tell me."

He took a deep breath. "I just told you how I feel about people spreading rumors. I don't have any hard information, just suspicions. When I have proof of anything, you'll be the first to know."

She examined him closely. The hard set of his jaw told her she wouldn't get any more from him. "I can respect that. What are you asking of me then?"

"To be kept in the loop. Tell me where you are with the investigation."

She considered keeping the details to herself, but the sheriff had basically bowed out, and she couldn't afford to turn down help. Maybe if she gave Randy some information, he'd open up and share with her.

Quickly, she gave him the details of the sabotage, then explained about the four suspects and her progress investigating them.

When she finished, Randy rubbed at his goatee, the dark brown whiskers speckled with gray. "Okay. I'll check out my theory tomorrow and let you know what I find."

"Are you sure you can't tell me anything now?" she pleaded.

Randy thought for a minute, then shook his head. "No. I've got to make sure on this one. The one thing I can tell you is I don't think Wally is involved."

"Why not?"

"He's been up there for years. As far as I know, he just wants to be left alone. Why would he start something now?"

"Good point." Lenaia bit her lip in frustration. Randy wanted her to dismiss Wally but refused to share any more information. She had no leverage to make him talk, so whatever Randy was hiding would stay hidden until he was ready to share it.

CHAPTER 14

Lenaia caught sight of the green address sign at the last second and turned, kicking up gravel on the driveway and leaving a cloud of dust behind her. Morgan Marshall hadn't been at his house in town so she and Griffin were checking his second home at the winery.

The driveway meandered for a hundred yards past rows and rows of vineyards with wooden trellises, before ending in a circular turn around. She parked at the apex of the circle near the door to the pristine ranch house.

Wally's tip about someone walking down to the campground hadn't amounted to anything. Griffin had checked the campground cameras and no vehicles had parked there the night of the sabotage. So Morgan Marshall was next on their list to investigate.

Griffin shifted in the seat beside her, his eyes glued to the complaint report. He hadn't been the best of company, but at least he'd agreed to come. Assessing Morgan's reaction to Griffin would give her an idea of how serious the complaint was. He handed her the papers, and she searched his face. No sign that he was worried about being mentioned in the report.

The sheet in her hand stated that an unknown person had told the Cascades Volcano Observatory that Morgan Marshall made inflammatory remarks against Griffin Wall. Morgan called the geologist a "waste of taxpayer's money and a drain on the oxygen reserves of the planet." Nothing that would get him arrested, but perhaps Mr. Marshall had enough anger left for sabotage.

She folded the report in half, got out, and walked a few paces down the driveway, away from the house. The grove of trees next to the culvert struck a familiar chord. She glanced back at the house, then at the trees again. Of course, this was the property she'd seen on the news, where Morgan had pleaded for the city to go out searching for his wife. She'd have to tread carefully here to avoid being insensitive to what Morgan was going through.

A screen door slammed shut behind her with a thwack.

"Can I help you?" Morgan stood, framed by the doorway. His spotless jeans, dress shirt and perfectly groomed hair seemed out of place for a farmer, but not for a council member.

Morgan focused on her and a broad smile stretched across his face. Then, his eyes found Griffin and the smile fell. The subtle lift of the man's head told her he knew this wouldn't be a casual visit.

Morgan crossed the porch and gingerly descended the steps, putting two feet on each one. "Forgive my awkward gait. My sciatic nerve flares up every once in a while." He said sciatic with too much emphasis on the 'a.'

As he drew closer, she moved to meet him. He stood several inches taller than her, over six feet, and looked younger than she'd first thought, probably in his later thirties. He carried himself erect, sweeping his eyes from her to the driveway. Had he been expecting someone before they came?

"Who might you be?"

At least, he didn't seem to recognize her from when she'd stood next to Zayden as Morgan accused him. She stuck out her hand. "I'm Lenaia Talavera. And this is Griffin Wall."

Morgan answered without a glance at Griffin. "Him, I know."

He took her hand in both of his. "What a beautiful name. It just rolls off the tongue."

She pulled her hand back. This guy was a classic politician. "Thank you. I'm a volcanologist, working on an assignment for the USGS, and I have a few questions for you." She lowered her head, but kept her gaze fixed on him. "But first, please let me say how sorry I am for your loss."

"Thank you." He swept a hand toward the house. "That's why I'm out here. Too many people have come to my house in town to give condolences. I just need time to grieve."

"Of course."

He scanned her from head to toe with an expression she couldn't read. "I'm sorry about my manners. Please, come in." He took a step back. "What kind of questions would a volcanologist have for me?"

She took in the house, an ordinary ranch style with cream-colored wood siding and burgundy shutters. Perfectly normal for the area, and yet an uneasy feeling settled over her. She pointed at some chairs set up on the porch. "It's a beautiful day. Why don't we talk out here?"

Morgan dropped his arm. "Whatever makes you comfortable."

He waited for her to go up the steps first before he followed slowly. She sat in a white wicker chair at the end, placing the folded report on the ground next to her. Griffin stood on the top step and leaned against the railing, feigning a lack of interest. She'd asked him to let her do the talking and for once he hadn't argued.

"Mr. Marshall—"

"Please, call me Morgan." He gave her a smile and stomped a foot on the porch, causing a wooden board to vibrate. "Now, I'm being rude again. Can I get you something to drink? Lemonade, maybe?"

"No, thank you. I'm here because I understand you've had some issues with park staff in the past."

Morgan ran his thumb along his bottom lip. "Not park staff exactly." He glanced at Griffin. "The USGS aren't employed by the park."

"Yes, sir. You are correct. Can you tell me what problem you've had with USGS personnel?"

"Like many people around here, hunting is one of my passions. So, I have a problem with someone telling me not to carry a weapon when that man doesn't know an elk from a snowshoe rabbit."

Griffin opened his mouth, then clamped it shut after a warning glare from her.

"Hunting in the park is illegal, sir."

"I know that, but it's a ridiculous rule. The animals on Mt. Rainier will just run somewhere outside of the park and I'll kill them. It's not like they know Mt. Rainier is a safe zone."

She turned to face him a little more. "I think the rule is not so much for the animal's safety as for the safety of other park guests."

Morgan lifted his chin. "See, Griffin should explain things like you do. I should talk to Sherry and ask her to replace him with you."

Morgan's not so subtle flirting and his jabs at Griffin unnerved her. Was he simply the type of man who enjoyed conflict or was he trying to distract them from asking more questions? "So you and Griffin argued about hunting, then?"

"Not exactly. Like I said, we argued about my gun." Morgan put his palms up. "I wasn't hunting with it. I carry it for protection. He didn't believe me and said he would report me."

She glanced at Griffin. He stared out at the vineyard with his jaw clenched. Good. He was staying in control. She turned back to Morgan. "Are you still angry with him?"

"Of course, not." Morgan scooted his chair around until he faced her, putting his back to Griffin. "This occurred several months ago and we've reached an understanding. Why are you asking about this now? Is something happening on the mountain?"

She ignored the question to ask one of her own. "What kind of an understanding?"

"It's more of an agreement to live and let live. We all stress too much about the little things in life." He turned his eyes down. "My wife used to say that."

"I'm sure you miss her."

"Of course." Morgan rubbed his thumb along his bottom lip. "Such a sad event."

Event? It was an odd word for murder. She stared out at the greenery and wooden trellises of the winery. Rachel would likely have enjoyed the view. Did she think of this special place as she was dying? Probably not. Her thoughts would have been of her son. Lenaia thought about asking Morgan how the boy was adjusting but shook away the question. Her priority was the sabotage. As much as the man seemed to want to talk, she sensed Morgan might shut down if she delved too deeply into his family life.

Turning in her chair, she locked eyes with Morgan. He'd been staring. He might have also been wondering who killed his wife, but Lenaia wouldn't ask. That was a question for the sheriff. "When did you last go up on the mountain?"

"Hmm. I guess it's been a while. Rachel recently asked me to go up there with her, but I was too busy with council business."

Lenaia kept an even tone. "Do you have any reason to commit destructive acts on the mountain?"

Morgan's eyebrows dropped and his jaw tightened. "I knew there was something going on up there."

Griffin suddenly looked over at Morgan, and she felt the same excitement. Finally, they were getting somewhere. "How did you know?"

Morgan glanced from her to Griffin several times before

answering. "Rachel told me she saw a man digging in a meadow on the southeast side of the mountain. It seemed suspicious."

The southeast side. On the other side of the mountain from the STAR station. Her hopes dropped. She stood, eager to end her time with this confusing man. "Thank you for answering my questions."

Morgan also stood and captured her hands again. "A pleasure to meet such a lovely woman. I hope we meet again under more pleasant circumstances."

Where was the distraught man who'd wailed about losing his wife while pointing a finger at Zayden? Apparently, he thought nothing of charming other women mere days after his wife had died. She pulled her hand away. "Goodbye, Mr. Marshall."

Morgan looked over at Griffin, acknowledging him for the first time. "Bury the past, Griffin. What your mom and that crazy pastor did has made you stronger than most." His tone was almost affectionate. "Do what you must to show everyone how strong you are."

Turning on his heel, Morgan opened the screen door and went into the house. After the screen snapped shut, she faced Griffin. "Weird that he brought up your mom."

Griffin had a faraway look in his eyes. He blinked a few times, then focused on her. His eyebrows dipped into a scowl. "I don't want to talk about it."

He took the porch steps two at a time and strode toward the car.

Why had Morgan brought up Griffin's mom? There must have been something more to how she died. Under normal circumstance, she'd respect Griffin's privacy. But if Morgan felt it was important, and if he was the saboteur—admittedly quite a lot of ifs—then it could be related to the sabotage.

She walked down the steps and got in to the car next to a sullen Griffin. This trip hadn't helped at all. Now she had questions about both Morgan and Griffin. Much as she didn't care for

Morgan, she didn't have any evidence he was involved in the sabotage. She should probably rule him out, but their interaction had left her feeling like a bug under a magnifying glass. She didn't know what was up with him, but at least she had a good idea of where to get answers on Griffin. She had an appointment with Pastor Doug tomorrow.

TRAVIS TUGGED on the sides of his dress pants where they had stuck to his warm legs. On a warm, spring day like this, he'd normally wear shorts, but today felt like a formal occasion.

He wiped a bead of sweat off his brow and pulled open the door to Steppler's Jewelry Store. A nervous tremor ran through his stomach as he stepped inside. This was a decision that would change his life forever ... and Lenaia's too.

Although he knew Lenaia loved him, she'd been pulling away lately. Every time he wanted to talk seriously, she ran off to another part of the country and buried herself in work. He'd tried to give her time and space, but maybe that wasn't what she needed. Maybe she needed to know how strongly he felt about her.

A woman in a tailored skirt and blouse approached him. "Welcome to Steppler's. My name is Mary. May I help you, sir?"

Travis glanced around at the numerous polished display cases before answering. "Yes, I'm looking for a ring."

Mary nodded, her short dark hair bobbing forward. "Any particular occasion?"

"I'm sorry, I meant an engagement ring." He swept a hand through his hair.

"Our selection is right over here." Mary led the way to a counter in the back. She motioned for him to sit on a low cushioned chair in front of the glass, while she went behind the counter.

He sat with his knees doubled over, waiting, while she worked the lock on the glass case. When the key finally turned, she lifted the top of the case completely off. He peered inside to see row upon row of sparkling diamonds. The tremors in his stomach intensified. How would he choose the right one?

"Do you know what you're looking for in terms of cut and clarity?"

Thanks to the mineralogy course he'd taken during his geology undergraduate degree, he had an idea of what made a good diamond. He just wasn't sure what Lenaia would want. "Can I see something in the colorless to near colorless range with just a few inclusions?"

She smiled, apparently pleased with his knowledge. "Any particular cut?"

He paused for a moment. Maybe he should have asked Lenaia what kind of rings she liked. But then it would ruin the surprise. Only in the surprise could he gauge her uncensored, true feelings toward him. "I'm not sure what she prefers. Can I see some different ones?"

"Of course. Did you have a carat weight in mind?"

"Not really. My budget isn't huge, but I care more about how it looks than how big it is."

She pulled out several round, oval and princess cut rings and put them on a small shelf in front of him. He leaned over and one by one cradled each box in his hand. They all looked beautiful to him, but would Lenaia like any of them? He rubbed at his chin and gave the woman an awkward smile. "I'm not sure how to choose."

"Oh, wait. I have more."

She placed boxes with pear, emerald, and even a heart cut diamond on the shelf. He picked up each box, running his thumb over the shiny gems. If Lenaia said yes, she'd have to look at this ring for the rest of her life. He tried to ignore the big *if* at the beginning of that thought.

Tugging one ring free from the box, he pinched it between his thumb and forefinger. The shape of the ring didn't matter as much as what the ring stood for, right?

He glanced at Mary. "My girlfriend is a geologist. I think the emerald cut looks the most like a natural rock, so maybe she'd like this one. What do you think?"

"Emerald cut is always a solid choice. It's very traditional and conservative."

He inspected the diamond again, then glanced back at the saleswoman. "What if she hates it?"

The woman smiled kindly. "Keep your receipt. She can bring it back and exchange it for something else."

Travis blew out a breath. This was the biggest decision of his life. If he took this step, he didn't plan on ever going back. He was ready—in fact, he'd been ready for months. This was one way to find out if Lenaia felt the same way.

Lenaia pushed though the unlocked door of the visitor's center. Even though no one was allowed in the park due to the government shutdown, Griffin should be more careful with locking up. The air inside languished as still and stale as when she'd arrived here last week. Lenaia tried to imagine it the way she remembered, packed with visitors crowding over the displays of history and potential dangers of the mountain. She ran her fingers over a cross-section model of Mt. Rainier, lingering on the orange straw-like column of lava, leading from the mantle plume to the summit. What the model didn't show was any sort of lava dome. No bulge pushing and straining at the surrounding rock. Could there be one out there now? Maybe even close to the pressure needed to explode? Without data, she had no way to know.

She walked down the dark hallway to the computer room. The

door to the office stood slightly ajar. She grabbed the handle just as the door swung inward and stumbled along with it.

Zayden caught her around the waist, saving her from hitting the front desk. "Sorry. I was just leaving."

She looked up into his face. His eyebrows drooped and dark circles had formed under his eyes. He let her go. She stepped back to lean against the desk that she'd almost fallen onto. "Is everything okay?"

He gave a half frown. "You mean other than possibly losing my job?" His dark hair fell across his forehead as he looked down. "Or never seeing you again after you leave?"

All hope of a response escaped her. She loved Travis. And yet, the connection she'd always had with Zayden tugged at her at the worst possible times and a voice inside whispered about how he'd changed. But so what if Zayden was a different person now? She was too, and she wouldn't get caught up in the *what if* game of what might happen if her heart were free. "Why are you in the office?"

"I came to see Randy. He left me a weird message. Something about the old guy on the mountain."

Her mouth fell open. "He found something from the lead he was following and he's planning to tell you, not me?"

Zayden shrugged. "Randy and I are in a men's bible study at church. I guess he feels like he knows me better."

She bit her lip. "If he tells you anything about the sabotage, you need to tell me."

Zayden raised his eyebrows. "I *need* to tell you?"

She stuck her chin out. "Yes."

Smiling, he took a step closer. "Is it worth dinner?"

"You're bribing me?"

"If I have to."

She averted her gaze, focusing on the carpet. She remembered the first time he'd pursued her; full of passion and fervor. His persistence wasn't surprising, but this situation was different, and he was pushing too close to her personal boundary lines. "I can't go out on a date with you. I have a boyfriend."

He smiled as if he'd expected the argument. "Okay, how about this? Some night before you leave, we'll sit down to dinner and talk about everything honestly. That's not a date."

No, but it sounded just as dangerous as a date. Still, she'd like to leave on better terms this time. "Fine. Let me know when you find Randy."

He walked to the door, then turned back. Squinting, he tilted his head in her direction. "Why are *you* here?"

"Also looking for Randy. I was hoping to talk to him about our most recent suspect interview."

Zayden gave her a quizzical look.

"I have four suspects from a trip I took to CVO. One of them is the old man on the mountain, which is why you need to tell me what Randy says."

He grabbed the door handle. "I have bible study tonight. Maybe I'll see him there."

After he left, she took in a deep relaxing breath. Zayden at bible study was still a real mind bender. No doubt, he'd changed, but that didn't mean they had a future together. Maybe if they sat down and talked, Zayden would realize it as well.

She turned to go, but then turned back. Odd that Griffin wasn't here working. She'd dropped him off here a few hours ago and he'd said he had work to do. She should call him. Perhaps he was on the mountain.

While she was thinking about phones, she needed to call Sheriff Conklin to update him on her investigation. She threw her backpack onto the desk and rummaged through it for several minutes looking for her phone. It wasn't in there. Maybe she'd left it in the car.

She picked up the office phone instead and dialed the sheriff. The dispatcher patched her through and he answered in a low voice.

"Hi, Sheriff. It's Lenaia. I just wanted to keep you updated on the sabotage."

"Of course. Fill me in."

She spent ten minutes updating him on her interviews, spending most of the time on Morgan Marshall. The sheriff listened quietly. When she finished, he gave an amused snort. "That sounds like Morgan. He pushes people as far as he can."

Maybe there was more to it. "Does Morgan have any other connection to Griffin or his family?"

"Not that I'm aware of. Honestly though, Joni Wall's death hit everyone in this town hard."

She had to ask, but didn't want to sound like a gossip. "Any idea who the man was that caused Joni such guilt?"

"No. Joni left a note, but it didn't name any names. I don't think it would have anything to do with this anyway."

"You're probably right." She sat in one of the office chairs and propped her legs on the desk. "What about the old man on the mountain?"

"You are wise not to rule him out. He's never done anything to cause problems, but he's got to be a little crazy to live solitary like that."

She smiled. Sheriff Conklin didn't pull any punches and she appreciated his brutal honesty.

"Good investigative work. You know, I tried to call you a few minutes ago, but didn't get an answer on your cell phone."

"Yeah, I must have left it in the car. Did you have something to talk to me about?"

She heard a rustling sound.

"I'm holding a bag with a torn piece of an orange sweatshirt that was found in the back seat of the excavator. I think I know who it belongs to."

She remembered seeing the orange sweatshirt, but hadn't really looked at it.

"The tag has a University of Michigan logo."

Her stomach dropped. Zayden had attended university there. And in a small town like Mayim, there couldn't be too many people who went to school in Michigan.

"Did Zayden ever have a sweatshirt like that?"

She felt herself nodding, then quickly realized the sheriff couldn't see her. "I've seen him with one. You found it on the excavator?"

"Yes. Do you remember what he was wearing that day?"

She tried to remember. "I know he wore jeans and a polo. It was too warm for a sweatshirt. Maybe it's not his."

"Maybe not, but I've got to follow up on this."

"I understand." Her hand quivered on the phone. This was a mistake. Zayden wouldn't sabotage the levee he helped to build. Would he?

CHAPTER 15

 *L*enaia flopped into the chair across from Pastor Doug's messy desk. "I need to ask you about Griffin Wall."

He gave her an indulgent smile, but she caught the layer of tension hiding underneath. He didn't want to talk about this. Even so, she needed to know if something in Griffin's past would cause a person like Morgan to seek revenge. What better motive for sabotage than to make Griffin look incompetent and get him fired?

"Pastor, I'm not asking you to break a confidence. Just tell me what's common knowledge. If I were someone who'd lived in this community my whole life, what would I know about Griffin's past?"

His shoulders relaxed a little. "This is for your investigation."

"Yes, I think someone might want to hurt Griffin."

Pastor Doug ran a hand over his face. "I'm going to tell you because I know you're not a gossip. As you said, these things aren't secret, but I'm sure Griffin wouldn't want to discuss them."

"I understand."

Pastor Doug steepled his fingers together. "Griffin's parents, Art and Joni Wall, were members of Christ's Devoted Church."

Her eyebrows raised. The church led by Pastor Marty.

"I knew Art because he came to see me a few times on personal matters. He wasn't comfortable at Christ's Devoted, but his wife insisted they attend church there. Art figured having Griffin in any church was better than not, so he went along." Pastor Doug paused and took a deep breath. "Except this was one of those times when he should have put his foot down."

"What do you mean?"

"We've already talked about how Pastor Marty takes passages of the Bible out of context. Any time you misrepresent the Bible, you run the risk of causing a lot of pain. Pastor Marty preached a strict definition of the scriptures in Matthew 5, verses 28 and 29. Those verses say if your eye causes you to sin, better to gouge it out than let your whole body go to hell. And if your hand causes you to sin, cut it off and throw it away."

She crossed her legs and folded her hands in her lap. Where was he going with this?

"Pastor Marty taught his congregation to take the scriptures one by one and apply them literally to their lives. He honestly believed the scripture meant that if a part of you sinned, you should offer the offending body part as a sin offering to God."

She scrunched up her face. "What do you mean offer up the body part?"

Pastor Doug stared at her for a moment.

She caught his meaning. "Oh, my."

"Griffin's mom, Joni, died because of that teaching."

She almost didn't want to ask, but she had to know. "What happened?"

"Tragedy." He drummed his fingers on the table. "Joni touched a man in a lustful way. Then, after a heated sermon given by Pastor Marty on those verses, she tried to cut off her own arm. She didn't succeed, of course, but by the time the paramedics arrived she had lost too much blood."

Lenaia stared at him, stunned. How could Joni have believed

God would want her to mutilate herself? "It must have been horrible for Griffin."

"And for Art. He couldn't handle it. Just walked off, leaving everything behind, including Griffin. I never heard from him again."

"Effectively making Griffin an orphan. I can imagine he'd hoped and prayed for someone at church to adopt him so he could stay in his hometown and his school. It must have been hard for him to suffer such loss. He would have felt so alone."

Pastor Doug nodded. "But he was never alone. Just as you were never alone when your father died. God takes better care of us than our earthly fathers ever could."

Oh no. This was the part where Pastor Doug would bring up her trust issues, assuring her she could trust God even when He felt untrustworthy. It should be a comforting thought, but it wasn't.

Instead, Pastor Doug scratched at his beard like he was deep in thought. "I think you were right when you said Griffin was drawn back to this place. He needs to make peace with what happened."

She thought of Griffin's brooding attitude. He needed peace all right. At least now she understood why. And also why Morgan would throw Griffin's painful past in his face, except the comment hadn't seemed like a jab. It had seemed like encouragement. As if Morgan thought he was spurring Griffin on. But how far would Morgan go to push Griffin? Would he be willing to cause Griffin even more pain? Like jeopardizing Griffin's job?

CHAPTER 16

Zayden lay on the bench, staring up at the dirty, gray ceiling of the holding cell. The sheriff had promised a nicer cell later where he would spend the night. As if he would look forward to a cleaner version of captivity.

"Visitor," the deputy yelled back.

Zayden flipped his legs down and sat up. He could tell it was Lenaia from her steps—fast and purposeful, muffled by the rubber of her hiking boots.

She stopped in front of the cell door, the bars splitting her image. "They won't let me come in. Regulations or something."

"Of course not." His voice sounded sharper than he'd intended.

"Do you need anything?"

"Yeah, for the judge to do the bail hearing so I can get out of here."

"Sheriff Conklin said sometime tomorrow morning."

She leaned her forehead against the bars. Strands from her ponytail swung through. He longed to draw close to her, but he wouldn't. Not when she hadn't shown any interest in getting back together with him. All he could do now was hope she'd change her mind.

"What's going on, Zayden?"

His jaw clenched. She was questioning him. And why wouldn't she? They hadn't seen each other for five years and then he ended up in jail. "I wish I knew."

"How did your sweatshirt get in the back of the excavator?"

"I don't know. Several months ago, I lost it while hiking on the mountain."

"Which part of the mountain?"

"One of the Paradise trails near the visitor's center, I think." A bead of sweat rolled down his forehead. He swiped it away with the sleeve of his shirt. "What is this? You're grilling me like the sheriff."

"I'm just trying to understand."

He gripped the sides of the bench and hung his head. "Me, too."

"Do you think somebody put it in the excavator on purpose?"

"To frame me?" He blew out a breath. "I keep trying to come up with a less dramatic answer. Maybe someone picked it up after I lost it and by coincidence they stole an excavator while wearing it?" He glanced up at her, hoping she'd tell him it made perfect sense.

She sighed. "Hard to believe that's the less dramatic answer."

He stood and took a few steps toward her. From two feet away, he noticed faint worry lines around her eyes. Was he the cause of her worry?

She lifted her head off the bars. "Did you find Randy?"

"No. I couldn't reach him on his cell. His message said he was going up the mountain."

"Could he have gone to see the old man up there?" she asked.

"I suppose."

"I'll go look for him tomorrow. Maybe he found some answers. Speaking of cell phones, I can't seem to find mine. You don't remember seeing it yesterday, do you?"

"No." Somehow it felt good to talk about something as

mundane as a cell phone. He reached out to tap one of the bars with his finger. "I can tell you it's not in here with me."

"I thought it was in the car, but it's not."

She tugged at the strands in her ponytail and shifted her feet. Why was she nervous? "Do you have something else to say?"

She swung her ponytail over her shoulder. "I have to ask. How angry are you at the town for trying to fire you?"

"No, you don't *have* to ask." He folded his arms across his chest. "But to answer your question, it stinks. I'm angry, but only at those who are spearheading this."

"Like Morgan Marshall?"

And then he understood. The buildings that would be hardest hit by flood waters if the levee failed were the wacky church and Morgan's house. Couple that with Rachel's death, and Morgan's insistence Zayden was involved, and the circumstantial evidence grew into a mountain.

"You think I'm involved in this." He slid his feet backward and sank down to the bench.

She stepped forward to grip the bars in tight fists. "I'm not saying that."

"And how far does it go, Lenaia? I suppose I sabotaged the geologic equipment, hoping they'd call you to come back? Maybe Randy was on to me and that's why he's disappeared also? Or is that not a part of your Zayden-is-responsible-for-everything theory?"

She let go of the bars and her shoulders slumped. "I'm not accusing you. I'm trying to figure out what's going on."

"Then figure out who else is doing this so I can get out of here." He crossed his arms over his chest and lay back down on the bench. He'd answered enough questions. It was time for her to get out there and find the truth. Right now, she was the only one who could.

LENAIA PACED in circles around Wally's shack. The place was dead silent. No Randy. No Wally.

She'd already stopped by the hospital. Marge had been expecting Randy to return to have lunch with her, but he hadn't come back. And Marge had confirmed, Randy still wasn't answering his phone. But she had found his green truck parked along the Westside Road, so he had to be somewhere on this vast mountain.

If Randy had come up here and couldn't find Wally, where else would he go? Perhaps to the tiltmeter to search for clues. It was worth a try. She turned northeast, hiking back to the Wonderland Trail. A few hours later, she came out of the tree line onto the Puyallup cleaver. She couldn't see St. Andrews Rock from here. The only way to know if anyone was up there was to climb.

The hike strained her legs, but at least her lungs handled the altitude better now. After another hour, she crested a small rise, giving her a view of the STAR observation station. No one up here either.

She looked down at the gray rock under her feet. A myriad of footprints swirled through the dust. She couldn't get a fix on which prints belonged to whom. They could be hers and Griffin's from their first trip. Or maybe the saboteur's.

She paced in a circle, from the face of St. Andrew's Rock as it rose above her and around to the edge of the path where it sloped down toward the Tahoma Glacier. On her second pass along the edge, a crumbled rock a few feet down the slope caught her attention. It had a large footprint in what remained of the crushed rock. Someone had gone off the path on the way to the glacier. Maybe Randy had come through here.

With careful sidesteps, she followed the prints downslope until she found another set of footprints, barely visible in the dust. They were smaller ones, although still bigger than hers. Two people had come this way.

She continued sidestepping down until she reached the

margin of the glacier. There, the clear footprints morphed into a jumble of disturbed dirt. She searched the dusty ground for a few minutes, then found the same two sets of footprints moving parallel to the glacier. The feet were spaced farther apart. Perhaps they were running.

She followed as the larger set stayed close to the glacier's margin. The other set swung wider. Then suddenly, both sets disappeared.

Although, the footprints didn't have the telltale tread of ice spikes, the only place they could have gone was onto the glacier.

She stopped and stared at the white expanse. Not far out, she saw a large area of torn up ice. Something gray and dull lay on the pale surface. She took a deep breath and stepped out onto the slippery ice. Sliding her feet one by one, she inched closer to the object.

When she was a few feet away, she recognized it as a park ranger's badge. Picking it up, she read the name. *Randy Turnbuckle.* Dread flooded through her stomach. He'd been out here running after someone or from someone.

Looking around, she searched the area for more signs of him. Nothing.

What could she do? She didn't have a phone to call anyone and Randy could be hurt waiting for help. But where?

She decided on a search path along a straight line from where she found the badge. Stretching her arms out for balance, she slid her feet over the ice, mimicking some sort of wounded bird. After about a hundred yards, she spied another dark object.

She shuffled her way over to pick up a hat with a National Park logo on it. It probably also belonged to Randy.

Where had he gone? She slid a few more feet and was about to take another step when an anomaly caught her eye. Instead of an unbroken sea of milky white ice, a gray stripe appeared. She pulled back, assessing the threat at the same time. Less than two feet away gaped the opening of a crevasse, a large crack, nearly invisible in the sea of slushy ice.

She wriggled out of her backpack, and then lowered down to lie on her stomach. Using her hands like flippers, she pushed against the ice and inched toward the open air of the crevasse.

As her eyes cleared the edge, she peered down. A strangled cry escaped from her mouth. The crevasse wasn't as deep as most, but it was deep enough. At the bottom, Randy lay unmoving. His salt and pepper hair was matted with a dark stain that flowed from his head like the tendrils of a red ink blot.

She thrust herself back from the edge, jumping away from the horror below, but her feet slipped. She spun backward and fell. Pain sliced through her skull, forcing her vision to a pinpoint, before it faded to a black haze.

TRAVIS HUSTLED DOWN THE SIDEWALK, dodging slow college students and holding his cell phone tight against his ear. "Lenaia, this is my fourth message and I'm starting to get worried. I know you get busy with work and you can't always get cell service, but not hearing from you is making me nervous, honey. Please, call me if you get this message."

He ended the call and shoved the phone in his back pocket. He'd gone days without hearing from Lenaia before, but this felt different, and not just because he'd thought about flying out there to surprise her. It was Sunday night and he'd last talked to Lenaia on Thursday, more than three days ago. She would want to know how the phone call to Bristol College went, but he hadn't been able to tell her.

He veered onto another sidewalk, the one that led to the river walk. He needed a brisk run in the evening air to clear his head. The whole day had gone by in a blur of keeping himself busy, trying not to think about why she hadn't called.

Frustration formed a solid rock in his gut. Nothing he could do now except wait for their boss, Jayna, to check things out through her contacts. For now, he needed to work out some nerves. He started at a light jog, letting his leg muscles stretch out the tension he'd built up since yesterday. He'd only gone a few miles when his phone vibrated in his arm band. He tapped the device to answer. "Jayna, what have you found?"

"Lenaia was seen on Thursday at the Cascades Volcano Observatory."

"But not over the weekend at all?"

"Not by anyone I talked to. With the government shutdown it's hard to get people on the phone out there. Have you tried the sheriff?"

"Every time I call, I get a recording."

Jayna's tone was smooth. "Okay. Is there anyone else out there we could contact?" She was trying to soothe him, but it wasn't working.

"Lenaia went to a counselor a couple of times. A pastor, I think. But I don't know his name. I'll see if I can look it up and give you a call back."

He ended the call, then pulled up the internet browser on his phone. Two churches in town and only one of them had a pastor whose name sounded familiar. He located the number and held his breath as he waited for an answer. Voice mail picked up.

Ugh. Travis hung up without leaving a message. He called the sheriff's office again. Someone had to pick up eventually.

After six rings, a female voice answered. "Pierce County Sheriff's Office. May I help you?"

"Hi. My name is Travis Perego. I'm Lenaia Talavera's boyfriend and I'm having trouble reaching her."

"Oh, my. Well, I know the sheriff talked to her just the other day."

"When, exactly?"

"Hold on a minute. I'll ask him."

Before he could agree, easy-listening music came over the line. Thankfully, he didn't have to wait long.

"This is Sheriff Conklin. Who's this?"

"Sheriff, I'm Travis Perego, Lenaia's boyfriend. I'd like to know the last time you spoke with her."

"We talked on the phone yesterday."

Travis frowned. Yesterday? Why hadn't she called then? "Was she on her way somewhere?"

"She was in the middle of interviewing people about the sabotage."

"*She* was doing that. Isn't that a job for your office?"

"I've been involved in a death investigation. One of our local women was murdered."

Travis held the phone tighter. "Murdered? Lenaia hadn't told me that."

"We still have a missing woman so solving this case takes priority for me."

"Should I be worried?"

"I'm sure Lenaia is fine. She's probably just busy on the mountain. If I hear from her, I'll tell her to contact you."

Travis's legs felt weak. He ran a hand through his hair. "Thank you. I appreciate your help."

Travis bent over and put his head between his knees. There was a killer in that town. Lenaia could be in real trouble and he had no way of knowing. What if she was hurt, crying out for him to come help her? Or trapped somewhere at the mercy of a sadistic monster, waiting for rescue?

Dear Lord, help me to know what to do here. Does she need me or am I freaking out for nothing?

He straightened, tapped his phone, and selected Jayna's number. Although, he wanted to think positively, to assume she was fine, he couldn't shake the sense of dread draping over him like an ominous cloud. A killer could have her in his grasp right now and Travis couldn't just wait on the other side of the country to find out.

After two rings, Jayna picked up. "Did you find out anything?"

"Yes and I'm afraid it's not good." He explained what the sheriff had told him.

Jayna blew out a breath. "I called the bed and breakfast where she's staying. The person who answered said the owner is in the hospital and they didn't know if Lenaia has been around."

Travis turned and began to walk back toward his car. "I just have this feeling I need to get to her."

Jayna went silent for a minute. When she answered, her voice sounded concerned but determined. "Okay, the microfossil project can wait. Go find her."

CHAPTER 17

Zayden stared around the courtroom in disbelief. This wasn't the way he wanted to spend a Monday morning. How did he get here? Two weeks ago, life had chugged along with little to no excitement. Now his job was on the line and he could be facing jail time for a crime he didn't commit.

The judge paraded down the aisle in a robe too big for his lanky frame. He stepped up to sit behind the wooden platform, and folded his hands in front.

"You may be seated," the bailiff called out.

Judge Cunningham, a middle-aged former lawyer, leaned forward in his seat, eyed Zayden up and down, and then looked at the sheriff. "You may read the charges."

"Yes, Your Honor. Zayden Planke is charged with theft of a farm machine, specifically an excavator, trespassing, and tampering with public property, specifically the Puyallup River levee outside of Mayim."

"And how does your client plead?" The judge turned his head toward Zayden and his lawyer, whose name Zayden had already forgotten.

The lawyer rose halfway out of his seat. "Not guilty, Your Honor." He sat back down.

"So noted," the judge said with a flat expression.

Sheriff Conklin stood and walked close to the bench, looking up at the judge. "Before you make a decision on bail, Your Honor, the prosecuting attorney asked me to read a brief statement from him."

The judge leaned back in his chair and narrowed his eyes. "If he wanted to make a statement, why isn't he here?"

"I believe he's in the middle of harvesting berries on his farm."

The judge picked up the gavel and swung it in a circle in the air. "Since this is only a bail hearing, I'll allow it, as long as it's brief."

What? The prosecutor didn't bother to show up, but he got to speak his piece. Zayden was fighting for his freedom and his lawyer had told him not to say a word. Where was the justice in that?

Sheriff Conklin pulled a folded piece of paper from his pocket and began to read. "Zayden Planke should be denied bail on the basis of strong circumstantial evidence."

Zayden stared at the sheriff in shock. Denied bail? The evidence to prove he'd stolen the excavator wasn't strong. No way was he going to rot in a cell for one more night. He turned to his lawyer. "You've got to be kidding me."

The lawyer put a finger to his lips.

Sheriff Conklin ran a hand over his spiked crew cut as he continued reading. "The theft of the excavator and attack on the levee was a premeditated effort to harm one person, Morgan Marshall, whose house would be flooded if the levee failed. Morgan had garnered enough support from the town to eliminate Zayden Planke's position as Evacuation Planning Coordinator." The sheriff cleared his throat. "This gives Zayden Planke motive to commit the acts he's accused of. In addition, Rachel Marshall was abducted and killed approximately one week ago. It's possible, Mr. Planke committed this crime as well. For these reasons, I believe bail should be denied until the extent of the crimes committed by Mr. Planke become clear."

All of Zayden's blood drained down to his toes. Now they thought he'd killed Rachel? This was getting out of hand.

"I don't know." The judge rubbed the gavel along his cheek. "It seems like a leap to go from theft to murder with only motive as evidence."

He let out a relieved breath. At least the judge had some common sense.

"However, I feel I need to consider all the information before rendering a decision. Expect my decision in a few hours. Court adjourned."

Judge Cunningham slammed his gavel down with gusto before standing to leave the courtroom.

Zayden sat in stunned silence. His head was spinning.

The sheriff walked over and stood in front of the table. Zayden glared up at him. "You know this is wrong."

Scowling, the sheriff grabbed Zayden's arm and pulled him out of the chair. "Those weren't my words. I'm obligated to assist the prosecuting attorney when he can't attend. I'm just doing my job."

Zayden didn't respond. He let the sheriff drag him out of the courtroom, moving his feet mechanically along the corridors, out to the sidewalk and back to the sheriff's station. Back to his cramped jail cell.

"I'M NOT CONVINCED your girlfriend is missing." Sheriff Conklin tapped a fast beat with the eraser on a pencil.

Travis tried not to glare at the man who sat on the other side of the desk. After having already checked the visitor's center and the bed and breakfast for Lenaia, his next stop had been the sheriff's office, but the frustrating man had only caused his tension to grow. He rubbed at a tight spot in his chest. "She's not answering her cell phone."

The sheriff poised his pencil over a yellow legal pad. "As far as I know she's still investigating the sabotage. She went to see Councilman Morgan Marshall about it on Saturday."

"Has anyone heard from her since?"

The sheriff's eyes narrowed beneath his closely trimmed eyebrows. "Why didn't she mention you?"

Travis held back a frustrated growl. Lenaia was a private person. She didn't have to work his name into every conversation. "Have you heard from her?"

Sheriff Conklin dropped the pencil and scratched at his day-old stubble. Then, he got up and left without a word.

Time crawled by at a snail's pace, but Travis resisted the urge to hit the intercom button and demand an explanation. He needed the sheriff's cooperation if he wanted to find Lenaia.

When the sheriff returned, he again sat at the desk and resumed tapping the pencil. No apology. In fact, for a full minute he merely stared at Travis with an unreadable expression. "My deputy saw her yesterday. She came to see Zayden Planke, who until an hour ago was in my holding cell."

"Who's Zayden Planke?"

"A friend of hers from when she used to live here." He drew out the word "friend."

"And by friend you mean ... ?"

Sheriff Conklin angled his head and lifted his brows. "They used to date."

"I see." Travis shifted in the seat. Now, she was spending time with an ex that she'd never mentioned. Who was this guy? He couldn't be a real winner if he'd been in jail. "What's this man's crime?"

The sheriff pressed his lips together before answering. "Zayden was charged with theft and destruction of property. Lenaia came to visit him because she thinks he's innocent."

"Where is Zayden now?"

"Likely at home. He was released on bail this morning." The sheriff flipped the pencil and scribbled something on the yellow pad, then ripped the sheet off at the middle. "To save you the trouble of looking it up in the phone book, here is Zayden's address. Maybe he can help you."

Travis took the paper. "I'm sure you can understand why I'm worried given what's been happening in the area." That was another question he couldn't answer. Why hadn't Lenaia told him about the murder? Probably because she didn't want him to worry. But couples were supposed to do that—share their problems and work things out, together. He loved her more than he'd ever thought he could love anyone. And yet, he couldn't be there for her if she wouldn't fully let him in. "I hope I don't sound callous for asking, but are you making any progress on the murder investigation?"

The sheriff leaned both elbows on the desk. "Not yet, but I will. It's my job to get justice for the folks living here." He dipped his head and twisted his lips. "And for the ones who die here too. Rachel Marshall worked as a secretary in this office before she got married. She was a great lady, and I'm going to find out what happened to her. Understand that I'm only meeting with you because I had my secretary check you out. You seem like a steady guy, but don't try to interfere with this investigation or you'll also end up in my jail cell."

Travis nodded. The background check explained the long wait from earlier. At least, the sheriff looked after his own and he seemed to consider Lenaia as one of his own.

"Don't worry too much. Lenaia knows how to take care of herself. She's probably with Zayden or with Griffin, the USGS coordinator, up on the mountain continuing her own investigation."

Travis's heart skipped a beat at the sheriff's assumption that Lenaia might be with her ex. Ever since he'd met her, he'd always admired Lenaia's independent nature. After all, who wanted a woman to cling to your side every moment of the day? But he was starting to feel like he didn't know his own girlfriend.

Sheriff Conklin stood, a strange look on his face, somewhere between irritated and compassionate. "If you can prove to me Lenaia is missing, then I'll look into it. Right now, all I have is a girl who's been spending time with her ex and who's not calling her boyfriend back. I can't investigate that."

Travis left without another word, his head reeling. Was that the best-case scenario here? That Lenaia was hanging out with another man and didn't want to talk to him?

CHAPTER 18

*P*ainful noise stabbed daggers into Lenaia's head. Somebody shuffled about. A voice talking, but not to her. Lenaia tried to open her eyes, but the light assaulted her. She squeezed them shut.

What happened? She tried to grasp the memories, but they slipped like water through her fingers. Ice. She'd been on ice.

"Are you awake?"

Too loud. More stabs of pain through her temples. The voice sounded familiar, and yet she couldn't place it.

She rolled onto her side and groaned.

"You needed to sleep through the night for your head, but I think you've got quite a day ahead of you."

Summoning all of her determination, she forced her eyelids open. Crusty, or rather Wally, bent over her. She looked around. His makeshift bed supported her.

She bolted upright. How had she gotten to his shack? Her head swam and the room shifted. She fell back against the thin mattress.

"Come on, now." Wally put a moist paper towel on her forehead. "You've got to do things slowly. You hit your head pretty hard."

Bits and pieces came back to her. She'd fallen. Whacked her head on the ice and blacked out for a second. When she'd regained consciousness, a migraine had taken over and her skull felt like a hive of a hundred angry bees. She'd tried to get back to the road, but partway down the mountain, she dropped to her knees, cradling her head with her arms. Only sleep could vanquish the migraine.

Then, Wally had appeared. He'd put a cool cloth on her forehead and everything had started to sway. She probed the back of her head. A crusted knot throbbed along the right side of her skull. She'd fallen after ...

The rest came back in a rush. The ice crevasse. *Randy.* Blood around his head, mixed with the ice, frozen into a crimson slab.

She pressed her fists into her eyes. This was no time for a breakdown. She couldn't help Randy, but she could find out what had happened to him. Rolling onto her side, she stared at Wally's face. This close up, he didn't look quite as old, just weathered. His hazel eyes were bright, his gaze intense. "How did I get here?" she asked in a raspy voice.

He jutted his thumb toward the corner. A carved wooden sled with a rope attached rested against the wall. "I usually use it for sledding, but it worked."

"You pulled me on that?"

"Didn't have a choice. I heard your scream. Through my binoculars, all I could see was you lying there. It was getting dark, so I grabbed my sled. By the time I got to you, you'd gotten up and made it partway down, but you couldn't open your eyes. I rolled you onto the sled and pulled you home."

That wouldn't have been easy. If he hadn't helped, it would have been a cold, long night out there for her. "And I slept here all night?"

Wally nodded. "Didn't sleep well, though." He pointed to a

blanket in the corner. "From my spot on the floor, I heard you talking. Something about not being able to help."

Great. She was having arguments with God in her sleep now. Better not tell Pastor Doug about that.

She slowly pushed herself to a sitting position. Her head took a moment to stabilize. "Why did you say I've got quite a day ahead of me?"

"You told me about Randy ... "

A gentle sigh escaped from her lips. "Did you know him?"

"Sort of. I haven't talked to him in years."

"He didn't come to see you in the last couple of days?"

"Nope."

Lenaia furrowed her brows. Randy had wanted to talk to Zayden about this old man. Was Wally telling her the truth?

"I figure you'll want to go tell somebody what happened to him."

"You haven't told anyone?"

"Oh, no. I don't go anywhere near town."

Probably for the same reason he wouldn't divulge earlier. Maybe he would open up this time. "Why not?"

Wally shut his eyes. A moment later, he opened them, walked over to the far side of the room and lifted a bowl off the floor. "Hungry?" He returned and offered her blackberries.

Apparently, he hadn't changed his mind about confiding in her. "Yes." She ate the whole bowl, then felt guilty. "Sorry."

"No need to be sorry. But I'll ask a favor. Keep me out of this whole mess. I prefer my solitude."

Could she do that? *Should* she do that? He might have helped her last night, but his motives were suspect, especially since he wouldn't answer her questions. Maybe he wanted her to keep him out of it because he was involved.

She inched her way off the bed. "I need to get going."

"I can walk you to the four-wheeler."

She gave him a sideways glance. He seemed to know everything but wouldn't tell her anything. She didn't trust him completely, but she might as well accept his help. If he wanted to hurt her, he'd have done it by now. "Okay."

Wally held her under one arm and supported half of her weight as they took careful steps down Emerald Ridge. Her body felt fine, but her head still throbbed and dizziness would sporadically swamp her.

When they finally made it to the vehicle, she turned to Wally. "Thank you for the help."

Wally scratched at his dirty beard. "You're welcome. Be careful. This might sound strange coming from a guy like me, but there's some weird stuff happening on the mountain, right now."

"Like what?"

Wally didn't answer. He nodded, like she knew already, and then headed back up the slope.

Lenaia took the four-wheeler to the end of Westside Road where her car was parked. She threw her backpack in and leaned against the door, casting a tentative glance at Randy's truck. It still sat, waiting patiently for an owner who would never return. She averted her eyes and climbed into her car.

Resting her head against the steering wheel, she debated which direction to go. To the right toward Mayim to tell the sheriff about Randy, or to the left to call from the visitor's center? Getting to the visitor's center would be much quicker, and less time driving. Better to be safe, at least until the pain in her head lessened. She turned left.

A few minutes later, the trees along the side of the road swayed. It had to be her head. She stopped the car. A shaking began at her toes, then worked its way up her legs and through the rest of her body. She grabbed onto the armrests, but they vibrated, as well.

Not her head, but an earthquake. It wasn't a huge one but bigger than those typically felt on Rainier.

A few seconds later, the world calmed. Good thing she was

headed to the visitor's center. She could check on the earthquake, as well.

When she pulled into the parking lot, a lone black truck told her Griffin was inside. She climbed out of the car and walked to the door in slow motion, judging each step according to her shifting equilibrium. After resting at the door and once on the stairs, she made it to the office.

As she entered, Griffin looked up from his computer. "What happened to you?" He held her elbow and guided her into the nearest chair.

Randy's chair.

She fought to keep the tears from exploding out. Marge would be devastated. If only Randy had confided in her. *Lord, why didn't you let me help him?*

Griffin swung a chair over and sat with his elbows on his knees. "Did something happen to you during the earthquake?"

She shook her head and winced. "No, I was in the car."

"Then what happened?"

"I found Randy." She sucked in a heavy breath. "He's dead."

Griffin sat up straight. "What?"

"He fell into a crevasse on the Tahoma, or maybe somebody pushed him. I don't know."

"An ice crevasse? What was he doing up there? And why would you say somebody pushed him?"

"Randy wouldn't have been running around on a glacier by himself." She lowered her head. "I saw two sets of footprints to the edge. Randy is at the bottom with blood all around him."

"You're sure he's dead?"

"With that much blood, I don't see how ... " She coughed to choke back a sob. If she let herself cry, the full impact of Randy's death would hit and knock her to her knees. A solitary tear trailed along her cheek. She smashed it with her palm. "His face was pasty and gray. He's gone."

Griffin stared at her, unblinking.

"I found him last night. Then, I fell and hit my head. The old guy on the mountain took me to his house."

The chair squeaked as Griffin leaned back in it. "You stayed on the mountain last night in some old hermit's shack?"

She looked up at his skeptical tone. Why was he focused on that instead of Randy dying? Even though Griffin had only worked with Randy for two months, he ought to be a little more rattled. "I had a migraine from hitting my head. I couldn't walk."

"Have you told the sheriff about this?"

"No, my cell phone is missing."

"Okay. I'll call him." Griffin glanced at a list of town phone numbers, then picked up the phone on his desk and dialed.

She stood and shuffled to the door, not wanting to hear the details again as he called it in. "I need some air."

She held the handrail tight on the trip down the stairs, just in case, but her equilibrium seemed to be slowly returning to normal. The cool air outside refreshed her. She found a wooden bench, sank down, took a deep breath, and let her head fall back. The pain had faded to a dull ache, mainly centered around the bump on her head.

A short time later, Griffin came out. She lifted her head and shot him a questioning gaze. He shook his head. "I got the answering machine."

"Should we call 9-1-1?"

"No. As hard as it is to say, Randy's not going anywhere. I'll head into town and go to the office myself."

The bench shook as he sat down next to her. "Lenaia, have you considered the possibility that Randy might have sabotaged the equipment?"

"No way." Although, Randy had been acting strange and secretive. She shook her head, then winced at the pain. "I can't believe that."

"Think about it. Randy's close to retirement. The government has been messing with pensions for years. Maybe the shutdown pushed him over the edge and he took out his frustrations on a tiltmeter that probably cost more than a month of his salary."

She shook her head again, this time slower. "If Randy broke the tiltmeter, then why would he go back up there?"

"To see if we'd replaced it?"

"Then how did he end up dead?"

"An accident, I'm sure. Maybe he saw someone coming, took off down the ice, lost his footing and fell."

A plausible scenario, and yet it didn't ring true. What about the second set of footprints? If Randy wasn't the saboteur and had gone up there to figure out who was, then the saboteur might have killed him. But how would the real saboteur know Randy was up there investigating?

She gasped. The camera.

Griffin nudged her arm. "What?"

"Have you looked at the camera footage recently?"

"No, why? Oh, you're thinking we might have gotten a look at the guy." Griffin jumped up. "You stay here and rest. I'll go look."

She nodded, slumping down on the bench to relax.

The thwap of the door signaling Griffin's return startled her. She must have fallen asleep. He flopped onto the bench beside her. "Randy passed through the camera once, left for fifteen minutes, then passed through again. No one else was on the footage."

Another dead end. "Could someone else access the camera file?"

"I checked. Someone did yesterday, but there's no way to tell from which computer."

The office had three computers, all of which could access the network they'd put the camera feed on. Griffin's was password protected.

"Who has access to the other two computers?"

"Randy has a password on his, but I could never get him to change it from his name."

She lifted her brows. "Randy's password is Randy?"

Griffin shrugged. "He was old-school."

She grimaced at his use of the past tense. "And the third one?"

"An open computer used by anyone who has reason to be in this office. Lately, Zayden's been using it."

An unexpected twinge ran through her at the mention of his name. Was Zayden still in jail? Surely, he'd noticed that she'd missed the bail hearing? "Why would Zayden be using the computer?"

"He didn't say and I didn't ask." Griffin twisted his body to face her. "Are you feeling okay?"

She sat up straight. "Better, yeah." So, this was what it took for Griffin to play nice—head trauma. Pulling on both ends of her ponytail, she tightened it before realizing how much it would hurt. She rubbed at her temples. "I'm just confused. Nothing seems to add up."

Her head felt more stable and she forced it to think. Someone had sabotaged the tiltmeter but left the camera intact. Either they hadn't seen it or they left it on purpose to secretly keep an eye on the area. Did the saboteur want to know when the tiltmeter was replaced?

But that would mean Randy wasn't the culprit because he would have known they hadn't replaced the equipment. So then, Randy was up there looking for something else. But what?

The idea of Randy looking for evidence took root and held like a stubborn weed. He must have found something. If she wanted to figure this puzzle out, there was no way around it. "I need to go back up on the mountain. You'll contact the sheriff?"

"I'll try again in a few minutes, and if I don't reach him I'll head to town." Griffin stood and walked back into the building.

She pushed off the bench and gazed up at the solitary peak. The answer was up there. It had to be.

CHAPTER 19

The sun bounced off the slushy ice of the Tahoma Glacier, blinding Lenaia. Her head still ached, but the dizziness had subsided at least. She trudged on, following a nagging feeling that wouldn't go away. Randy was out here looking for something.

The crevasse came into view as a shadowed line, barely visible in the ice. At least she'd remembered her ice spikes this time to prevent her from slipping. She approached the edge, but couldn't bring herself to look over. Hopefully, Griffin would speak to the sheriff soon and they could get Randy out of there.

The footprints from yesterday were now obscured by blown ice and surface melting, but she began to search in a path parallel to the fissure. In two-hundred-foot-long swaths, she scanned the ice for anything foreign, the same way she would look for geologic anomalies.

After two hours, her eyes burned from the brightness and she'd found only a few candy wrappers and animal feces. Returning to the STAR tiltmeter, she shoved the trash in her pack to throw away later and pulled out lunch—a granola bar. She lowered herself down onto the rock ledge and glanced around at the expanse of ice she'd just searched.

Maybe this was a waste of time. There was nothing over there. But if Randy wasn't the saboteur, and she didn't think he was, then he had been up here for a reason. Probably to get the proof he'd talked about, but without knowing what she was looking for, the search was futile.

She reached down to take off her ice spikes, then stopped. What if she'd been thinking about this all wrong? If Randy had been chased, maybe that person chased him *away* from whatever they wanted to protect. Maybe she'd been looking in the wrong place.

She straightened and walked to the other side of the STAR rock. The Puyallup Glacier stretched out to the northwest, its pristine whiteness similar to how she'd imagine the frozen terrain of Neptune. The ice curved as it followed the contours of the mountain.

Might as well try the same search grid. She walked parallel to the STAR rock, searching the ground in front for anything unusual. The pale tundra passed under her feet with little change.

After six long rows of searching, Lenaia climbed on top of a small ice dome to rest. She closed her eyes to escape the blinding landscape and sucked in several deep breaths. Her persistent nature might be getting the best of her. She should probably give up and go check on Zayden.

Instead, she opened her eyes and scanned the icy surface to the south. Nothing unusual. She turned around and scanned the portion behind her. As her eyes roamed the ice, they stuck on a spot in the distance. Perhaps fifty yards away, a tiny black dot marred the perfectly uniform expanse of ice. A rock? Or maybe a trick of her tired eyes? Only one way to find out.

She slid down the dome and crunched across the ice. The black spot grew as she approached to the size of a hamburger. A chunk of dark basalt.

She picked up the hardened lava and rolled it around in her hand. *Where did you come from, sweetheart?*

A careless tourist could have tossed it from the cleaver or maybe a bear had used it for a Frisbee. She was about to turn back when her eyes registered a void in front of her. The rock had been covering a hole in the ice—a bore hole.

Of course. From the drilling project. Kneeling down, she caught sight of a thin wire, like fishing wire, coming out of the hole. It stretched a few feet onto the glacier.

She peered into the hole. It went deeper than she could see without a flashlight, deep below the snowpack and into the true glacial ice made as hard as stone from years of pressure from the snowpack. Even if she had her phone, the flashlight probably wouldn't shine all the way down.

She tugged on the string. It caught on something, pulling taut at first, but then came loose. A subtle resistance on the line told her something weighed it down. Carefully, she pulled the line up, hand over hand. Every pull brought out more string with seemingly no end in sight.

Her arms burned with exertion as she kept pulling. After several minutes, hundreds of feet of string lay splayed on the ground. As she brought up the last stretch of wire, a black cylinder about a foot in length dangled from the end.

Her heart raced and the dizziness returned. She'd seen one of these during her internship on a mining site. It was an explosive device.

But what was it doing up here?

She laid the cylinder gently in the snow and took several steps back. As she did, her boot caught on the other end of the fishing wire, pulling another section from under the surface ice.

As the snow fell away, it revealed a tiny, square box with a red light on top that flashed in rhythmic beats.

She stared at the box and swallowed hard. Attached to the explosive device, it could only be one thing—a remote detonator.

ZAYDEN RANG the doorbell on Randy's house again. No answer.

He knocked on the door. Silence from inside.

Something wasn't right. His numerous calls to Randy, and Lenaia, too, had gone unanswered. Both of them were likely on the mountain somewhere but where? Randy said he had discovered proof of who committed the sabotage. They were supposed to meet to talk about it, but then Zayden had gone to jail.

A sick feeling settled into the pit of his stomach. Randy wouldn't just disappear. He would have at least called back. For that matter, so would Lenaia. She'd said she lost her phone, but surely she'd found it by now. Or she would have found another way to contact him.

Could they be chasing a lead together? He sat on the front stoop. If he could find out what Randy knew, maybe he could figure out where they were. The sabotage of the tiltmeter and the sabotage of the levee were too similar to be a coincidence. They had to be connected and Randy knew how, which meant Randy could be in trouble. Zayden had to find him.

He took two steps toward the four-wheeler sitting in the driveway, then hesitated. Entering Randy's house when he wasn't home might be unnecessary. Or it might be the only way to find out what was going on. He flipped open the storage compartment of the four-wheeler. Just as he expected, the garage remote rested inside. Hopefully, Randy would understand later. He pressed the button, watched the door rise, and then placed the remote back in the vehicle. At the entrance door from the garage, he paused with his hand on the knob. He'd gotten out of jail today—had just washed the stench of it off his skin—and now he was breaking and entering. Actually, no breaking, only entering. Trespassing to be precise. No big deal, right?

He opened the door and stepped into the narrow entryway. Although, he'd been here several times for prayer meetings, the group had met in the living room. Cringing at the silence in the house, he wandered around until he found a home office tucked into the back corner.

Double doors swung into a neat work space complete with a computer, two metal in-boxes, and a printer, all of which sat on an ornate wooden desk. Randy's taste for delicate things had always seemed a little at odds with his large, mountain-man exterior.

The one exception was the oversized office chair where comfort must have outweighed taste. Zayden sank down into the chair and tapped the computer keyboard to turn it on. The screen asked for a password. He didn't have a clue.

Turning his attention to the desk instead, he opened one drawer after another, gently rifling through the contents. On the bottom right, the drawer held stacked hanging files. Most had innocuous names like bills and taxes, but as he flipped through them he caught a glimpse of a manila folder laying underneath.

He tugged it out carefully and opened it. A single sheet of paper rested against the stiff cardboard. A receipt from March 12th.

The description of the merchandise listed one 30-count box of pre-packed ammonium nitrate fuel oil in three-inch diameter plastic cylinders, an unspecified amount of conductive wire, and detonators.

ANFO was a powerful explosive used in mining and the military. Randy wouldn't have ordered this. It had to be the evidence he'd talked about.

Zayden flipped the paper over. A name was handwritten on the back. *Griffin Wall.*

Dread hollowed out a pit in his stomach as the pieces of the puzzle snapped together. Griffin's history with the town. The drilling project under his control. Weren't ice cores usually about four inches in diameter? And the explosives with all that wire.

Zayden stuffed the receipt in his back pocket and darted out to his truck. Lenaia had been right. The answers to this mystery were up on the mountain.

CHAPTER 20

The address the sheriff had given Travis led him to a two-story house painted a deep ocean blue with windows framed by white shutters. He got out of the car, disappointment weighing heavily in his chest. No vehicles in the driveway and the garage door was closed.

Staying hopeful, he walked along the landscaped walkway to the front door. He knocked three times. Waiting, he tapped his shoe on the welcome mat. *Come on. Please answer.*

The distant bark of a dog sounded from inside. It must be kenneled in a back room somewhere. A clear sign no one was home.

What now? Zayden wasn't around and the sheriff didn't want to help. Travis could try the mountain again, but he'd seen no vehicles at the visitor's center.

Lenaia could be hurt somewhere. With a killer on the loose, it was time to start his own investigation. He jogged back to the car and sped in to town. Small town or not, they had to have a library. The sheriff wouldn't share any information, but newspaper reporters had a way of getting it anyway.

On Main Street, he parked in the same spot he'd parked in half an hour before. A quick look around and he spied the library, two doors down from the sheriff's office.

Travis hustled to a row of computers in the far corner. He passed by a few curious people, but no one said anything to him. He searched for local news and two newspaper articles came up. The first one from today. The second from a week ago. He started with the older one that contained a picture of a young, blond woman.

LAST NIGHT, *Summer Planke, a resident of Mayim, Washington, went missing. Summer is the wife of Dan Planke who died a month ago in Hawaii. Her eight-year-old daughter is being cared for by her uncle, Zayden Planke, until Summer can be found. Police are still investigating her disappearance. To report any information on Summer's whereabouts, contact the Pierce County Sheriff's Department.*

THIS WASN'T the woman the sheriff had mentioned. He clicked on the second article. The accompanying picture showed a lovely dark haired woman standing next to a serious older man.

A PARK RANGER *discovered the body of Rachel Marshall on Mt. Rainier last Wednesday. The coroner released his report this morning, which states the cause of death as strangulation. Rachel Marshall was the wife of Morgan Marshall, owners of Puyallup River Winery, and both were residents of Mayim. When asked to comment on his wife's death, Mr. Marshall expressed both grief and appreciation for the police who have questioned a person of interest, Zayden Planke of Mayim. As of today, no charges have been filed against Mr. Planke.*

. . .

Travis's pulse raced. The sheriff hadn't said anything about Zayden being involved in a murder. This guy could be a killer and Lenaia had been seen with him recently. But if it were true, why hadn't the sheriff filed murder charges? Was he still building his case? Maybe trying to tie Summer's disappearance to Zayden?

Travis rubbed his ice-cold hands together. Checking up on Zayden hadn't worked. The man might have skipped town, but Travis had one more lead. Morgan Marshall.

Maybe Morgan knew something about his wife's murder. Or better yet, maybe he would know where Zayden had gone.

Travis looked up the name in the telephone directory. No Morgan Marshall listed. After trying two more searches, he found the winery's full address on the Mayim City website. He wrote the address on his hand. It was a good place to start.

Twenty minutes later, he turned at a sign marking the winery. The gravel driveway led to a clean, white ranch house, surrounded by rows of trellises. Travis parked at the apex of the circle drive, got out and walked to the door. He only got in one knock before the man from the picture flung the door open.

"Can I help you?" Dressed in khaki pants, a pale pink button down shirt and a white apron, he appeared almost domestic. A thin layer of flour coated his hands.

"Morgan Marshall?"

"Yes, but I'm working on dinner, so please state your business." Morgan blocked the door, keeping Travis from seeing inside.

"My girlfriend is missing and I'm trying to find her." He cleared his throat. "I wanted to ask you a few questions about Zayden Planke and what might have happened to your wife."

A frustrated growl rumbled in Morgan's throat. "You're a reporter."

"No, sir."

He raised his thin eyebrows. "With the sheriff's department?"

"No, sir."

Morgan dipped his head. "Why do you think I know where your girlfriend is?"

"I don't." Travis met the man's eyes. His defensive attitude could be justified if reporters had hounded him. "I'm trying to follow any lead I can. You know ... " He hated to say it. "Just in case."

Morgan nodded, but his gelled hair never moved. "Just in case she was taken." He moved aside. "Come in. I'll tell you what I know."

Finally, someone who was willing to give him information. Travis followed the man into a small eat-in kitchen. Painted a deep green with owl figurines on the counter, the room reminded him of the pine forest outside, beyond the winery.

"So, what's your girlfriend's name?"

"Lenaia."

"Ah, yes, Lenaia Talavera. Such a pretty name. I remember."

Travis took a step closer. "You've seen her?"

"Yep, and I'll tell you all about it, but I must watch my manners. Would you like a glass of lemonade?"

"No. Thanks." All he wanted was to find Lenaia.

Morgan went to the refrigerator and pulled out a pitcher. He poured the liquid into a glass. "Everybody likes lemonade. I'll give you extra sugar since I don't put much in."

This guy was persistent. Maybe if he drank some, showed himself to be sociable, then Morgan would be more likely to open up. "Okay." Weird that Morgan didn't use much sugar. Perhaps he had diabetes.

Morgan pried the lid from a plastic container and scooped two spoonfuls into the liquid. He handed the glass to Travis, along with a spoon for stirring, then he returned to his preparation of breaded chicken on the center island.

"Thanks." Travis took several quick drinks. "When did you see Lenaia?"

"A few days ago. And only briefly. She came here with a friend."

Please, not Zayden again. "Who?"

"Griffin Wall."

The name sounded familiar. "Isn't that the geologist?"

"Yes. Apparently, Griffin didn't appreciate some comments I made about him."

Travis sipped some more of his drink. Why had Lenaia come here? Did she think Morgan had committed the sabotage? Or was this about the missing women? Morgan continued smoothing a flour mixture over the chicken breasts.

"Did she ask you about the other woman who went missing?"

Morgan rubbed his bottom lip, smearing flour along his chin. "You know, I think we talked about it a little."

"Did she ever mention Zayden?" He seemed to be the link between both women.

"No. We talked about how Griffin and I fought about hunting. But now we get along very well."

The green walls shifted as a wave of dizziness engulfed Travis. He shook his head and it passed. Morgan seemed not to have noticed. Travis ran a hand through his hair and refocused his thoughts. "How did you work out your issues?"

"Actually, I'd tell you, but then I'd have to kill you." Morgan slapped the counter and chuckled as if that wasn't the oldest joke in the book.

The owl figurines on the counter spun as another wave of dizziness hit Travis. Sweat broke out on his forehead and his upper lip. The cup started to slip from his hand. He tightened his grip and stared down at it. A tiny amount of yellow lemonade coated the bottom along with a feathery white substance. It didn't look like undissolved sugar.

The urge to throw up wrenched through his stomach. He closed his eyes and doubled over.

"Are you feeling all right, Travis?"

He forced his eyes open.

Morgan leaned over him, his face framed by white ceiling tiles. Travis's head ached and his back pressed into the hard floor. How had he gotten down here? He fought to keep his eyes from closing again, but he couldn't stop them from sliding shut. His lids blocked out the light and he slipped away into darkness.

CHAPTER 21

*L*enaia hurried down the rocky slope, purposeful with every step on the loose rock. If only she had her cell phone, she would call someone for help, or at least she would have tried. Cell service on the mountain was spotty, but sometimes she could get a weak signal in open areas.

The sun had already started its race toward the horizon, sapping its warmth away with every degree of descent. She zipped her jacket and pondered what to do next. She wouldn't have time to get to town and bring someone up here to disarm the explosives. But who knew when the person with the detonator would decide to detonate it? If they did and it triggered a mudflow, the town could be at risk.

About a third of the way down, she came around a bend in the trail and swerved out of instinct to avoid someone. She caught herself against a tree before she looked back to see who it was.

"Lenaia." Griffin appeared relieved to see her.

Relief also flooded through her. "Do you have your phone? We have to call something in."

"No need. I finally heard back from Sheriff Conklin. He said he'll meet us at the STAR station as soon as he can." Griffin pulled a camera case out of his backpack with one hand. "He told me to take pictures of the scene for him."

She scrunched her nose. The idea of taking pictures of Randy's dead body turned her stomach. She looked up the slope of the mountain, then back at Griffin. "You don't understand. I found something else up there."

"What?"

Lenaia pushed off the tree. "An explosive device with a remote detonator."

Griffin's mouth dropped open. "Where?"

"Near the STAR station."

Griffin's face went slack and he blinked at her a few times. "How much did you find?"

"One device. I guess I don't know how much was in it." Her contact with explosives was limited to her summer internship at a mine in Arizona.

Griffin returned the camera case to his backpack. "Then, we have to get up there to take pictures now."

She gnawed on her lower lip. Griffin seemed a little too eager to get up close and personal with explosives. He was either brave or crazy. "You know, remote detonation means it could blow at any time."

He gave her a look that said 'duh.' "That's why we have to get pictures. If the charges go off, the evidence will destroy itself."

He was right. The type of explosive and detonator could give police a lead on who had put them there. But did she want to risk her life to save the evidence?

She thought of Travis. He wouldn't want her to go back up on the mountain where she could be blown to bits, but she'd left the device on the ice. If they gave it a wide berth, and took pictures from a distance, they would be relatively safe. She nodded and headed up the path with Griffin trailing behind her.

More than an hour later, Lenaia climbed up to St. Andrews Rock again, gasping for breath. This was more hiking than she'd done in a long time. Thankfully, Griffin had been quiet the entire way up, so she hadn't needed to make conversation. Now, he stood as still as a statue, staring out into space. His expression was unreadable, at first, then his eyebrows began to droop and he seemed anxious. He had probably just now grasped the gravity of what they were up here to do.

She glanced out at the Tahoma Glacier, unable to keep her eyes from roaming to where Randy lay. Something about this whole situation gnawed at her, but she shook off the feeling. Thankfully, now it wasn't her job to figure this out. The sheriff could do that when he got here.

Griffin followed her line of sight, but said nothing. After unzipping his backpack, he pulled out the camera with its case. "Well, let's get this over with. Where did you find the device?"

"You want to take pictures of that first?"

He tossed the small camera bag over his shoulder and shrugged. "I figured it would be best to get that done in case it went off."

His voice was flat. He didn't seem concerned at all, just stared at her, waiting for her to take the lead. She opened her pack, tugged out her ice spikes, and fitted them over her boots, flipping the strap to secure them. As she stood, she put a hand on the rock behind her for balance and almost dislodged the video camera they'd installed nearly a week ago.

The camera. That was part of what was bothering her. Randy's killer had likely seen him through the camera, hiked up the mountain, and killed him to keep him from finding the explosives.

She trudged out to the device with Griffin following behind. Stopping ten feet away, she stared and crossed her arms over her chest, thinking.

Not many people had access to the camera footage. Although one of the computers was unsecured, only two people besides Randy were known to be in the office: Zayden and Griffin. She glanced at Griffin out of the corner of her eye. But why would one of them want to cause an explosion in such a remote area? "I don't get it. Why right here, over the possible lava dome? Blowing it up probably wouldn't do anything, unless ... "

Griffin lifted his eyebrows and waited for her to go on.

"Unless the earthquake today shook up the gases in the lava dome. Then it might be primed to blow." She bit her bottom lip. "If an explosion causes even a small eruption, most of this glacier would melt, generating a massive mudflow. With the levee compromised, Mayim is hit full force by a devastating lahar."

He blinked a few times before giving her a skeptical look.

"Except they would probably need a whole lot more explosives to blow the lava dome. Maybe they used all of the drill holes from your project." As the words left her lips, the truth hit her full force. Zayden might have known about the camera and the drilling project, but not the lava dome, at least not before she'd told him. Despite the innocent act, there was only one person who knew about all three and had the opportunity to insert the explosives —*Griffin.*

She sucked in a quick breath and deliberately ignored him, moving to the explosive device instead. If she was right, there could be many more of them out here, but she might have a chance to disarm them. Her summer internship had taught her that removing the blasting cap would separate the remote detonator from the explosives. She would do her best to disarm as many as she could before Griffin got wise.

"What are you doing?"

"Just looking." Keeping her back to him to block his view, she pried the blasting cap off and dropped it to the snow, covering it with her foot. But it took too long. He had come up behind her.

"I really think you should wait for the sheriff."

What she needed was a knife from her pack to cut the lines quicker. Especially since she knew Griffin probably wouldn't let her pull them all up, she had to try. She scooped her backpack up from beside him. "Let's look for more."

The devices would probably be in a grid ten to twenty feet apart, but how long would he keep up the ruse?

"If we get too far off track, the sheriff won't be able to find us," he said.

He might have a point, except she had a feeling he had never called the sheriff. "I think we should look in this direction." She turned her back to him and headed north.

After several steps, she chanced a glance over her shoulder. Griffin was bent at the waist, rummaging around in the camera bag. When he looked up, he locked eyes with her. No nervous blinking this time. A muscle clenched along his jaw. "How about we don't do anything?"

His hand emerged from the bag holding a dull, black handgun.

CHAPTER 22

"Put the device back in the hole, Lenaia." Griffin held the small barrel of the gun pointed directly at her chest. His eyes reflected the same steely gray as the metal of the gun.

She sucked in a deep breath. Her heart hammered in her chest as her mind raced to the inevitable conclusion. Griffin would kill her to accomplish his plan.

"Now." His voice was a menacing growl.

She picked up the wire and lowered the device gently down into the bore hole, grinding the detonator into the snow just outside the hole. At least one of the devices was disabled.

The melodic sound of the song "My Lighthouse" reverberated through the air—her phone's ringtone. It came from the camera bag. Griffin had taken her phone.

He grunted and pulled over the camera bag, fumbling with the front zipper. Once he got it open, he extracted her cell phone, but the ringing had stopped. "From Zayden. How cute."

The peppy ringtone began again. It was a miracle that her cell even had reception up here.

"That guy doesn't give up." Griffin shoved it in her direction. "Talk to him for a minute. On speakerphone. And don't say anything about me."

With trembling fingers, she swiped the screen to answer, then tapped the button for speaker mode. "Hello?"

"Lenaia, are you okay? I've been calling all day."

"I'm sorry. I ... " Her voice sounded strained. She cleared her throat. "I'm fine. Just exploring up here at the STAR station."

"Have you found anything?"

"I ... uh ... " Griffin raised the gun to point it at her head. She flinched. "Nothing that you need to see."

Zayden huffed out a breath. "Okay. Just stay there. I'm on my way up to you."

Griffin glared at her. If Zayden came up here, Griffin would kill him. "What did you say?"

"I'm on my way to you. I'll be there in an hour."

She had to talk him out of coming. "That's not a good idea. It's only a few hours before dark."

Zayden's tone was decisive. "I've got to check something out and it can't wait. We can help each other make the climb down in the dark."

Griffin circled the gun in the air. He wanted her to wrap it up, but she couldn't let Zayden walk right into a trap. Who knew what Griffin was capable of?

"Please, don't come up here."

"Why not?"

Griffin raised the gun and placed the barrel against her cheekbone. The cool circle bit into her skin. The message was clear. If she warned Zayden, she would die. She closed her eyes and tried to think clearly. What would keep Zayden from coming up the mountain? "I'm starved. I'll come down and we can get some dinner. We'll come back tomorrow."

"Tomorrow will be too late."

She stifled a gasp. Too late for what? What did Zayden know? Griffin grabbed the phone from her but kept the microphone near her mouth. He silently mouthed the word *finish*.

"Okay." Lenaia sighed in defeat. Nothing she could say would change Zayden's mind. "I'll see you when you get here." Griffin pressed the end button to kill the call and with it her only hope of protecting Zayden.

Griffin lowered his arm and paced in frantic lines on the ice. She backed away a few steps and breathed a little easier now that the gun was pointed away from her. But her stomach clenched tight at what she'd done. He could easily ambush Zayden along the trail.

Griffin stopped pacing, blinked at her, then closed the distance between them. The gun still pointed at the ground, but his face hovered six inches from hers. "Why is he coming up here?"

She bit her lip. "I have no idea. He's talked about us getting back together." She was grasping at straws, but she'd try anything to keep him from labeling Zayden a threat.

Griffin furrowed his eyebrows until they knit together into one. Turning away from her, he began to pace again, muttering to himself. "This changes things. I can't blow the mountain until tomorrow and we can't descend. We'd never get past Zayden." He stopped and advanced on her. "Does he carry a gun with him all the time?"

She hesitated. If she told him Zayden carried his gun all the time, would he think twice about an ambush? "Usually in his car, yes, but I don't really know his habits anymore."

"I could surprise him, but if he has a weapon, it's better not to take the chance." He pulled at the top of his dark hair and stared at the massive peak. "I guess there's nowhere to go, except up."

He couldn't be serious about wanting to go up the mountain at this time of day without equipment.

Using the barrel of the gun, he pointed to the east, farther up the slope. "Let's go. We need to make some progress before it gets dark."

He gestured for her to pick up her backpack while he stuffed the camera in his, then slung it over his shoulder. He left the empty camera bag behind and gestured for her to lead the way. Not long after, he directed her to turn northeast and cross over onto the Tahoma Glacier.

She glanced back at him, hoping to distract him so she could leave a breadcrumb. "Why wait until tomorrow?" Not that she wanted him to blow it now, but she was curious. He ignored her question and turned away. She seized the moment to scratch her leg, surreptitiously dropping her keys at the same time.

Griffin kept walking. His refusal to talk was probably a bad sign. He didn't want her to know the whole plan.

Her sharp ice spikes gripped the rough ice with each step, helping to keep her balance. When Griffin started to slip, he sat down to put on his own ice spikes, keeping his eyes on her and the gun within inches of his hand.

What else did he have in his pack? Surely, he wouldn't try to summit the mountain without the proper equipment. He must have a different plan in mind. But if he intended to detonate the explosives tomorrow, where could they go to be safe from the blast? Dread snaked through her stomach. Unless this was a suicide mission.

As they continued to hike, the slope of the ice increased and the air thinned out. Two hours later, he stopped to take a rest. He shrugged off his pack and pulled out a long ice ax. No doubt he hadn't packed an ice ax for her. She'd have to go up the mountain without one.

He took a long drink from a water bottle, keeping his eyes focused on her. His expression was resolute. If only she could control her emotions as easily. During the entire hike, images of Travis filled her mind. What was he doing at this moment? Would he be devastated if she didn't make it? He'd grieve, of course, but Travis was resilient. Much more so than her.

She threw off her pack, then reached for it. Griffin held the gun higher. She slowly pulled out her water bottle and drank several long swallows.

"That's enough. Let's go," he ordered.

"Where exactly are we going?"

Again, he didn't answer. She pushed her feet forward, steps mechanical. This was her fault. She should have figured it out earlier. He must have been planning this for months while he was drilling the ice cores. Then, when he'd found the lava dome, he decided to use it to give the explosion an extra boost while at the same time compromising the levee with the excavator. But she still didn't understand exactly why. Or if it had anything to do with the missing women.

They trekked on. As the slope grew steeper, Griffin used the ice ax as a walking stick. Without an ax, she had to lean farther forward and dig her ice spikes in to keep traction.

They passed by the point where they would have met the tip of the crevasse that Randy had died in. She shuddered. Had Griffin killed him in cold blood or was it an accident? And what would he do with her in the end?

At least the crevasse didn't extended this far up. But as the ice continued to thaw from winter, it would become more friable, making crevasses more likely. She strained her eyes in the fading light to search the ground for danger.

More than an hour later, they came to a nearly vertical wall of rock covered by ice. The blue-green ice tumbled over the narrow rock ledge in a waterfall of frozen tendrils.

Griffin walked to the bottom, dropped the gun in the snow, then his pack, and started pulling out equipment. He threw a harness in her direction.

"Put that on."

Apparently, he'd prepared for this situation. "What are you, some sort of evil Boy Scout?"

He gave her a look filled with such rage that she backed up a step. Definitely not the Griffin she was used to dealing with. As a warning, he placed his hand on the gun, pressing it into the snow.

She put two hands out, palms toward him. Her sarcastic coping mechanism might get her killed. "Okay. I'm getting ready."

Slipping her feet through the leg loops, she tightened the belt at her waist. She'd climbed more than one mountain and was familiar with multiple techniques, although she wouldn't consider herself an expert on ice. Hopefully, Griffin knew more than she did.

He finished rifling through the pack and stood. "Here's how this is going to work." He tied a threaded figure-eight knot with yellow rope around the harness hook at her waist, then he took two plastic zip ties and secured the rope to the harness. They were hooked together, and even if she untied the rope, the zip ties were too tight for her to pull the rope through. "I'm going up first. I'll place ice anchors for you to hook on to and then I'll help pull you up." He waved the gun in her face. "Don't think about trying to pull me over the edge. The anchors would catch me, and then I'd have to shoot you. I'm not ready to do that yet, but I will if I have to."

Yet? He might not want to shoot her right now, but it sounded like he would eventually. Why was he keeping her alive?

Griffin spiked the ax into the ice about a foot above his head. Digging his ice spikes in a few feet above the ground, he held himself by the handle of the ax. When his feet were set, he pulled the ax out and thrust it higher on the wall. One by one he moved his feet until the spikes had a secure hold, then he transferred his weight to his feet and moved the ax.

About five feet up, he placed an ice screw hammering it in with the other side of the ax. He hooked in a carabiner, unscrewed it, threaded the rope through, and screwed the carabiner closed.

She watched as he continued up the wall, placing ice anchors every five feet. The rope around her waist played out as he climbed. If she tried to pull him off the wall, he'd fall only about fifteen feet before the anchors caught him. The gun rested snug in the side pocket of his backpack within easy reach. If only it would break free and fall down to her.

The third and final anchor he placed two feet from the bottom of the ledge. After hooking his rope to it, he raised his ice ax, dug it in and scrambled over the top of the ledge.

"Come on up," he yelled down.

"Throw the ice ax for me."

"No way. You can make it without."

He tugged hard on the rope. With her heart racing, she approached the wall. She had no choice. If she tried to run, he'd pull her back with the rope and if he decided to shoot, she'd be an easy target down here.

Digging her front ice spike into a spot two feet up, she stepped and reached for the first screw. It wasn't ideal to put all her weight on the screws—they were meant as a backup to catch a person in the event of a fall, not as a primary climbing tool—but she didn't really have a choice there either.

He pulled up the slack in her line as she climbed. She stretched and clawed her way up the ice. Her legs burned and her feet ached by the time she reached the last ice screw. She grabbed onto it and it almost came out under her weight. She flailed and grabbed for a nearby knob of ice. It held.

She looked up. He was only two feet above her, but because of how far the overhang stuck out, he couldn't see much of her. This could be her one chance.

She ripped the screw out the rest of the way and slipped it into her jacket pocket, but doubt edged into her mind. Could she really use it to hurt or kill another person? He had kidnapped her, threatened to kill her, and planned on blowing up the mountain. Yep, she could do it.

He tugged on the line. "Put a hand up. I'll pull you over."

She lifted her right hand. He grabbed it, dragging her over the ledge. As her feet came over, he slipped and they both fell backward, landing in a tangle of limbs. She rolled away from him and glanced back.

The gun wasn't in his hand. Now was the time.

She tore the screw from her pocket and lunged at him, swinging her arm toward his chest. He raised his right leg and kicked, throwing her off balance. She fell to the side, but recovered quickly.

She pitched forward for another swing. He rolled away and the screw connected with bare ice.

"Drop it." Griffin's order cut through the air, slicing through all hope of freedom.

She didn't have to look up to know he now stood above her with the gun.

"On second thought, throw it over the edge."

She got to her feet and turned to face him, cringing at the cold impersonal glint in his eyes. Pure rage or no emotion. She didn't know which she preferred.

He raised the gun a few degrees. "Drop the screw over the edge."

She arced her arm back and threw it, watching as the only weapon she had tumbled into the snow at the bottom of a thirty-foot cliff.

Holding the gun still pointed at her, he reached into his bag, removed a square package, and tossed it at her feet. "You get to build the tent."

"We're camping?"

He gestured at the sun sinking lower in the west. "Can't climb in the dark."

She unzipped the package and pulled out the thin, one-piece tent. While she wrestled with their sleeping accommodations, he pulled some beef jerky from his pack, not offering her any.

"Why are you doing this?" She cringed at the tremor of fear in her voice.

"Not so bossy when I've got a gun, are you?"

He was in charge now and he wanted her to know it. She pursed her lips and swallowed another sarcastic retort.

"Well, you weren't in my original plan, but it got scrapped because of you, so this seems fitting." He quirked one of his eyebrows. "What did you think? That this was *God's* plan?"

She glared at him before turning back to her task. The tent was flat and the wire supports were already inside. Lenaia picked up a stake and held it steady while kicking it into the ice with her foot. If only she could do this to his face. Instead, she needed to play nice, to keep him talking so she could figure out how to stop him. "Really, Griffin, I don't understand why you're doing this."

He paused, as if letting her anticipation build, and then he laughed. "You saw the note—probably even figured out the biblical reference."

He had written the note? Did that mean he killed Rachel as well?

"The earth is going to commit murder for me." His matter-of-fact tone sent shivers down her spine. "All of the people at Christ's Devoted were only devoted to their own comfort. They wouldn't help a kid who just wanted to stay in his hometown. As of tomorrow all of their kids will be orphans like me."

The earth will punish them. The note wasn't about Rachel at all, but about Griffin's fantasy to punish the church. "What happens tomorrow?"

"A church-wide members' meeting for adults only. They will all leave their kids with their babysitters while they drown in a massive mudflow. Sure, a few houses with kids might be hit, but most will survive. An entire church of orphans."

"Not everyone in the church would have been here at the time when your mom died. Doesn't this seem like overkill to you?"

"That's how you get away with murder, Lenaia. When the

police don't even know it's murder." He clenched his jaw. "It was supposed to look like a natural disaster. I could have convinced them the lava dome broke the equipment. But then they called you in to investigate the sabotage and I needed a new scapegoat."

"But why kill Rachel? What did she have to do with this?"

"Wrong again. I didn't kill her, although I did give him the note to put on his next victim. I just didn't realize the next one would be his wife. Stupid, really." Griffin rubbed his hand down his scruffy cheek. "The police haven't connected the women disappearing in Seattle with this area yet, but it's all the same guy."

"Morgan is killing women and you're helping him?"

"Didn't have much of a choice. He saw me burying one of the explosive devices and threatened to call the sheriff if I didn't help him dispose of his leftovers. Plus, he promised me he'd take some of the future ones from my old church." He swung his arm around in a circle. "I was doing them both a favor. What better resting place than on a majestic mountain?"

She gaped at him in shock.

"Don't look at me like that. It's not like *I* killed them. And I couldn't let Morgan ruin my plan, so I improvised. Just like I've had to do since you came to town. But as it turns out, you provided an even better scapegoat than Mother Nature."

Her stomach twisted as she pondered what he might mean.

"Now, I'm using both you and your man."

"What?"

Griffin smiled with a mischievous gleam in his eyes. "I'll bet you thought I didn't call the sheriff. But I left him a detailed message saying I found evidence on your phone that you helped Zayden obtain some explosives to get back at the Mayim Planning and Zoning Committee for firing him. When you disappear, your phone disappears, and the glacier explodes, everyone will think Zayden did it and got rid of his accomplice."

Lenaia shook her head. "Nobody will believe it."

"They will when they find the explosives I hid in Zayden's

shed." He took on a serious tone. "It's a small town, but he really should get a lock for that thing. Add that to what the sheriff already suspects from the sweatshirt I planted on the excavator and the town will blame him. They'll never go looking for another explanation. Really, I should thank you. This way actually works out better." He looked up at the darkening sky. "Almost God ordained, don't you think?"

She stomped in another tent stake with her foot. "No."

He pointed in the distance where she could see the outline of a few buildings in town. "I'll bet Christ's Devoted Church would think so."

Lenaia stuck the last peg of the tent in the ice and threw all her anger into pounding it in. They would have shelter for the night, but the accommodations would be cramped. No chance for her to get away from this lunatic.

"Ladies first."

She glared at him, then the gun, before climbing through the small flap.

"Lay down all the way to the right side."

The side farthest from the tent door. With a sigh, she complied. The temperature had already dropped considerably, so she zipped her jacket higher under her chin as she curled into a ball to keep Griffin as far from her as possible.

He curled onto his side facing her with his backpack under his head as a pillow and the gun tucked under his arm, the barrel pointed in her direction. Not a comfortable way for either of them to sleep and she wouldn't be able to get the gun without waking him up.

"Oh, yeah. We can't have you sneaking out in the middle of the night."

He sat up and zipped the flap of the tent down tight. Slipping a zip tie into a circular hole on the flap, he connected it to a ring in the floor of the tent. She wasn't going anywhere.

Taking a deep breath, she folded her arms under her head and tried to focus on sleep, but terror buzzed through her system. Griffin had aided a serial killer, killed Randy, was prepared to commit mass murder, and would have to decide what to do with her tomorrow. Her heart refused to calm down. More than likely, sometime tomorrow she'd end up as a casualty in his quest for judgment.

CHAPTER 23

Zayden woke with the first rays of dawn. As he folded back the flap of his sleeping bag, the crisp morning air stung his face. It had been cold last night, but that didn't explain why he hadn't slept much. He was worried about Lenaia. He stood and stretched, leaning against the dark mass of St. Andrews Rock beside him, but the loosening of his muscles didn't relieve the fear settling like a heavy rock in the bottom of his stomach.

He'd climbed up to the STAR monitoring station yesterday, only to find Lenaia gone. All of his calls to her cell phone now went straight to voice mail. After searching in the dark along the cleaver for any sign of her with no luck, he'd bedded down for the night. But images of her alone on the mountain haunted his dreams.

It was an unusually clear day up here with no steam from the summit and no rain clouds. Piercing rays of sunlight bounced off the white ice. He reached for his sunglasses and slipped them on, then strapped on his ice spikes. Today, he'd either find Lenaia or find out if his hunch was right. He stood, slung his backpack over his shoulders, and stared between the two glaciers for a moment.

About a month ago, Griffin had mentioned his ice-coring

project on the Puyallup Glacier, bragging about how deep he'd drilled into the ice, about 200 feet down, almost to the bottom of the glacier. Could that be where Griffin intended to use thirty cylinders of explosives?

Zayden turned around and circled St. Andrews Rock before stepping out onto the Puyallup. The glacier stretched out in front of him in immense whiteness. He started the search by walking west.

Ice crunched beneath his steps, sounding louder than usual, either due to the silence surrounding him or the thinner air. His eyes scanned the uniform surface of the packed snow. Other than a few knobs and valleys, it never changed.

When he stopped to rest, he pulled out his cell phone and tried Lenaia's number again. A recorded message sounded in his ear. What had happened to her? If she'd changed her mind and gone down the mountain, they would have met on the trail. He suppressed an urge to call the sheriff. Without an indication of what happened or proof of explosives, the sheriff couldn't do anything. Besides, Zayden was at the top of the sheriff's suspect list.

Switching to another wide swath, he continued for a third pass. As he reached the end, he turned around, then looked out ahead at the unending white ground. But it wasn't all white. In the distance, a small dark object sat on the ice.

He raced to it as fast as he could without slipping. As he approached, the black object grew until he recognized a camera bag. Next to it, a wisp of a thread, curled up, blowing in the breeze, the other end disappearing into a bore hole.

He pulled on the wire and dislodged a small box with a blinking red light on top of it. What else was attached to this? He tugged on the portion of the wire extending into the hole, hand over hand, until coils of wire were spread in a circle around him. Finally, at the end, he pulled out a long, cylindrical tube. This had to be the ANFO canister, which made the box most likely one of the detonators.

Thank you, Lord, for helping me find this. But now what?

Could he disarm it? Looking closely, he realized it didn't have a cap. A quick search and he found the cap smashed into the snow. This one was safe, but there could be others.

One bomb probably wouldn't do much to a glacier. There had to be more in Griffin's bore holes. Assuming he would drill in a grid, Zayden headed due north. The next hole sporting a wispy thread and black box sat twenty feet away. He pulled up the wire until the device dislodged from the bore hole. Gripping the cap with his fingers, he took a deep breath. This might require a steadier hand than he had right now. He tried to calm his racing pulse, but couldn't. Instead, he whispered a prayer and yanked it off.

Nothing happened. He breathed a thankful sigh.

The cap in his hand held a piece of what looked like silly putty in it. The rest of the tube held dry powder. The two probably needed to be in contact to explode, so he kept them separate. The black box still blinked at him so he dug out his Swiss Army knife and used the small pair of scissors to cut the wire attaching the detonator to the cap. The red light went out.

After grabbing several plastic bags out of his pack, he placed the detonator, cap and explosive powder into three separate bags, and stowed them in isolated pockets of his pack.

He drank deep from his water bottle while wiping off a thin layer of sweat running down his face. Disarming a bomb wasn't so bad.

The receipt from Randy's house had listed thirty containers, which Griffin could parcel out as he wanted. Had he used all of them?

Zayden stowed the water bottle and headed north again. Hours of searching brought him several more. He disarmed them and placed them in the bags. After he found the last device in a northerly direction, he headed west to work the next block of the grid. His work sped up as he became accustomed to the spacing and the fastest way to disarm the devices.

When he had completed four passes, he traveled back to the starting point to take a closer look at the camera bag. It was left out here like a beacon and its presence was nagging at him. The bag didn't look familiar, but someone had left it for him to find. Or maybe they didn't have time to hide it.

He examined the ground around it. Two distinct sets of footprints left from the area, heading up the glacier—one small and one large pair. Could one of them be Lenaia's?

He followed them for several hundred yards before the tracks turned eastward, toward the Tahoma Glacier. He scanned the area.

A hint of color in the distance caught his eye. Something green. He ran to it and picked up a set of car keys with a rental car logo attached to the key fob. His stomach clenched.

Lenaia had come this way but with someone else. And not likely of her own volition. If she was forced, then the other set of footprints could only be one person. *Griffin.*

Zayden stared ahead at the vast field of snow and ice. *Thank you, Lord, for miracle number two. I've found her. Now, please let her still be safe.*

Zayden glanced back at the glacier behind him. He'd collected a total of about sixteen devices. There could be another fourteen remaining. But every second Lenaia was with Griffin, she was in danger. He had to go after her. Hopefully Griffin hadn't used all of the devices he'd ordered.

After quickly hiking back to the STAR rock, Zayden pulled out the bags containing the explosives and stuffed his sleeping bag in his pack. He left the disarmed explosives in the bags on the rock. If he didn't make it back, maybe the sheriff would find the evidence and use it against Griffin.

As he turned to go, he hesitated. If he left now, he had no way of knowing if he'd gotten all of the explosives. As the Evacuation Planning Director, he had a responsibility to warn the town and start an evacuation. And yet, without seeing the proof, the sheriff probably wouldn't believe him. He stood still for a moment in indecision.

No one in town trusted him right now, except for one person. He took a photo of the explosives, then dialed as he walked.

Pastor Doug picked up on the second ring. "Hello?"

"Pastor, it's Zayden. Forgive me for burdening you with this, but I don't think anyone else will believe me." He told Pastor Doug what he'd found. "I'll send you a picture of the evidence. You need to convince the sheriff or the mayor to evacuate the town."

The pastor's voice sounded heavy but determined. "I'll probably try the mayor first. He's got a little less on his plate right now. How long do you want to evacuate for?"

"Just until we can get someone up here to make sure all the explosives are disarmed."

"Okay. You're coming down, then?"

"No, I'm going up. I can't find Lenaia and I'm afraid Griffin might have taken her up the mountain."

"Griffin? You've seen him?"

"No, but I found something of hers plus two sets of footprints going up. I'm assuming one of them is his."

"Be careful. Don't underestimate a desperate man."

"I won't, but I'm just as desperate to find Lenaia. Pray for me, Pastor."

Zayden continued northeast until he picked up their tracks again, crossing over the cleaver and onto the Tahoma Glacier. Although he hadn't brought any mountain climbing equipment, he couldn't wait. He had to go after her.

Following the tracks where he could find them, he hiked for hours. The gradient increased sharply, as he climbed several hundred feet in elevation, and he thanked God for his ice spikes.

Another two hours of hiking went by in a blur of climbing

over knobs and descending into small valleys. He'd just come over a knoll when his progress was stopped by a high wall of ice.

The smooth surface rose over thirty feet. A row of ice screws, spaced every five feet, told him someone had been through here recently. Probably Griffin and Lenaia. How far behind was he?

Something silver glinted by his foot. He kicked at it. A fallen ice screw. He scanned the wall and found one missing near the top.

He tucked the screw into the side pocket of his backpack, then pulled out his small ice ax. He dug the ax into the wall and began to climb. Why had she gone with Griffin? Did he threaten her or was she still fooled by him like everybody else? It appeared that their goal was the summit, but Zayden didn't want to think about what Griffin would do with her once they reached the top.

Zayden pushed the terrifying thoughts away. Worrying wouldn't help. Praying and climbing would. *Dear Lord, protect Lenaia. Help me get to her. I need Your strength now.*

His body took over the climb on autopilot, his mind only vaguely aware of his gloved hands gripping the screws, his shoes spiking into the ice, and his arms thrusting the ax.

THE CRUNCH OF SNOW, the blinding white ice, the effort needed to push her ice spikes in to get traction—all of it became monotonous. Lenaia had slept for only a few hours. The lack of sleep combined with the thin air had caused her pounding headache to return. She rubbed at her temples with one hand, keeping the other out for balance. The slopes they'd traversed today had gradually increased in angle. Now, she was connected to Griffin by a rope, even while they walked. At least they hadn't come across any more ice walls.

He held the gun by his side, its presence a constant reminder of this forced march. Would he blow the mountain today?

"I need to rest. My feet are sore and my calves are killing me," she said. They'd been walking since before dawn.

"Nah, we'll make the summit in a couple of hours. Let's just get there."

So, they *were* going to the top. She'd suspected as much with the distance they'd traveled today. But the sooner they got there, the sooner he would execute his plan, and she had no way to stop him.

"What if I don't go, Griffin?"

He answered without turning around. "You should go."

"You're going to kill me anyway. Here or there, who cares?"

He shook his head as if dealing with an irritating gnat. "If you want to die right now, then fine." He raised the gun, gripping it tight. His face was expressionless, but his white knuckles betrayed his true emotions. This was difficult for him. And yet, one look at his eyes, now turned murky green, and she had no doubt he'd kill her now, if necessary.

She put her hands up. "Okay, I'm going."

He relaxed his grip on the gun but didn't lower it.

She picked up her feet and took the lead. "Would your family want you to do this?" She said it over her shoulder in almost a whisper.

"You don't know anything about my family."

"I know a little. Pastor Doug told me."

"That old coot needs to mind his own business."

"Speaking of Pastor Doug, did you know he has a son at home? Scott's not much younger than you."

"I vaguely remember."

She glanced back at him. "He had an accident and is paralyzed from the waist down."

"Nope, didn't know that." He circled the gun in the air. "Keep moving."

"If you blow the glacier and trigger a mudflow, he won't be able to get out of the house fast enough. He'll be killed."

"Too bad for him."

She stopped and turned to face him. He met her gaze, his face as hard as granite. "You can't mean that."

He gestured again for her to get moving. "It's not like I want him to die, but really, what kind of life does he have anyway?"

She resumed walking. "You mean because he's paralyzed?"

"Of course. He's half a person already."

Fury boiled through her veins. "How can you—"

The ground dropped out from under her feet. Her legs swung over empty space and her arms grasped for anything to hold on to, but found only air.

She plunged downward, falling until the rope jerked her to a stop. Her body swung in a wide arc before slamming into a solid wall of ice. She grunted with the impact.

Below her, empty blue space stretched down. No bottom in sight. Pure horror froze her heart solid. She was dangling inside an ice crevasse.

PASTOR DOUG SHUT the garage door to his house as he entered. "Ethel? Are you here?"

Ethel Murphy stayed with Scott every Monday and Wednesday afternoon so his wife, Carol could volunteer at the community center while Pastor Doug led a men's group at the church. She came out from the kitchen, wiping her hands on a towel. "Pastor, what are you doing home?"

"I canceled the men's group. The town is evacuating. You need to get up to the community center right away."

She tilted her white bobbed head. "Why?"

"A possible lahar."

She raised one eyebrow. "But the sirens haven't gone off."

"I know. There is a danger, though. Trust me."

"Okay. Can I go home first to pick up a few things?"

"Only if it takes you less than five minutes." They had to be running short on time. It had taken hours to find the mayor and convince him to start the evacuation based on Zayden's word. But Pastor Doug had put the town before his needs, praying all the while that he would have time to get Scott out.

She pointed up the stairs. "Scott's reading in his room. You'll be okay here?"

"We're not staying. I'll get Scott into the car and to the center. I told Carol to stay up there."

Ethel nodded and grabbed her jacket off the coat rack. "Be careful, Pastor."

After Ethel left, he climbed the stairs. His son lay propped up against the headboard. The copy of *War and Peace* on his chest moved up and down rhythmically with his snores.

Pastor Doug smiled. Scott had always been a deep thinker, but even he couldn't stay awake while reading Tolstoy.

He touched Scott's arm. "Wake up, son."

Scott's lids opened and he searched the room in a daze for a second. Pastor Doug quickly explained to Scott the full reason why they needed to evacuate. The totality of the information would have sent Ethel into a tizzy, but Scott merely nodded and pushed back the covers.

"Where's Mom?"

Pastor Doug rolled over the wheelchair. "Already there."

Scott grabbed both his legs and swung them off the side of the bed. When he released them, they flopped down like a sack of rice.

Pastor Doug put an arm under Scott's shoulders. With his support, Scott used his arms to transfer himself to the chair. They'd never had to evacuate before and he prayed this process wouldn't take as long as normal.

He wheeled Scott to the chair lift where they used the same system to transfer him to the small electronic chair. Scott fastened the waist belt, then pressed the button to turn it on.

Nothing happened.

Scott tried again. Still nothing.

Pastor Doug flipped the switch for the hall light. Nothing. "Oh no."

"What?"

"I forgot. Part of the evacuation procedure is to turn off the electricity in town." It might lower the risk of fire, but it didn't help them right now.

"What do we do?"

"How about we lower you down each stair?"

Pastor Doug helped Scott climb out of the chair and onto the first step. Scott lifted his weight from behind with his arms and Pastor Doug yanked on his legs. Scott jerked down a step.

"Sorry, I'll lift next time, not pull." Pastor Doug brushed sweat from his brow and patted his generous stomach. "I guess this would be easier without my extra."

Scott laughed. They tried again and the process went smoother. They repeated the motions over and over until they were halfway down.

"I need to rest for a minute, Dad."

"That's a good idea."

Balancing on one step, Pastor Doug tugged his phone out of his back pants' pocket. He checked for messages from the mayor. None. Hopefully, the rest of the evacuation was progressing. He scrolled through his new texts and moved his thumb to clear the screen. After sticking the phone back in his pocket, he spun around to face Scott again, but his tired back muscles protested at the movement and over-rotated. Momentum carried him to the edge of the step. He stepped down but couldn't regain his balance.

His body tumbled down, twisting as it hit each step.

Scott screamed.

An impact forced the breath from his lungs, then blackness overwhelmed him.

CHAPTER 24

Travis's mind first registered cold dampness ... and darkness.

No, it wasn't dark. His eyes weren't open. He tried to open them, but the lids wouldn't budge.

He sucked in a breath, steeled his resolve, and tried again. They opened a fraction, only to fall closed again.

Relying on his ears instead, he heard no sounds, except his own breathing.

What had happened? He sifted through the sparse images stored in his memory. He'd arrived at Morgan somebody's house. The last name? He couldn't remember. It didn't matter.

He'd stood in the kitchen, drunk some lemonade, then nothing. Was he still at Morgan's house?

His neck ached as if his head lay kinked back against something. He shifted and his head flopped forward, his chin smacking his chest. He put all his effort into opening his eyes. The right one cracked opened first, and then the left.

A view of his lap. Moving his head seemed like too much work. Instead, he moved his eyes around. Supporting him was a plastic saucer chair, the kind found in bowling alleys, only this one must have had a higher back since his head had rested on it.

Slumping forward a little more, he examined underneath the saucer. The lone metal bar under the chair was bolted to the floor.

He shifted attention to his body. His arms were secured with handcuffs laced through holes drilled in the side of the chair. He moved one wrist, expecting a metallic clanking sound, but the noise was muffled by the plastic.

He tensed his shoulders, then his neck muscles in order to flip his head back. A wave of dizziness hit him as his head hit the back of the saucer-chair. When it passed, he opened his eyes again. The ceiling was made of concrete. A few naked light bulbs hung on wires. It smelled musty like a basement.

Tipping his head to one side, he stretched as far as he could see. A concrete wall flanked by a row of wooden work benches. Various tools rested on top and some hung in racks on the wall. Hammers, screwdrivers, and cordless drills, all waiting to be used. Why would someone keep all these tools in a basement instead of the garage?

A wooden door he hadn't noticed yet swung open and slammed into the wall with a sharp crack. He leveled his head, eyes squinting at the loud noise and brighter light.

Framed by the door, Morgan stood with his hands in the pockets of his dress pants. One pocket bulged out from its contents. A gun?

"Looks like the drugs are running their course," Morgan said.

"What did you give me?"

"Only a sedative."

Travis shook his head to clear away more of the cobwebs. "Like Rohypnol?"

Morgan leaned against the door frame. "I don't use anything quite so exotic. Too expensive. Besides, I want people to remember their time with me."

Morgan had drugged him. Why? His foggy mind was already

piecing together the answer. A woman from town was dead and he'd stumbled onto the killer—her husband. And based on this set up in the basement, she probably wasn't Morgan's first victim. Lightning bolts of terror sparked through his stomach. Lenaia had met with this killer, and then disappeared. He could ask what happened to her, but did he really want to know? "You want them to remember you right up until you kill them?" His voice sounded groggy.

Morgan gave a forced laugh. "Sorry, I don't kiss and tell."

"I thought people like you enjoyed talking."

"People like me? Are you afraid I'll be offended by the word sociopath or even serial killer?"

So Morgan *had* killed more than just his wife.

Morgan cocked his head to one side, studying Travis. "I've never had a man to talk to about this. Well, of course, Griffin knows, but he prefers not to hear about my activities." Morgan leaned against the door, his hands clasped in front, as if they were two friends chatting about the weather. "It's not about getting my baser needs met. Any decently charming man can find a woman to use. But to have control over their very life. You can't understand the power, what it feels like to hold someone as they die."

His stomach lurched. He did know what it was like to hold a dying person. He'd held Lenaia's uncle in Costa Rica and watched as the man took his last breath. "Not all it's cracked up to be."

Morgan didn't seem to hear his answer. "There's a moment when they're dying and they know it. When their eyes see things we can't see. A glimpse behind the veil of the other side. I try to get them to tell me about it."

Had Lenaia already gone to the other side at the hands of this madman? "Great, this is where you tell me there's some sort of otherworldly purpose to what you're doing." He almost smiled. Lenaia would be proud of his sarcasm.

Morgan shrugged. "There's a purpose for me, yes. For them, not so much."

Travis wanted to punch him in the face. Instead, he swallowed hard and fought for composure. His fear was turning to anger, and thankfully pushing the last of the drugs out, but if he lost control, he'd have no chance to escape. "What about your wife? Surely, she told you about the other side."

Morgan cast his eyes to the ground. "I didn't want to know what she saw. I regret that she had to pay for my mistake."

"I'd say you've made a lot of mistakes."

Morgan's eyes flashed with anger, but then he smiled as if remembering the sweetness of a first kiss. "I had told a friend I wasn't here at the winery the night Summer disappeared. My one mistake. I tried to get Rachel to lie for me, but all along I knew she wouldn't. She was pure. It's why I married her."

"So, you killed her to save yourself."

Morgan laid a hand against his chest. "Unfortunately for her, I'm not so pure."

Travis opened his mouth, then closed it. He needed to know about Lenaia, but could he stand to hear it if Morgan had done something to her? He doubted the man would tell him the truth, but maybe he'd know from the way Morgan reacted. He rattled the handcuffs binding him to the chair. "Is this what happened to Lenaia?"

Morgan twisted his lips to one side. "You really love her, don't you?"

He hesitated. Of course, Morgan already knew that. The man was toying with him. "I love her very much."

Morgan wrinkled his forehead and sighed. "To honor the memory of my Rachel, I will tell you the truth. She never came inside this house."

"That doesn't mean you didn't do something to her."

"I might have if she'd have come alone, but I was distracted by Griffin."

His heart ached. He wanted to believe Morgan more than

anything. Was it possible Lenaia was still alive? If so, then where was she?

Morgan shrugged. "Believe me or don't. It's up to you." His face turned sour. "Do you think this is any fun for me? This room was made for women." He spread his arms out in a circle, like a peacock. "Soundproof, of course, not that I have any neighbors to hear the screams. I built it myself. I've thought of bringing a man here, but it wasn't you."

He didn't want to ask Morgan about his next intended victim, but maybe then Travis could find a way to warn him. That was, if he could get out of here. "Who?"

Morgan let out a long sigh. "Griffin." He took a step closer. "He's the only other person who knows my secret. We have an agreement that I'm supposed to make orphans of children here in Mayim, especially from that weird church, but I don't like blackmail, even if it's mutual blackmail. Besides, we have a history together, although I'm not even sure he knows it."

Travis scrunched his brows and waited for Morgan to go on.

"Griffin's mom committed suicide after touching a man." Morgan's grin revealed perfect rows of teeth. "That man was me. And I wanted a lot more than just rubbing up against her. Who knew she'd flip out when we'd hardly done anything?" He brushed a hand over his stiff hair. "Recently, I've gotten it in my head that it would be fitting if I made him my first man. Kind of like a legacy thing. Joni killed herself because of me and Art left because of me. If I kill Griffin, I've destroyed an entire family—what a rush that would be." Morgan slowly shook his head. "But I wasn't going to do it until after he completed his plan. It's more ambitious than what I've done. I can't wait to see what the town looks like after a huge mudflow hits." He tapped a finger on his freshly shaved chin. "You and I will miss it way out here. Even so, I've got to do something about you."

Travis snorted. "How about you let me go?"

"Problem is, I've got another issue to worry about next door. I can't have either of you found near my property or it would raise too many questions." Morgan grabbed the door and swung it halfway closed. "Don't worry. I'll search for somewhere out of the way and peaceful. No one will ever find you."

LENAIA HEARD Griffin yelling from above but couldn't make out the words. The sound bounced off the icy planes surrounding her, jumping away from her ears. Would he try to help her up or would he cut the rope at any minute?

She dangled for several seconds, finally deciding not to wait for him. Hopefully, he had set an anchor with his ax to keep the rope tight or else her efforts would pull him over and they'd both plummet to the bottom. The fall would crack her skull. Or worse, she could be corked—wedged into the narrow bottom with no way out, waiting for starvation to claim her.

Without an ax or anything else to help her climb, she had to do it the hard way. Gripping the rope in both hands, she placed her ice spikes flat on the smooth wall. She shifted her body to spread her weight horizontally and began pulling herself up the rope, digging her spikes in as deep as possible with each step.

She climbed hand over hand, fighting the downward pull of gravity. By the time she reached the top, her arms burned and her legs shook.

Griffin grabbed the rope at her waist, hauled her over, and threw her face-first to the ground. She lay in the snow with no energy to move while he stood over her.

"Try not to do that again," he said in a flat voice.

She twisted her head to look in his direction. Wet strands of hair stuck to her face. "I'm surprised you didn't cut the rope."

He took a few steps away from her. "I considered it. But I still might need you. You're the bait. In case your boyfriend decides to track you up here, once he discovers you're gone."

"He's my ex-boyfriend."

"Whatever. It's obvious he's never gotten over you. Not that I blame him." Griffin ran his eyes along the length of her body. Her coat wouldn't give him much to leer at, but she suddenly wished she was wearing thick snow pants instead of tight jeans.

She bit her lip, forcing herself not to respond. Griffin was toying with her, enjoying his power. Let him get comfortable while she looked for an opportunity to escape.

She crawled to her feet and moved away from him but couldn't go far. The rope kept her close.

"You make a great distraction, and if he comes up here, I'll only need to distract him for a little while. Until I can execute the plan."

"But if Zayden follows our tracks, he'll find the explosives."

Griffin grinned. "I don't care if he finds the *one*."

Shivers coursed through her body. He discussed destroying the mountain and killing people in Mayim with no emotion. "And after you blow the mountain, then what about us?"

"Everything in Mayim will be buried, so when they can't find you, the police will assume all of us were victims of the lahar you both started."

She gazed up at the summit, just a few hundred feet above them. The only thing up there was rock and ice. He couldn't throw her into a pit of lava or anything. At least, not on this mountain, unless ...

Her body trembled. He planned on taking them into the caves. One of the most dangerous places on the mountain.

A muffled ding came from Griffin's pack. He swung it off his shoulders, pulled out her phone and read the display. "Go figure. It's your lover boy, again. A call wouldn't go through so he texted you." Griffin looked at her for a second like he might tell her what the text said, but then he shrugged and tossed the phone into the ice crevasse. "We don't need that anymore." He gestured for her to walk parallel to the fissure. "Let's go. It looks like the crevasse tapers off over there."

She forced her aching body to walk. It took a few steps before her muscles stabilized and her legs stopped shaking, but her hands never did. It wasn't just muscle fatigue; primal fear was seeping into her veins. If she didn't get out of this mess alive, she'd never see Travis again on this side of heaven. Never have the chance to stand in awe as he got down on one knee, to gaze on his smile as she pledged her life to him, to see him tenderly hold his first precious child. Travis would make a wonderful father. All of the things she'd been afraid of, had been avoiding, now haunted her.

Leading the way, she followed the crevasse for fifty yards, until it narrowed enough for them to jump over. He forced her to jump first, so she did, landing unsteadily on the other side. She turned back to face him, separated by only the chasm. Maybe she could pull hard on the rope and get him to fall, but then she'd fall, too, with no way to cut the rope.

Before jumping, Griffin flipped the safety on and strapped the gun to the back of his pack with a carabiner. Another, more promising, idea formed in her mind.

He took one step, then leaped over the open air, his ice ax outstretched in one hand. As he came to her side of the divide, she put her hand on his back and helped carry his momentum forward. He landed face-down. She stepped on his pack to hold him there, as she worked to unhook the gun.

He struggled, pushing her off just as the gun broke free. It flew from her hand, toward the crevasse, stopping inches short of the edge. They both scrambled for the weapon.

She reached it first, flipping the safety off as she curled her finger over the trigger. She turned and raised her arm.

Sudden movement came from her left. The blunt end of the ice ax was on target to hit her face. She ducked, but it connected with the tip of her chin, slicing her skin and spilling blood in the snow.

His knee came up before she could react, hitting in exactly the same spot. Pain knifed through her jaw. She fell to the snow, dazed.

He ripped the gun from her hand.

She lifted up on her arms, one hand pressed to her chin. He knelt next to her and put the gun to her head. His hand shook, his teeth ground back and forth.

"Go on. Do it," she yelled as her fear turned into anger. "You're going to kill me anyway, so let's ruin your masterful plan."

His jaw relaxed. He leaned back on his heels, dropping the gun to his thigh. He bit his lip, stretching it through his teeth. She watched his anger fade, replaced by grim determination. "Get up. We're almost there."

She swiped her sleeve over her chin and got to her feet, walking ahead of him up the slope and along a narrow path toward the summit. One of these times her attempts at escape would probably get her killed, but she had to try.

After another hour of hiking, Columbia Crest, the highest of the two cones on Mt. Rainier, came into view. It was a circular mass of steam and ice, like a porcelain bowl full of hot soup, but the source of the heat came from deep down. Gases and steam snaked through the neck of the volcano along the same conduit that carried magma during an eruption.

He gave her a shove. "Keep going."

She willed her feet to move again. Snow had worked its way into her boots some time ago, probably during one of her scuffles with Griffin, and her feet were numb.

She trudged up the slope with a heavy weight in her chest. The closer they got to the top, the faster she approached her fate. Maybe it didn't matter, in the end. She couldn't change the outcome. She'd fight for her life, but God would do what He wanted. She was surprised to feel a little less bitterness and a little more peace with that thought.

As they neared the top, she had to walk hunched over at the waist, digging handholds in the ice to make it up. Inside her gloves, her fingers were completely numb. She stopped to rub them, turning around to lean her back into the mountain for balance. Glancing up, she caught her breath at the magnificent view of the valley below. Beyond the glaciers, the Puyallup River swept through thick trees until the ground flattened and green fields stretched out in all directions. A stunning vista where Mayim sat peaceful and ignorant in the middle.

Ice crunched under her back as she shifted to peer at Griffin. "We're here. Now what?"

He gave her only a cursory glance as he circled around the cone, stabbing at the jagged ice with the blunt end of his ax. She knew what he was looking for. An opening to the steam caves, deep tunnels where steam had carved the glacial ice into caverns. The caves were one of the most unstable places on earth because the weakened glacial ice made them prone to collapse.

The steam caves led to a lake beneath the snowcap. All of it was notoriously perilous, akin to a labyrinth of death traps. Few climbers braved the tunnels and even fewer made it out alive. In her five years on the mountain, she'd never been in them. She took a deep breath and tried to gather her strength.

He punched a hole in the ice with his ax, then shoved the ax around in a circle to clear it out. He peered inside. "This could be good, but a more level spot is over this way." He moved ten yards to his left, dragging her with him. After punching another hole, he swiped the snow away and looked inside. "Perfect."

She moved with him because of the rope tethering them together, but otherwise she ignored him. Her legs ached and the thinner air stole her breath. "Why are we here?"

"You mean besides the obvious fact there's nowhere to run?"

He didn't know her very well. She'd be willing to take her chances running through the steam caves. "Besides that."

"This is the safest place on the mountain to ride out the explosion."

Really? An explosion rocking the already friable ice caves didn't sound safe to her.

He walked over and kicked her foot. "Come on. You're going in first."

She glared up at him.

He tugged on the rope. "Or I'll throw you in."

She rolled to her stomach and pushed herself up to a bent position, then scooted along the snow to the opening he had created in the ice. The drop was around fifteen feet. She could survive it but would probably break a leg.

He kicked at the opening, widening it, until he reached thicker ice. Apparently satisfied the bottom part would hold the rope, he hammered in a dead man snow anchor to distribute her weight, strapped a carabiner to her harness, and threaded the rope through it. Finally, he released her from the rope that tied them together when she had nowhere to go but down.

"Lean over the edge," he said.

She turned around at the opening and leaned back until the rope supported her weight. He played the rope out as she sat back into it, letting her feet swing over the edge, dangling in space above the floor of the cave.

He let the rope out foot by foot. At the floor, she put her feet down and slipped, landing on her rear end.

"Untie the rope so I can pull it back up," he yelled from up top.

She got back to her feet. And if she didn't, he'd probably start shooting.

As soon as she untied the figure eight knot, he pulled on the rope. She watched it slip through her hands, before turning her attention to her surroundings. The steam cave she'd landed in was more like a large room painted in celestial blue. Light shimmered across the ice, throwing cascading shades of blue everywhere.

In the back corner of the room, a blackened spot marked where someone had built a small fire. A dangerous practice in an already deadly place.

An arched opening led farther into the tunnels. She thought about making a break for it, but Griffin had the gun trained on her as he lowered himself down. He landed next to her with his feet spread wide to keep from falling.

She unzipped her jacket and stripped down to her zippered sweatshirt, grateful for the steamy warmth provided by the mountain. Her body began to thaw, but her heart remained ice-cold. They'd made it to Griffin's goal and now he would use her to lure Zayden up here, kill them both and leave their bodies in the steam caves.

He must have noticed her expression because he looked over and studied her. "It won't hurt." He said it almost gently.

She wanted to punch him in the face. "How would you know?"

He took a step toward her. "I meant that I'll make it as painless as possible."

"I suppose you want me to thank you for that. How can you talk about people dying like you don't care?"

"Because only the goal matters. Those people deserve to die."

"And the rest who are caught in the mudflow? And me? And Zayden? Do we deserve it?"

"Look, I know you believe in all that God stuff, like you have something you're supposed to do here on earth." He put on a calm expression that she found condescending. "The truth is, there is no great plan."

Inside, she cringed. If only she was as confident in a divine plan as Griffin supposed. No, her will to survive came from a deep, primitive fear of dying and of leaving Travis behind, not so much the desire to fulfill her God-given destiny. Her stomach clenched, then quaked with nausea. She had completely stopped trusting God without realizing the extent of it.

"When you die, you're just gone. One less animal in the human species." He tucked the gun into the waistband of his jeans. "You won't exist anymore and the good news is, you won't know it. So, as long as there's no pain, it doesn't really matter."

"Why don't you believe?"

"In God? First of all, there's no proof. Quite the opposite, in fact. The world is consumed by evil, especially in churches, supposedly God's house."

"But that evil comes from people. You can't blame God for it."

He shook his head as if again dealing with a gullible child. "I don't blame Him. He isn't there to blame. You're right. People are the ones who do evil. And that evil needs to be dealt with here and now."

"Repaying evil for evil only puts more evil in the world."

He gave her a sideways smile. "Not if you call it justice."

"Where's the justice for the innocent people who might die so you can have revenge?"

"They'll get the same mercy given to my mom." He paused, staring at the icy ceiling, as if thinking about something far away. "She doesn't exist anymore. She's not in heaven somewhere looking down on me. That's a fairy tale told by those who are too weak to accept that death is final: the end, no coming back—do not pass go, do not collect two hundred dollars. The game is over for you."

"What if you're wrong?"

"If I'm wrong, I won't know it until I'm dead and by then, I'm pretty sure I won't care."

His answers sounded clinically logical. She had to try an emotional line of reasoning. "Would your mother want you to do this?"

He stopped and turned around, his hand balled into fists. "Do you know what she did to herself?"

Lenaia didn't answer. The little that Pastor Doug had told her was awful.

"She tried to cut off her own arm." He made a slicing motion across his bicep. "Because she touched a man with lust in her heart. Pastor Marty taught her to literally cut sin out of her life." Griffin grabbed the rope, turned his back on her and looped it around an icy knob in the wall. "I found my mother's cold body covered in blood, lying next to her journal. The last line she wrote was, 'May Pastor Marty forgive me.'" He snorted. "Not God, but Pastor Marty. That tells you where her mind was. She didn't believe in God, either."

"Maybe she did. Sometimes people just get confused ... " Lenaia's voice trailed off as she realized how accurately the words applied to her. She'd been confused for more than a year now. During his life, Uncle Jim had tried to get her to turn her back on God. Now, it was clear that what he'd failed to do in life, he'd accomplished in death. As she'd fought God's sovereignty over her uncle's death, she'd destroyed her trust in Him.

And not just because of her uncle. With all the death surrounding her lately—Dan, Randy, Rachel—she should have turned to God in desperation, not shut Him out. Her fear of a future *she* couldn't control had led her to this point where she was facing no future at all.

"Oh, she was confused, all right." He sat on a ledge of ice sticking out from the wall. "She put Pastor Marty on some sort of pedestal. Like he had superpowers. The same way you do with Jesus. It's crazy to believe in lunatics who claim to be more than they are."

She let the comment go. He was either trying to poke at her or distract her. Arguing with him wouldn't help. Instead, for the first time in a long time, she prayed.

Dear Lord, I've drifted so far in my anger. I blamed You for the choices Uncle Jim made. I should have known that You loved Uncle Jim more than I did. But I gave up. Just like Griffin's mom, I gave up living a life defined by You. I stopped participating in the plan You have for my life. Please, forgive me.

Inside of her, something shifted. She knew she'd been forgiven as soon as the words had gone through her head and she also knew she couldn't give up on this situation. She said the name of

Jesus over and over in her head as she spoke her next words. "Not that I'm anxious to die or anything, but what are we waiting for?"

"Two things. The church meeting starts at five o'clock. I'll wait until 5:15, to account for stragglers."

"And the other thing?"

"Zayden. If he's following us, he's probably hours behind, but he might get here before I'm ready."

Lenaia dropped to the floor of the cave, closed her eyes, and silently prayed for Zayden to turn around.

CHAPTER 25

I can't have either of you found. Morgan's words echoed through Travis's mind. Morgan must have another victim here. Had he lied about Lenaia?

Travis had to escape, not just for his sake, but for Lenaia and whomever else had been caught in this monster's lair. The more he moved, the more his body woke up. He scanned the basement room again. All concrete, no windows, which left the door as the only avenue of escape.

He pulled at the handcuffs. Morgan had put them on tight. No way to slip his hands out of them.

Shifting in the chair, he heard it creak. Morgan claimed he'd designed this room for women. Travis leaned forward and examined the whole of the chair. The plastic seat, keeping him trapped like an egg in a carton, fed into a metal pole that was one solid piece and flattened into a plate on the floor. The plate was bolted down.

Maybe the plastic would be the weak point. Rocking back and forth, he threw his full weight forward and backward at each extreme. The chair protested with creaks and pops. Hopefully the room was truly soundproof and Morgan didn't have a camera in here.

After several minutes, dizziness overcame him and he gave up. Where the plastic met the base must have been reinforced. Morgan was no amateur.

When the spinning calmed, Travis returned to examining the chair. He leaned all the way to the right. The hole for the handcuffs was about the size of an orange, cut into the seat of the chair below the area where the plastic folded over into a tiny armrest. Even if he yanked a handcuff through the base plastic, he probably couldn't get it through the doubled over armrest.

He bent over to the other side. This hole had been made slightly higher in the side, cutting a little into the armrest. If he could get a crack started there, it might propagate.

Slumping first to his left and holding his arm up, he quickly shifted his weight and pulled. The handcuff scraped against the plastic. He repeated the motion, pulling even harder.

His arm stayed tethered, but he leaned over to look. One small crack in the armrest.

Resuming the position, he pulled again as hard as he could. The handcuff cut into his wrist. Blood trickled down, smearing along the plastic and onto his jeans.

He leaned over to check his progress. The crack had lengthened just a little. He rested for a minute, then tried again. Ignoring the pain, he pulled with all his strength.

The crack grew but not enough.

He needed more leverage.

Blinking, he tried to clear his head. What else could he use?

His gaze fell to his feet. They were unshackled. He pulled his long legs up. The chair was too cramped to push much, but he wedged his knees in as extra pressure on the plastic side.

He pulled his wrist and pushed with his knees.

After several minutes of struggling, at last, he heard a satisfying crack. The armrest split. His right hand, still handcuffed, swung free.

He listened for a moment. No sound of footsteps, but he probably wouldn't hear Morgan coming in a soundproofed room. Either way, he had to keep trying to get out. Not much chance he could break through the other armrest. Instead, he swung his body over the chair and stretched toward the workbench. A clawed hammer sat on the edge.

He spread his legs wide, reaching with his right hand. Tiny spherical drops of blood hit the floor from his bleeding wrist.

His fingertips brushed the handle, but he couldn't quite get it. He jiggled the handcuff still tethered to his left wrist. It straightened and gave him another half-inch. He reached again. It still wasn't quite enough. His fingers circled the handle, grabbing for traction, but the hammer slid past and fell to the floor with a clang. Too far away to grab with his hands.

He leaned back and stretched both legs as far as they would go. His left hand protested at being smashed into the metal cuff. He kept scooting forward until he was splayed out like a rubber chicken. But his toes stopped two inches too short.

In frustration, he jumped at it with both feet. He fell on his tailbone. Knife-edged pain shot through his back and down his arm. His handcuffed wrist burned.

The pain took some time to ebb. When it faded into a dull ache, he turned his attention back to the hammer. At this level, his legs would stretch out farther. He rolled onto his side and reached a leg out. It connected with the hammer, slowly pulling it closer. He slid it inch by inch until it was close enough to grab. He scooped it up and held it against his chest. Relief flooded through him.

Shuffling along the floor, he inched back to the chair, ignoring the shooting pain in his wrist. He put the clawed end of the hammer into the underside of the hole above his left handcuff and pushed the handle up full force. The plastic buckled at first, then split up the middle. The brittle crack of breaking plastic had never sounded so sweet.

He stood and made a quick circle around the room to confirm there were no windows or other avenue of escape—only the door. The thick wooden door was held in place by one deadbolt. The hinges were on the outside. He'd have to bust the lock.

Grabbing a screwdriver, he placed it in the lock, then took a hammer and hit the screwdriver. The clang of metal against metal rang out. He hit again and again. The lock didn't budge.

He returned to the workbench. The drill should work, although it would be even noisier. Morgan hadn't come down yet. He might be pushing his luck, but he had to try.

With his heart thrumming, he plugged the drill into an outlet, took it to the door, and turned it on. Metal screeched against metal as the rotating bit churned, destroying the locking mechanism. Minutes later, he stood to the side and pulled the lock out of its hole, half expecting Morgan to shoot at him through it.

He waited a few seconds. No sound of movement. Nothing.

Maybe Morgan had left. Travis turned the handle and opened the door to the rest of the basement. On his left was another doorway with a lock as formidable as the one he'd just drilled out, to his right sat the stairs, and at the other end he saw a window. He quietly moved to the dirty glass, peering out at the circle driveway.

His rental car was gone. Morgan must have left in it.

There had to be another vehicle around here. Otherwise, Travis would have to walk out. But first, he needed to know if anyone else waited behind that door.

He crept quietly over, although he wasn't sure why. Near the crack, he used a loud whisper, "Hello?"

A muffled response.

He tried again louder, "Who's in there?"

Another incoherent jumble of words. Maybe this room was

soundproof as well. He quickly plugged the drill into an outlet in the main room, and went to work on the lock.

Minutes later, it fell out and he pulled the door open. A woman in her twenties with reddish-blond hair sat on the ground, a long chain handcuffed to her ankle. Her expression held amazement. "You're getting me out of here?"

He nodded as he pulled the drill over to her foot. "I'm Travis."

"Summer. Thank you so much. I have an eight-year-old daughter." Her eyes teared up. "He's a monster. He said he took me on purpose because my husband died a month ago. His goal is to make my daughter an orphan. Who does that?"

Realization hit. This was one of the women Lenaia had been searching for. "Hold still. I need to get this off you and get us out of here before Morgan comes back."

Her eyes went wide as she took in the knowledge they were still in danger. "I thought I'd be dead by now." A tear escaped from her right eye. "But he said he had to wait. Something about another woman being found."

Morgan must have meant his wife. Travis focused on her chains, drilling them out in only a few minutes, then he took another minute to do the same to his handcuffs.

When he finished, he took her hand and headed for the stairs. He dashed up the steps, but stopped at the landing. All was quiet. Towing her along, he rushed through the house to the place where he thought the garage would be situated.

After opening a few doors, he found the garage where a black Escalade sat unlocked. He found the keys hanging on a hook on the wall. Kind of trusting for a killer. Or maybe just overconfident.

Travis punched the button to open the garage door and slid behind the wheel. Using the backup camera, he backed out of the garage and around half of the circle, then put the car in drive and hit the gas.

The car accelerated, spitting gravel behind. He struggled to straighten out the wheel. He had to calm down or he'd run them off the road.

As he came around the circle, he looked up and his eyes landed on a person in the road ahead. Morgan stood in the center of the driveway, shaking his head. He held a gun, currently pointed at the ground. Travis's first instinct was to ram him, but he didn't want to kill him. Morgan might be the only person who could tell him what had happened to Lenaia. Hopefully, the man would jump out of the way.

Travis revved the engine. The car fishtailed on the gravel.

Morgan raised the gun and fired.

Bullets cracked through the windshield dead center, below the rear-view mirror. Travis ducked, keeping his eyes just above the dashboard.

The vehicle barreled down the driveway, ever closer to Morgan. The man didn't move but continued to fire.

Travis felt a sting in his right bicep, like someone had pinched his arm in a vice. Summer screamed.

Morgan stared him down with eyes of steel. He wasn't going to move. It was a game of chicken. But if Travis killed him, they would both lose. Travis would never know what happened to Lenaia, and he could end up in prison.

Travis spun the wheel to the right. The vehicle dipped as it went off the driveway, then lurched across the uneven ground, slamming him into the side window. The vehicle plowed through rows and rows of trellises, upending them like toothpicks. Travis banged back and forth between the steering wheel and the door while Summer continued to scream in his ear.

With the momentum finally spent, the vehicle pitched forward and came to rest in a small drainage ditch, just short of the trees.

Travis groaned. Everything hurt. He twisted his sore neck to look around. Something red oozed down the seat next to him. It came from his arm. He held it forward to examine it. A bullet had passed through, taking with it a chunk of his flesh. Summer groaned beside him, her eyes closed.

The car door swung open and he instinctively drew back, but had nowhere to go. Morgan stood with feet spread wide and one hand against the door to prevent it from falling closed. In the other hand, he held a gun pointed at Travis's forehead.

Morgan cocked his head at the long, bumpy path the SUV had made through the vineyard. He seemed strangely calm, almost excited. "Nice try. Now get out. You're bleeding all over the leather."

Travis twisted around in the car seat to follow his gaze. At least, the trenches in the vineyard were evidence that he'd been here.

He swung his legs out and pushed off the seat, making sure his bloody arm drug across the steering wheel. He'd leave behind all the DNA he could. As he climbed out, he saw a chance to escape. After he passed by, Morgan would be under the weight of the forward leaning door for half a second, while Travis was free. It might be their only chance.

He hesitated a second to make sure Summer was out of the car, then he ducked under the car door and twisted around, grabbing the door from behind. He swung it into Morgan, catching him on the hand. The gun fell into a pile of crushed wood and wire.

The car door trapped Morgan temporarily, but they didn't have much time. "Run!"

Travis bolted for the small patch of woods nearby with Summer following. At the edge of the trees, he dared a quick glance back. Morgan had freed himself and was now untangling wire from the gun.

"Keep going." He pushed Summer ahead of him, and they ran about a hundred feet before the trees started to thin. More rows of trellises appeared ahead.

He stopped and heard thrashing noises behind them. Morgan

couldn't be far away which meant they couldn't travel over exposed ground.

He searched frantically for a better option. The only cover was on the other side of the road where the terrain sloped up. But they'd have to make it across without getting shot ... again.

The thrashing came closer. "Cross the street. Now!"

Side by side, they sped through the tall, grassy plants along the drainage ditch and raced up the short hill to the pavement. Up here, they were sitting ducks but at least moving targets.

"Stop." Morgan sounded breathless.

A bullet whizzed by Travis's left shoulder and sunk deep into a tree in front of him.

"Go!" He pushed Summer ahead of him into the forest.

Another bullet streaked by, ruffling the hair by his ear. That one was too close.

As the cool shadows enveloped them, he grabbed Summer's hand and darted to the left. Going straight up would only slow them down, allowing Morgan to catch up. Instead, they skirted around the base of the hill, trying to move quickly, yet quietly—the way Lenaia had taught him in the jungle.

Lenaia. His heart flipped over at every thought of her. Those sweet, plum lips. Her hair cascading down her back like satin rain. Eyes the luminescent color of amber stained glass. Even angry, like the last time he saw her, her features were imperious and regal. Where was she? And could he escape Morgan long enough to find her?

A soft grunt came from beside him. He wrapped an arm around Summer's shoulder to assist her over a small creek. They both had scratches running along their cheeks and forearms from darting through the trees, but that wasn't his biggest concern. Since they'd entered the forest, she'd been stumbling over her own feet, and he worried she might be going into shock. Although he intended to do everything he could to get Summer home to her daughter, he couldn't stop wishing his arms were around Lenaia instead.

~

THE BAREST HINT of shuffling came from above, somewhere outside the cavern. Lenaia shifted her position on the floor, turning her ear in the direction of the noise. Griffin tilted his head as well. Had he heard it, too?

He sat with his back to their entrance hole on a wedge of ice sticking out from the wall. Over his shoulder, she saw a shadow darken the hole, then disappear.

Someone was out there. Zayden? Time to create a distraction.

"Do you really think Pastor Marty was responsible for your mom's death?" She raised her voice without being obvious, just in case the person hadn't seen their footsteps trailing off to the steam caves.

Griffin focused shadowed eyes on her. "He convinced my mom that she was no good. He broke her down until all that mattered was her sin. Doesn't sound like a pastoral thing to do, does it?"

"But your mother could have read the Bible. She could have seen for herself what God says. You were right when you said she didn't believe in the end." She stood, walked a few paces, and then turned on him. "Face it. Your mother just gave up. She committed suicide because it was the easy way out."

"You don't know what you're talking about." He tightened his grip on the gun resting on his right knee.

Lenaia paused. She needed to push him, but not too hard. If Zayden was outside, he needed time. She focused her attention on Griffin and resisted the urge to look at the hole above her. "Oh, but I *do* know. I've been doing the same thing. I gave up on God the minute after He let my uncle die."

"People die every day, Lenaia."

"Like your mom?"

Griffin narrowed his eyes at her. She got the sense he was dissecting her motives. She put on her best innocent face. Suddenly, he laughed and the sound echoed off the smooth walls. "So what? You think your uncle's in hell now or something?"

He was more perceptive than she'd given him credit for. "I don't know. I guess I wish I knew where he was."

"I can tell you. He's nowhere."

A small scraping sound, like grinding against the ice, this time farther away and from a different angle.

She looked at Griffin, keeping her expression flat. "Maybe I was afraid of that too. I prayed every day for my uncle to come to know Jesus. And then, to have my prayer answered with his death ... " She turned her back on him. "I decided God didn't care about what I wanted. He would do what He wanted no matter how I felt. I might not have killed myself, but I was like the walking dead."

"We're all walking dead, Lenaia. That's reality."

It was the response she was hoping for. In Griffin's mind, logic reigned. If she could convince him that his logic was flawed, maybe he'd give this up. She turned to face him. "If you believe that, then it really doesn't matter what Pastor Marty did to your mom since she was going to die someday anyway. Besides, her death is irreversible history."

Griffin blinked. Apparently, he hadn't expected this turn in the conversation. He slid the gun across to his lap. "Reality is what we make it. And I say he has to pay for what he did."

"But what if you're wrong? What if reality is what God makes it?"

"Seriously? If God exists then He killed your uncle. He could have stopped it, but He didn't. And you're okay with that? Sounds like you're the one not dealing with reality."

His words stung. Griffin was right. She hadn't been dealing with the reality of her uncle's death. It was time to let go of what happened and finally acknowledge God's truth. "The reality is that

God is loving. He loves me. He loved my uncle, and even respected him enough to accept his choice."

"What choice?"

She crossed her arms. "The choice to spend eternity *without* God."

Griffin rubbed the gun along the top of his jeans. "Is this the part where you say 'God loves you too, Griffin' and I break down in tears?"

Behind him, Zayden stepped through a small opening in the ice, poised to throw an ax. Relief washed over her, but she refused to let it show on her face.

"Nope, this is the part where I say put the gun down or you get an ax in the back." Zayden's voice held a combination of anger and strength she'd never heard from him before.

Griffin hesitated for a second. Would Zayden really do it? Griffin didn't look convinced.

In one quick move, Griffin spun around to his right and raised the gun.

Zayden let the ax fly, then ducked behind the ice bench as a lone bullet sped over his head.

Lenaia dropped to the floor and covered her face.

When no other shots were fired, she lowered her arm and looked around. Griffin stood staring at the blunt handle of the ax sticking out of his right shoulder. Somehow he still gripped the gun, the barrel pointed at the floor.

Griffin transferred the gun to his left hand.

Zayden jumped at him, sending them both hurtling to the ice floor. The ax fell and spun in her direction. She grabbed it with shaking hands.

The two men writhed on the floor, each one struggling for control of the gun. Griffin still clutched the gun in his left hand—the hand Zayden held pinned to the ice.

Zayden swung a fist at Griffin's face, but Griffin bobbed his head to one side. Zayden's fist slammed into the solid ice. He groaned, but kept his hold on Griffin's arm.

Griffin punched Zayden in the stomach. As they fought, they slid across the ice. Zayden kept losing traction, allowing Griffin to squirm away.

Lenaia circled around them until she held the ax over Griffin's head. "Give the gun to Zayden or I'll split your skull."

Griffin breathed heavily and eyed her suspiciously. He shook his head. "You wouldn't."

"Do you really want to find out?"

Griffin released his hold on the weapon. Zayden grabbed it and squatted to a crouched position, putting a hand out for balance. Griffin twisted away from him and lunged for his backpack. From inside it, he pulled out a skinny, black box with a small electronic display. It looked like a walkie-talkie, but she knew better.

"What's that?" Zayden asked.

Griffin took a step toward them. "The fulfillment of my plan. I'm not going to let you mess it up."

"The plan is over, Griffin." Zayden held the gun level. "I've already disarmed all the explosives."

Griffin squinted at Zayden. "You're bluffing."

Lenaia spied a twitch near Zayden's eye. He was bluffing, or at least he wasn't sure.

Griffin must have seen it too. He held the box straight out, but at an angle, inviting them to read it. A square electronic rectangle on the screen read 'detonate.' He shifted his gaze between the two of them, his thumb poised over the screen.

Zayden shook his head. "I already told you. I disarmed them."

"Let's find out," Griffin said as he pushed the electronic button.

CHAPTER 26

ravis relaxed a little once they had passed by the house and discovered Morgan was searching for them in the Escalade. As long as they stayed off the road, they had a chance to escape. They climbed for more than an hour before they came out of the trees near the top of a mini-mountain. He led Summer around to the northern side before collapsing on the ground. His lungs ached from the altitude and his legs burned. Summer lowered herself down next to him.

In a valley, straight ahead, Mayim sat with its streets leading in multiple directions at random angles, as if it had grown haphazardly out of the fertile volcanic soil. To their left, the peak of Mt. Rainier was framed by the other mountains of the Cascade Range. He couldn't identify them by name, but they stood as a reminder of the upheaval this area had seen in the past. A wondrous display of God's power. He understood why Lenaia loved it out here.

A deep, menacing rumble came from the mountain. The ground shook violently under his backside. Good thing they were already sitting.

When the shaking subsided, he scanned the horizon. A tendril of smoke rose halfway up the slope of Mt. Rainier, coming from one of the glaciers. As he watched, the tendril dissipated, replaced by a white wave of material, sliding down the mountain.

Underneath the white wall, steam erupted out of the rock. He squinted into the distance. Had the volcano erupted? He didn't see any lava, only the mass of flowing white.

The wave built on itself, darkening as it added forest material. Now, ice, water, and mud picked up speed as they moved downslope.

A lahar—a mudflow traveling faster than an Olympic sprinter!

By the time the mudflow reached the tree line, the sediment had turned it into a churning, brown mass. Seconds later, it reached the river valley, where trees fell like dominoes, bridges were turned into kindling and swept downstream, and the air was filled with a roaring rush. The water was a rabid beast that couldn't be stopped.

He clutched at his hair, digging his fingers into his scalp. There was nothing he could do. The lahar would overtake the town in minutes. In the distance, the piercing whine of sirens echoed the only warning the town would get.

Lenaia. Was she heading toward a shelter somewhere? What if she'd been on the mountain?

~

"Dad, come on. Wake up."

Pastor Doug opened his eyes and groaned as pain invaded his senses, radiating from his head and back. "How long have I been out?"

"A little while, but I'm glad you woke up because we have a problem. The sirens are going off."

Pastor Doug tilted his head and listened. A faint whine sounded outside the windows. A mudflow! Zayden was right. "How long?"

"They just started."

Pastor Doug sat up and blinked in confusion. Scott was sitting next to him. "You got yourself down?"

"I let gravity do the work for me." Scott touched his legs. "But I can't get out to the car."

Pastor Doug nodded, pushing past the fogginess and pain in his ankle. He'd worry about broken bones or a concussion later. Limping up the steps to the second floor, he grabbed the handles of the wheelchair and bumped it down the stairs.

Lifting Scott under the armpits, he dropped him into the chair and raced it out the front door. He leaned the chair all the way back and did a wheelie down the one step to the sidewalk.

At the car, he lifted Scott from behind, practically shoved him in, and slammed the door. A deafening roar came from the direction of the river valley. They didn't have much time.

He folded the wheelchair with practiced movements and threw it into the trunk. Then, he got in, started the car, and backed out of the driveway onto Randall Street. This route would take him closer to the river, but it was also the quickest way to high ground.

He drove straight to the river, then followed the curves parallel to the water, driving as fast as he dared on the meandering road. The roar of the advancing water was loud inside the car now.

They made it through the valley floor and started the climb up the tallest bluff near town where the city had built the community center and evacuation shelter. He floored the gas pedal. Thirty feet and they'd make it.

Halfway up the hill, advancing water rose like a brown wall in his rearview mirror. It was coming too fast. "Hang on."

A wall of water, as hard as concrete, slammed into the back of his vehicle. The car shot forward, catapulted by the force.

The front end slammed into the hill as water lifted up the back end. The car spun until it floated perpendicular to the road.

Another rush came, throwing them sideways into the road.

The car bobbed and swayed like a cork. Pastor Doug was helpless. What would he do if it tipped over? He could swim out, but Scott wouldn't have a chance in the raging floodwaters. If it came to that, he would die trying to get his son to safety.

Lord, help, please. Right now!

A wave spun the car around. He clung to the steering wheel. In the rearview mirror, he saw Scott clutching at his seat belt. At least, the car was still floating.

In his side mirror, something big and white caught his eye. He swung his head around to look.

A mammoth block of ice twisted in the current. An iceburg ready to smash their car in the middle of the flood.

The block slipped past the car's rear end. It might miss them.

As it cleared the bumper, another wave of water rushed in. When the turbulent current caught the block, it bobbed for a second before reversing course and heading straight for the rear passenger side door.

"Look out!" Pastor Doug yelled.

Scott looked up just in time to lean away. The iceburg crumpled the door across from him.

The impact launched the car over the crest of the hill. Pastor Doug grabbed the steering wheel again as they went airborne.

Two wheels touched down, then a jolt, and the other two wheels hit the ground, all of them in a full-blown skid. Pastor Doug whipped the steering wheel to the side, but he had no control. The car crashed sideways into the community center.

CHAPTER 27

The shock from the explosion rumbled in Lenaia's ears, echoing off the walls of the steam cave. The mountain shifted under her feet, and she fell to the ground.

Zayden stayed standing a second longer, but then he, too, dropped to the floor. The gun skidded across the ice, stopping a few feet away from Griffin who had grabbed on to an ice pillar to keep his balance.

A loud crack sounded above her head. She ducked and covered her head as jagged pieces of ice broke free from the roof and shattered next to her, sending daggers of ice into her hands and arms. Her arms were protected by her sweatshirt, but her hands stung with tiny cuts. When the ice settled, she unfolded herself and began crawling along the ice toward the gun. If Griffin got it first, he'd kill them for sure.

The shaking had stopped, but a loud crunching, crashing sound continued, like a freight train echoing through the ice tunnels. Had Griffin started an eruption, a mudflow, or both? Either way, it meant disaster for Mayim.

Griffin spun around on the ice pillar, spotted the gun, and pounced on it before she could stop him. His hazel eyes flashed delight and a slow smile spread across his face. Was he imagining the pastor of his old church drowning or anticipating the delight of killing her and Zayden?

Griffin pointed the gun at Zayden. The freight train sound drifted off into the distance. "How did you get in here, by the way?"

Zayden lay flat on his back, feigning defeat. At least she hoped he was faking it.

When he didn't answer, Griffin walked backward through the opening where Zayden had entered, keeping the gun directed at them. Griffin bent down to pick up something, then came back. After tossing Zayden's backpack on the ice, he opened the front pocket, and pulled out a cell phone. He threw it to the ground and smashed it with his ice spikes, the sharp edges crunching through the glass face. "It's too easy for them to track people with these things." He turned back to them. "I'm glad there's a better way out of here. Of course, I'll be the only one leaving. Get up."

Lenaia stood, brushing away the blood from her superficial cuts. This was it. All Griffin had left to do was get rid of them. When Zayden stood, he placed himself in front of her, then leaned back to whisper in her ear, "When he shoots, you run."

Griffin lowered the weapon a bit, his lips puckering into a frown. "I don't think anyone will find you, but just in case, it needs to look like a murder-suicide. I can't have one bullet going through both of you. Zayden, move out of the way."

Zayden planted his ice spikes. "Or what? You'll kill me? Give it up, Griffin. Your plan is ruined."

Griffin gave a short chuckle. "I don't blame you for trying, but we all heard the devastation. Most of Mayim is gone."

"You're wrong. I started an evacuation hours ago." Zayden crossed his arms over his chest. "People in town know what you've done."

Griffin wrinkled his brow, considering this new information. "Whatever. It doesn't matter. All three of us are going to disappear. Even if they believed you, they will think we're all dead. Except only two of us will be."

He raised the gun and extended his arm.

"Don't do this." The quiet, but distinct, voice came from directly behind Griffin.

Lenaia couldn't see the person, but she recognized the voice. *Wally.*

Griffin went pale before turning around. Wally stood in the small opening with his arms hanging by his side. "I know you're hurt and angry, but this won't change anything for you."

"Well, isn't this a surprise?" Venom dripped from Griffin's words.

"I know what you've been through and I'm sorry." The soft-spoken old man stared at Griffin with such compassion on his face. How had she once considered him a suspect?

She looked down at where he stood. He was still close enough to the opening to get out before Griffin could fire. "Wally, you need to go."

Griffin glared at her over his shoulder. "Wally? Are you kidding? *This* is the mysterious hermit you've been talking to on the mountain?" He turned back to Wally. "Of course, you wouldn't want anyone to know what you did." Griffin swung around to her again and gave an exaggerated bow. She winced as his gun hand flailed toward the ceiling. "Lenaia, meet Art Wall, my father."

Of course. She should have realized it earlier.

Wally, or rather Art, averted his gaze, focusing on a spot above their heads. "It's true. I'm Griffin's father, although I wasn't much of a dad." He brought his gaze down a fraction to meet Griffin's. "I left you when you needed me the most. I have no excuse."

"Nice to know you feel bad. I guess that makes up for all the years I spent thinking you were dead." Griffin spat out the words. "Tell me, *Dad,* if you cared so much, why did you disappear?"

Art retreated until his back rested against the wall of the chamber. "I let your mother down. I didn't keep her safe like a husband is supposed to do. I should have gotten her away from that pastor and his twisted ideas, but I was too weak to stand up to him. So weak that I was afraid to fail you, too. At first, I only meant to take a little time to figure things out. I knew your aunt would take care of you and I thought the time alone would help me work through the loss. But in isolation, the guilt only grew. I was so messed up. Eventually, I convinced myself you were better off with your aunt."

"You felt guilty? That's it?"

Art pushed off the wall and took a step toward Griffin. "After you went to live in Seattle, it was easier to let the days pass, to try not to think about anything. Until you came back here."

Griffin shifted on his feet like he couldn't decide whether to move closer or back away. The gun dangled limply in his hand. "I've been here for six months and you didn't have anything to say to me."

"I didn't know *what* to say. I thought you'd never forgive me. After what I've done, you really shouldn't, but you don't need to forgive me to listen." Art gestured to the gun. "Please, don't do this, Son. You'll only make things worse for yourself by hurting them."

"Don't call me that. And I'm not doing this for myself. Or for you." Griffin straightened his shoulders. "This is for Mom."

"Your mom's dead. It's too late to help her. She doesn't need your vengeance."

While Griffin was distracted, Zayden bent down and grabbed something long and pointed from the side pocket of his pack. An ice screw? That wouldn't do much good against a gun.

Griffin's hands trembled. "You of all people should be happy that Pastor Marty is dead."

Art hunched his back and stared at the floor. "I've imagined that man's death many times. If he's dead, Pastor Marty will pay for what he's done. And you will also have to deal with what you've already done." Art glanced at her and Zayden. "Please think about this decision."

Lenaia grabbed Zayden's arm and took a quiet step back, sliding him with her. For all of Art's pleading, it wasn't working. Griffin's posture had stiffened, his resolve strengthening. He would shoot them all soon if they didn't make a run for it.

Griffin shook his head in defiance. "No, what I've done is for the sake of justice."

"The police won't see it that way."

"Which is why I'm not turning myself in." Griffin raised the gun, pointing the barrel at his father. "I'm sorry." His voice was icy. "You've got some things to answer for as well."

Griffin pulled the trigger.

Lenaia screamed as a small circle opened in Art's forehead. The bullet went through his head and hit the ice behind, spraying chips around him like a halo. Art fell backward, a stunned expression on his face.

As the blast of the gunshot faded, she heard Zayden's low voice. "Run."

She forced her legs into motion, turning away from Griffin and ducking through the entrance to the next cave. A shower of ice rained down from a bullet hitting just above her head.

More bullets whizzed by. She could feel Zayden behind her but had no time to look back to see if he was okay.

She ran through a small cave and into the next where the floor suddenly sloped down. She lost her footing and slid uncontrollably down a ramp. She clawed at the ice with her fingernails, but it was too slick. She shifted her feet down, hoping to dig in with her spikes. No luck. She was going too fast.

Zayden slammed into her from behind. The collision propelled her faster down the slope.

A wall of ice stretched out before them. No way to avoid it. They were going to crash, but she had to keep Zayden from smashing her. She twisted her torso, changing her slide into a spin.

She spun in a full circle before hitting the wall with her back. The air was forced from her lungs and ripples of pain shot up her spine.

Zayden hit the wall a few feet to her left. She rolled over, trying to catch her breath.

Had they outrun Griffin or was he crazy enough to follow them down here?

A far-off grunt echoed through the cave. He hadn't given up so easily.

She tried to sit up. Her head and neck felt okay, but her back protested. Ignoring the pain, she rose to her knees.

Next to her, Zayden struggled to get up as well. But they had to keep moving before Griffin caught up to them.

She put one foot underneath to stand, but a long groan from above made her freeze in place. The ceiling of ice shifted. She looked up, eyes wide.

Chunks of ice fell from the roof of the cave. Glittering, icy splinters showered down on her head. She ducked and covered her head until the ice stopped falling.

When all was quiet, she opened her eyes. The ice had cut her skin everywhere, even through her sweatshirt. Blood wept from the gashes, but no serious damage had been done. She looked around and her heart skipped a beat.

Zayden was gone, buried under a mound of ice.

CHAPTER 28

*L*enaia dropped to her hands and knees, clawing at the ice. Would there be enough air for Zayden to breathe under there? What if he was crushed instantly? She grabbed a basketball-sized chunk and rolled it to the side.

The swooshing sound of fast movement came just before a spinning dark mass rocketed toward her. She jumped out of the way as Griffin hit the wall next to her. A shower of small ice fragments peppered them.

He rolled over and groaned. His hand still gripped the gun.

She searched for a place to run. A small tunnel beckoned on the far side of the cavern. She bolted for it, skirting around Griffin.

Sharp pain pierced through her scalp as she was yanked backward. Griffin had her ponytail in his fist. She landed hard on her side and a needle-like pain cut through the side of her calf. Had she nicked herself with her spikes? She shifted to look down. The ice screw Zayden had been holding when he'd struck the wall had grazed her calf.

Griffin let go of her hair and struggled to his feet.

She grabbed the ice spike in one hand and covered the dripping wound with the other.

"Get up, slowly." Griffin had his feet planted and the gun trained on her.

She glanced at the side tunnel. Only five feet away. A few seconds at a dead sprint would get her there.

Sliding her feet underneath, she got to her knees. She put one foot out, making a good pretense of getting up. The ice above them creaked again. Griffin briefly glanced at the ceiling. She seized the opportunity. She grabbed a handful of ice shards and threw them in his face.

Without waiting for his reaction, she dove for the opening, sliding through headfirst ... and sliding ... and sliding. She dug her ice spikes into the sidewalls to spin around. Now feet first, she picked up speed for another ten feet before the tunnel leveled out and her speed slowed a bit.

Unsure of what loomed ahead in the darkness, she split her legs and scraped her spikes along the sides of the tunnel to slow down even more. When she hit the wall of the next cavern, her feet buckled, causing her knees to hit first, sending a jolt through her already battered spine.

But she was stopped and alive. This room was much smaller than the last with only enough space to stand or lie down. This deep in the caves, only sparse light came from the shaft she'd just traveled down.

Her muscles tensed as the light dimmed above. Shuffling sounds came from the tunnel. Griffin had followed her.

She spun on the ice, moving to the side and searching for a weapon. She'd lost the ice spike in her swift descent, but it had to have ended up here somewhere.

A dark shape smashed against the ice wall just as her hand closed around the metal shaft of the spike.

The gun clattered down a second later, sliding to the other

side of the room. A gun was better than a spike. She jumped over Griffin to get to it.

He grabbed her foot, pulling her down on top of him. She smashed her knee into his chest. He moaned, but held onto her leg. She slashed at the back of his shoulder with the ice spike, slicing a gash in his back. He howled and twisted his torso, releasing her as his hands groped for the wound.

She grabbed the gun. Ice spike in one hand, gun in the other, she stood to confront him. Anger burned like acid through her veins. He had killed Randy, drowned a town, and shot his own father. Her finger itched to pull the trigger, but she wouldn't succumb to vengeance like him. "Get up."

He moved to a crouched position as if he were going to pounce on her. She gripped the gun tighter.

A tense second passed before she heard more noise in the tunnel. She debated about turning to look, but an instant later Zayden slammed into the ice wall, landing on his shoulder.

Griffin jumped on him, punching him in the jaw.

Zayden returned the blow by slamming his fist into Griffin's eye. The two men traded punches as they rolled along the slippery floor. She pointed the gun at them, but in the semi-darkness, it was hard to tell where one man's body stopped and the other began.

With the chaos and the lighting, she'd probably hit Zayden by accident. Her uncle would have shot anyway, calling Zayden collateral damage. Her uncle's advice on their many hunting trips could have been summed up as "Always get your target. If something else gets in the way, shoot through it." But she wouldn't sacrifice Zayden.

Griffin rolled on top and pushed against Zayden's shoulder where a dark stain covered his shirt. Was that blood? Zayden grunted in pain. Griffin pressed into the wound with his fingers.

Using his other arm, Zayden elbowed Griffin in the stomach. Griffin pulled back, and Zayden pushed him. They rolled sideways. Zayden fought hard, but his movements slowed, his strength waning.

She aimed with the gun. If she didn't take a shot soon, he might not survive the beating. "Zayden, move!"

Zayden pushed against Griffin's chest with his elbows, then he wedged his knees in between. A strong push with his legs sent Griffin reeling backward into the other wall. His body hit sideways with a jolt.

Lenaia held her breath and pulled the trigger. She would try to wound him, not kill him.

A hole opened in the right side of Griffin's chest. The impact pinned him back against the wall. He hung there for a second before slumping forward, half of his body landing on Zayden's feet.

She blew out the trapped breath. Had she killed him?

Griffin's face pointed at the ice. She couldn't see his eyes.

Moving to Zayden, she lay the gun on the ground to roll him over. Blood seeped from the wound in his shoulder. He closed his eyes and went slack. She had to stop the bleeding. She searched the small area for something to use as a bandage until her eyes fell on Griffin's sweatshirt. It would have to do.

She jumped to the other side of Zayden to crouch near the top of Griffin's head. Reaching to Griffin's waist, she grabbed the hem of the sweatshirt and tugged it up his torso. His arms flopped forward as she pulled the material over them.

A moan escaped his lips and his head shifted. He wasn't dead? Despite her hope to merely wound him, she wasn't glad to see him moving.

The sweatshirt came free in her hands, throwing her backward. Clutching the material, she got to her feet and stared down at him. His arm twitched. She might not have much time. She took a step toward Zayden, keeping her eyes on Griffin.

Griffin rolled onto his back. His eyelids fluttered.

She knelt and leaned over Zayden, then lifted his back and

began wrapping the sweatshirt around his shoulder. Before she could tie the sleeves to secure them, she glanced back at Griffin. He locked his gaze on to her and sprang to his feet, pushing her against the wall. She groped for the gun but couldn't find it. Even in the darkness, Griffin's eyes looked crazed. She shouldn't have shown any mercy. She should have gone for a head shot.

Griffin pushed, drawing her up until her back hunched under the slope of the wall. His fingers locked around her throat. As he squeezed, she clawed at his hands. He only squeezed tighter.

She stole a glance at Zayden, unmoving on the ice. He wasn't going to help. She thrust a knee into Griffin's crotch. He grunted, releasing her for a precious second, but then latched his hands around her throat again like a vise. She couldn't fight him off. There had to be another way out of this. *Lord, please, help!*

The gun lay useless somewhere near her feet. She splayed her hands out to the sides, seeking some hope of escape along the ice. The fingertips of her left hand dipped into a crevice. Was it big enough to lead somewhere? She slid her back along the ice. If only she could slip away from him, but he held fast, moving with her.

Her hand fell completely into the crevice and she sensed air movement. From the corner of her eye, the opening appeared only a foot wide. A tight fit, but she was determined to get away.

Pushing hard on Griffin to angle her body sideways, she used her last bit of strength to punch him in his injured shoulder. He let go for an instant.

She dipped her own shoulder and shoved into the crevice. Jagged ice scraped at her arms. Griffin's hands grabbed for her sweatshirt, but she broke through to the other side.

She stumbled forward a step, and almost went over the edge of a cliff. It was darker in here, but the sound of water met her ears. Not rushing water. More like water sloshing in a bathtub.

As her eyes adjusted to the low lighting, she examined the ledge she stood on, five feet above an enormous underground lake. The water cast a greenish glow over the underside of the ice above.

Behind her, she heard a low growl. Griffin sprayed ice around her as he tried to smash his body through the small crevice. She shrank back and clung to the wall. Maybe he wouldn't make it.

He peered out and found her. Glaring, he lunged the rest of the way through and grabbed her sweatshirt but then lost his footing. One leg went over the edge, the downward force dragging them both to their knees. Griffin tried to recover by pulling on her, but his extra weight tugged them both toward the icy water below.

His knee slipped a few inches.

He tightened his grip on the front of her sweatshirt. For a moment, they hung in a precarious balance—half his weight supported by her, the other half dangling over certain death. But they couldn't stay like this forever. Either he would put too much pressure on her and they would both fall or she had to somehow cut him loose.

His dangling foot pawed at the ice cliff, finding no footing. He yanked harder at her shirt. She had to do something.

Bending her neck, she opened her mouth wide and sunk her teeth deep into his hand. Griffin screamed and loosened his grip. She bit deeper, gagging on the blood filling her mouth.

He let go and fell forward, frantically clawing at the ice to keep from sliding into the lake. Blood from his hand smeared around him like crimson finger paints. She twisted to the side to spit his blood out of her mouth, then turned back.

They locked eyes for a second. His were almost black, full of evil, and also panicked, desperate to live. She could try to pull him up, try to save him, but he wouldn't stop until he killed her.

For the first time in her life, she chose not to save someone. She swung her leg out and kicked at his supporting knee.

He careened over the edge.

She waited to hear a scream, but the only sound was a splash. She peered over. Griffin bobbed up and down, splashing and gasping for air. He struggled to find a handhold, but the ice wall was too slippery and steep.

He disappeared under the surface, then popped up like a cork, panting and wheezing. There was no way out. Hypothermia would set in and he'd drown. His body would drop hundreds of feet to an icy grave.

She eased away from the edge. Even after all he'd done, she couldn't bring herself to watch him die.

The crevice was easier to go through now as she pushed back to the other side. She ran to Zayden who lay unmoving with his eyes closed. She knelt next to him and placed two fingers on his neck. He had a pulse and was still breathing.

Looking back up the shaft of the tunnel, she bit her lip. They were deep in the caves, he was losing blood, and she had no way to get him out.

CHAPTER 29

Travis gaped at the destruction surrounding him as he and Summer inched into Mayim from the east side. Broken trees had been strewn about like matchsticks. Iceburgs taller than him were stuck haphazardly into the ground and melting in the sun. Chunks of ice mixed with lava rock were buried in a matrix of thick mud. His boots sank deep with every step and he constantly had to help provide leverage for Summer to pull her tennis shoes out of the muck. Wherever he could, he led her to thick branches to use as stepping stones. They didn't talk except to guide each other around treacherous objects. Giving voice to the destruction seemed almost disrespectful.

The streetlights had toppled, their round orbs sticking up from the mud like watching eyes. Most of the water had drained away, but here and there small lakes filled in depressions. Once on Main Street, they weaved around several cars sitting in the middle of the mud-covered road. One had crashed through a front window and come to rest half in and half out of the library.

The door to the sheriff's office hung off its hinges. Travis peered inside. A thick layer of rocky debris coated the floor, but no signs of life. Did the residents evacuate? Or were they buried in the mud?

They trudged to the end of Main Street where he stopped, unsure of where to go. Turning in a circle, he spotted higher ground to the southwest. On top of a hill sat a large building. He squinted and saw movement. People!

It took a full hour for them to get to the bottom of the hill. Relief washed through him at the sight of a road going up. There was less mud, probably due to the angle of the slope, and fewer obstacles.

His legs burned, aching to stop, but he pushed them on. He was frantic to find Lenaia, and Summer had to be equally worried about her daughter. He dug through his foggy mind for the last remnants of his determination.

At the top of the hill, he sank to his knees in exhaustion. He couldn't take another step. Summer flopped onto her back on the grass.

"Hey, there's somebody out here." The voice came from his left. A large man knelt next to him. "Bring some water," he yelled back to someone else.

A cold bottle of water was pressed to his lips. Travis drank half the bottle quickly before glancing over at Summer. She had two people hovering over her.

"Easy now," the man said as he pulled the water out of Travis's hand. "If you drink it too fast, you'll just throw it up."

Travis grabbed for the man's arm. "Her daughter."

"Arielle is inside and safe."

Travis glanced back to see two men leading Summer inside. She'd be okay. He turned back to the kind man. "I need to talk to the sheriff right away."

"Okay. My name is Doug. We've all had a rough day. In fact, I had quite a wild ride getting up that hill myself. So, the sheriff's got a lot on his plate right now."

Travis summoned all his remaining strength and channeled it into his voice. "I need to see him, now."

"All right, then. I'll get him."

Doug walked away with a slight limp. Travis pushed himself to a sitting position, looked over at the building, and did a double take. The front end of a car was embedded in the wall. Was that the wild ride the pastor had mentioned?

Sheriff Conklin came out the door, spotted him and rushed over to squat in front of him. "Whoa. You don't look as good as the last time I saw you."

No kidding. His khaki pants were covered in mud from the knees down, his shirt was torn along the sleeves from running through the trees and stained with blood from his wrists. But none of that mattered.

"You need to go after Morgan Marshall before he gets away."

The sheriff squinted at him. A moment later, he stood and offered Travis a hand up. "Okay. Come inside."

The community center was packed with hundreds of people. As he entered, many of them were going outside to inspect the damage. Travis eased down into a chair and took another long drink of the water bottle.

Sheriff Conklin pulled a chair up next to his. "What happened?"

Travis related the entire ordeal of how he and Summer were kidnapped and hunted by Morgan, sparing no details. The sheriff's eyes continued to grow until they looked like saucers by the end. He called over a deputy, whispered a few words to him, and then turned back to Travis.

"We're going to pick up Morgan as soon as we can. You've probably saved a lot of women's lives by finding him."

Travis nodded, truly grateful to stop someone like Morgan, but ... "Problem is, I'm no closer to finding Lenaia."

Sheriff Conklin put a hand on his arm. "I might have a lead on that."

Travis's heart soared at first, but the sheriff's tone was flat. Was this good news or bad?

"Remember how I said she might be with Zayden? Well, she's not, but Zayden did hear from her. Last he knew, she was on the mountain."

Travis dropped the bottle to the floor and hung his head. This couldn't get any worse. "You're telling me she was on the mountain that just exploded."

Sheriff Conklin scooted the chair a little closer. "There's hope. Only the Puyallup Glacier blew. Most of the mountain is still intact. The last location we have on her was near the glacier, but we don't think she's still there. When Zayden called Pastor Doug about the explosives—"

"Explosives? You mean somebody did this on purpose?"

"That's the information we have from Zayden. When he called, he reported that Lenaia had gone to a higher elevation and he planned on going after her. We can't reach Zayden right now, but that's not surprising. Cell phone coverage on the mountain is spotty and one tower was taken out by the lahar."

Something was wrong with this. Lenaia was headstrong but not usually reckless. "Are you saying she went up the mountain by herself?"

The sheriff avoided his gaze, looking instead at the pale linoleum floor. "Actually, we don't know. Zayden saw two sets of footprints leading up the mountain."

The pastor and sheriff seemed to think Zayden had saved the town, but what if he'd masterminded the whole thing? Was this his way of kidnapping Lenaia and disappearing with her? It seemed unlikely, but Travis wouldn't dismiss any possibility at this point. "Did Zayden say why she was up there?"

"He thought she might be with Griffin ... against her will."

Griffin, the guy who had looked the other way while Morgan killed whomever he wanted. This situation just got worse. Who knew what Griffin would do to her? "I'm going up there."

"Not today. The sun's almost down and it's too dangerous once it gets dark. It will be hard enough in daylight. The blast took out the lower half of the Puyallup. We might still be able to go up on the cleaver or the Tahoma Glacier, but I'm not sure."

Travis glanced at the dim light coming through the windows. The man might have a point.

The sheriff rubbed his chin, and when he spoke, his voice betrayed the strain he had to be feeling. "We'll both go. First thing, tomorrow."

"ZAYDEN, you've got to wake up." Lenaia shook him for the third time. If he didn't wake up, she wouldn't be able to get him out of here.

His eyelids fluttered. He let out a groan.

She smacked him lightly on the face. "You have to help."

She touched the wound on his chest, and he winced, sucking air in quickly. The blood had stained a large circle on his shirt. She unbuttoned two buttons and peeled back the fabric. A jagged hole in his chest muscle still seeped blood. It wasn't a bullet wound. He must have been punctured by the ice when it fell on him. At least, it wasn't bleeding much. She dabbed at it with a clean portion of his shirt. He groaned again. "That's it. Come back to the land of the living."

As soon as the words left her mouth, she pictured Griffin drowning in a frigid lake. His halting gasps. His desperate flailing. She would have to find a way to live with that. For now, she needed to concentrate on getting Zayden out of here.

"Lenaia?" he whispered.

She bent close. "I'm here."

Finally, his eyes opened and stayed open. They searched for her. "You're okay?"

She gave a weak smile. "I'm fine. Better than you, I think."

He lifted his head. She supported his back to help him sit up. He glanced around as if looking for Griffin.

"Griffin's gone."

He nodded weakly. "Then, I've never felt better."

She twisted her lips. "You've got a hole in your chest. I'm pretty sure you've never felt worse. We have to get you out of here. Can you walk?" She glanced over at the opening. "Or rather, can you slide?"

He smiled. "I told you. Never been better. To wake up and see you alive is all the motivation I need to keep going."

Her cheeks warmed and she turned away. Leaning to the side, she picked up the ice screw. "All we have to get us out is this. I'll go up first, then I'll slide it back down to you. That way I can help pull you out at the top."

She helped him struggle to his feet. He stood hunched over in the small space, but steady enough. A trickle of blood still drained from the wound on his chest. She remembered Griffin's sweatshirt and saw where it came to rest on the floor by the crevice. After buttoning Zayden's shirt again, she folded the body of the sweatshirt, trying not to look at the bullet hole in it as she circled it around his shoulder, then tied the arms in the middle of his back. "It should help, at least."

At the opening, she dug her spikes in, boosted herself up, and jabbed the ice screw as high as she could get it. She used her arms to pull up, and then moved her ice spikes up. It was slow, exhausting work and it would only be worse for Zayden.

Toward the end of her climb, her arms burned and her feet ached from holding her weight at odd angles. As the reflected light grew brighter, she spied the entrance to the tunnel. One last heave and she spiked the ice screw over the edge, pulling herself out.

She scrambled around to peer down into the hole. Zayden's shadow darkened the other end. "I'm throwing the screw down now. Watch out."

Yanking the ice screw free, she placed it on the slick surface and let gravity take over. It slid easily until halfway down, when it hit a bump and pinged along the rest of the shaft. Hopefully, Zayden had stepped far enough out of the way.

Several minutes later, his dark head bobbed slowly up the shaft toward her. "Don't rush."

He looked up at her. Pain stretched the corners of his eyes and mouth, but he managed to make steady progress using his legs and one arm. He kept his eyes fixed on her.

About six feet from the top, he stopped and held his position.

"Are you okay?"

"Not exactly. My arm is cramping up and I can't give it any relief. Nothing I can do, except hold here and see if it passes."

"I can help." She swooped her thin sweatshirt over her head. Her jacket would have been stronger but hopefully this would hold. She tied a knot in the sleeve and lowered it down. "Wrap it around your arm and I'll help pull you up."

Using his teeth, Zayden wrapped the material around his good arm. When he put half his weight on it, she pitched forward.

"Hold on, I need a better stance." She lay down with the sweatshirt between her legs and her ice spikes planted solidly on either side of the opening. "Okay."

From the pressure on her makeshift rope, she felt every step as he continued to work his way up. When his head appeared in the opening, she kept her hold on the sweatshirt, grabbed his good shoulder with her other hand and pulled. He army crawled onto the ice beside her and collapsed. His breath coming in short gasps.

They'd made it over one hurdle, but they were alone and in need of help.

Zayden rolled over. "Thanks. I wouldn't have made it up without you." He put his hand on her bare arm.

She suddenly felt exposed and cold lying on the ice in just her tank top. "You're welcome, but we've got a long way to go, unless we can find a phone."

He squeezed her arm, then let go. "Did Griffin have one on him?"

She sat up, worked the knot out of her sweatshirt, and tugged it over her head. "If he did, it went to the bottom of the lake with him."

"Lake?"

"He chased me through the wall to a ledge above a lake. I pushed him in and he drowned." There it was. Confirmation that she had taken a life. Even though Griffin was disturbed, he needed help, not a shove into deep water. She'd done something to another person that she could never take back.

Zayden nodded, giving her a compassionate look. "You didn't have a choice."

"That's what I'm telling myself."

Lord, help me to live with what I had to do. I place Griffin's fate in Your hands.

Relief flooded through her. Giving Griffin over to God released her from the burden of having to understand why this all happened.

With new fight in her, she stood and helped Zayden get to his feet. "Let's go. I think the next ice ramp will be easier and then we'll be in the main cavern."

He took a slow step. His face was as white as paper. "And then what? Fly home?"

His sarcasm held too much truth to be funny. She didn't answer because she had no answer.

The second ice ramp was shorter and wider, allowing them to move side by side with Zayden holding onto her. As they came into the main cavern, it seemed amazingly bright compared to where they'd been.

Zayden sank to the floor. She knelt beside him and pulled back the sweatshirt bandage.

"You're still losing blood. Not much, though." She retied it.

He put his hand over hers. It was frigid. From the floor or blood loss? "You need to go, Lenaia."

"We'll go in a minute. I'm going to search Griffin's bag. Maybe I can find a phone."

"Just take the bag and go."

"I'm not leaving you here. No way."

"Always so stubborn." His smile was laced with pain. "Please, go and bring back help."

She shook her head. Bringing help back would take too long. He could die first and she wouldn't leave him here to die alone. "You're coming with me, like it or not." She stood and looked down at him, putting on a stern face. "And you're going to have to walk, so quit whining and get ready to move."

He gave her a half-hearted salute. "Yes, ma'am."

Suppressing a smile, she turned her attention to Griffin's pack. After rummaging through the contents, she found nothing of much help, except the tent and a few granola bars. She opened a bar and gave it to Zayden, then took one for herself. She ate with one hand, using the other to transfer the tent to her pack. To fill the small space left in her pack, she transferred all the useful items from Zayden's into hers. With his injury, they could only carry one pack anyway.

As she finished the bar, she glanced around the room. Two feet clad in dirty, worn boots stuck out from behind the ice shelf. She sucked in a breath. So much had happened, she'd completely forgotten about Wally. She ran around the shelf to kneel beside him. His head was twisted to the side, his mouth and eyes open. A pool of blood thickened on the ice next to his right ear. She felt for a pulse, even though she had no hope of finding one.

She walked back over to Zayden. "Wally's gone. I mean, Art."

Zayden pushed up to his knees, put one leg up and stood. "Ready to get out of here?"

She gently tightened her ponytail. "I've never before been so ready to leave a volcano."

"Let's go out the way I came in."

She swung her pack over her shoulders and headed for the far end of the cavern where sunlight poured through an opening in the wall about four feet above her head. A large chunk of ice had broken off to create the opening and now sat directly below the hole. A perfect natural entrance—and exit.

She climbed up onto the icy block and shimmied through the hole. Turning around, she stuck her head back through. Zayden had balanced on the block. His height gave him an advantage. He could lean through, rather than climb. He reached toward her, and she grabbed him under the good arm. "Jump. I'll pull."

Spreading her knees wide on the ice outside, she grabbed at his thin cotton shirt and yanked. The thrust of him coming through pushed her back. She lost her grip.

Zayden landed on his bad side, screaming in pain.

She gasped and rolled him over. "I'm so sorry."

He bit his bottom lip, offering her a shaky smile. "Never better, remember."

His bravado wasn't convincing. He needed a hospital as soon as possible. She supported his arm with her shoulders to help him stand. "It's cooler out here. Let's get our jackets on."

She pulled the two jackets from her pack, threw hers on, then slipped Zayden's on over the sweatshirt bandage. After she'd zipped his as far as it would go, she moved to pull away, but he held onto her. "Are you sure I can't talk you into going on ahead of me?"

"Not a chance."

He scowled and let her take the lead. It was unusual for him not to argue more, but he probably didn't have the energy.

They hiked slowly for more than six hours before they made it to her goal—the ledge where she and Griffin had camped. It was sheltered and flat.

Low clouds turned the sky pastel pink and orange. Less than an hour of daylight left. She stripped off her jacket and made quick work of setting up the tent while Zayden rested on the ground. He'd trudged down the mountain with wooden feet. Several times he tripped over rocks and fell into her, almost taking her down. They both needed some rest before tackling the ice wall.

After she kicked in the last anchor, she took a water bottle and ran it along the ground, gathering snow inside. She warmed the outside of the bottle with her hands until the snow started to melt. They'd done this for fresh water all day, but this bottle was for washing Zayden's wound.

She went over to where he sat, dangling his legs over the edge of the icy ledge. "You know that's not safe, right? Your body heat is melting the ledge you're sitting on."

"The least of my worries. You're the geologist. Isn't there rock under here somewhere?"

She shrugged. "Maybe. Or maybe not."

He folded his arms and gave her a tight-lipped stare. "Besides, I don't think you should be talking about my body heat right before we spend the night together in that." He hooked a thumb toward the tent.

"Just until dawn when we can see to get down this wall." She ignored the blush creeping up her neck. "And the only part of your body I'm worried about is your shoulder. Come over here so I can take a look at it."

He scooted back from the edge and stood. She slipped her hands under the jacket, untied the arms of the sweatshirt and slowly peeled it away from his shirt. A shiver shook his body. It was cool out here, but it hadn't gotten bitterly cold yet. She touched his forehead. Burning hot.

"Can you unbutton your shirt, please?"

He gave a self-satisfied smile and did as she asked.

The hole in his shoulder still seeped blood. She grabbed a cotton T-shirt from her pack. "I'm not going to wash it because the blood is flushing the wound and I'm not sure how clean this snow is, but I'd like to get the bleeding stopped." She pressed the cotton shirt to the wound along with the bottle of snow. "Hold this here."

He pressed his palm on it. She tied the sweatshirt tightly in the back again like a royal sash. When she came around to his front, his face looked pinched. "You don't have to try to be brave to impress me."

He pursed his lips. "I'm not. I can't do anything about how much it hurts. Complaining will just give me a bad attitude."

She furrowed her brow. He had definitely changed.

"What?"

"The Zayden I used to know would have gone silent and brooding by now."

She tried to turn away, but he grabbed her arm. "We've both changed. When you left, I felt lost. I knew leaving was hard on you, but it was much worse for me. I kept expecting you to call or come back. After a while, I realized you weren't going to because you didn't need me like I needed you. You had something else to cling to."

He paused to draw a long breath. "You had Jesus. At first, I was jealous. Can you believe it? Jealous of Jesus because He meant so much to you." Zayden rubbed his thumb along her elbow, then released her. "Eventually, though, it made me want the same relationship. Now, Jesus is my life. More important than my job, my house—I don't know if it's still standing anyway ... " He moved his hand to her face, cupping her cheek in his palm. "Even more important than how I feel about you."

She swallowed hard. This was what she'd longed for him to say years ago. A declaration of his own faith. Back then, it would have saved their relationship. She would've stayed in Mayim ... back then.

But now, even though the remnants of her feelings for him still sparked through her body like fireworks, it wasn't that simple. She had Travis, and his touch ignited an even greater reaction. His sweet, kind nature balanced out her hard-headed, driven personality. Plus, he had held on to her through the confusion of the last year. He refused to give up on her, even when she'd given up on almost everything besides her job.

She took a step back and rubbed her arms against the cooler night air. "We'd better get some sleep. I can see how tired you are from today. I'll help you get settled in the tent, then I'll crawl in."

Zayden knelt down. "I think I can get in okay." He scooted and shuffled until he lay on his good side in the tent. "Nice. You made snow pillows."

"Yeah." She'd pushed snow under the tent where their heads would lay. While harder than an actual pillow, it would work better than curling their hands under their heads all night.

She peered into the tent. He'd left as much room as he could, but it would still be close quarters. Sharing this tent with Griffin had felt just as awkward but for completely different reasons.

After she crawled in, she zipped the flap closed. They only had one sleeping bag, so she'd opened it flat to drape over them like a blanket. She lay on her side next to him.

She turned out the flashlight and her eyes adjusted to the darkness slowly. As his silhouette came into view, she was surprised at how his general form resembled Travis. Zayden's shoulders were a little wider but not by much. The one time she'd slept like this with Travis had also been out of necessity. They'd slept in a hammock in the jungle that kept closing like a fly trap and pulling them together in the middle. She remembered the anticipation—and even the fear—of that first kiss. Somehow she'd known one kiss from Travis was all it would take to sweep her away.

"Griffin said you and Travis have been dating for a year. Is that right?"

"About that long, yes."

"Can I ask a personal question?"

Personal questions from Zayden could lead her onto

dangerous ground. "If I say no, you're going to ask anyway, aren't you?"

"Probably."

"Go ahead."

"Why aren't you engaged yet?"

She tugged the ponytail holder out of her hair. "Whew, that *is* personal."

He continued like he hadn't heard. "Because I can't imagine him not wanting to hang on to you. He'd be a fool."

She let out a long sigh. "He's not a fool. He's hinted about asking me, but I've put him off."

"Why?"

The one-word question brought a solid lump to her throat. She'd been asking herself the same thing for months.

Fear.

The quiet word echoed through her mind. Fear had invaded her life like a swell of magma burning her from the inside out.

"Why not get married, Lenaia?" Zayden whispered.

She sucked air in through her teeth. Zayden was keeping his distance in the dark and she was grateful. "I guess I've been afraid."

"Of what?"

"Of messing up my life." But that wasn't really it. She feared losing her job and her independence and most of all, herself. She feared becoming all that someone else wanted her to be and none of who she really was.

And more than that, she feared tragedy. Her youthful innocence was gone. The worst thing could occur when she least expected it so she'd spent the last year of her life trying to expect it. Watching. Waiting. Her fear had crowded out any thoughts of a happy future.

"I know I'm probably pushing you too hard." Zayden shifted his good arm around to place a hand on top of hers. "I just don't want to do what I did last time. I let you walk out of my life."

She gently pulled her hand away. "We're both different. How

can you possibly know what you feel for me? You don't even know who I am now."

"I know that I've never stopped thinking of you in five years. Has it been the same for you?"

She didn't respond. It had been that way, until she'd met Travis. It was Travis who had protected her at all cost in the jungle, who had sat with her uncle as he died. Travis was driven to succeed like her, but never took himself too seriously. He could charm a smile out of anyone, herself included. And he even cared enough to push her when she became her own worst enemy.

On the other hand, Zayden was intense with an air of mystery. Zayden knew when to give her some space. But Travis never left anyone alone, if he thought he could help. The two men were opposites.

She scooted away until her back pressed against the tent wall. "Um ... I can't talk about this right now."

The adrenaline was wearing off. Her eyes were lead weights dragging her into sleep. Zayden didn't respond, at least not before she'd already fallen asleep.

CHAPTER 30

*L*enaia woke on her stomach, her hair plastered across her face and a heavy weight on her back. She rolled over to push it off.

Zayden flopped back, his arm smacking the floor of the tent. He didn't wake up. But he should have.

She raised up on her elbow and stared at him. His face was ashen, almost as white as the snow outside. Despite the cool air in the tent, sweat dripped off his brow.

"Zayden, wake up."

He stayed deathly quiet.

Pushing back the sleeping bag, she sat up and put a hand to his forehead. He was on fire. Had infection already set into his wound?

"Zayden." She couldn't shake him by his hurt shoulder, so she tapped him lightly on the face. He stirred.

She tapped a little harder until she was almost slapping him.

His eyelids fluttered. They closed for a second again, then opened wide. The pain must have hit him full force.

"How do you feel?"

"Awful."

"At least you're being honest this time."

"You've got to go on without me. Get help and bring it back."

"No. You can do this." She sat up and hit her head on the roof of the tent. "I just wish I had some pain medicine to give you."

"That would help." A small smile crept across his chapped lips. "Why don't you take the car down to the drugstore and get me some? I'll wait here."

"Very funny." The melted snow bottle from last night had worked its way loose and come to rest in the corner. She handed it to him. "Drink some water. We have to get going."

He drank for several minutes. When he handed it back, she shook it. Empty. "I'll get you some more."

"No, I'm okay. Get some for you."

She unzipped the tent and scooted out, expecting another clear day, but gray clouds hung low, draping her in cool, moist air. The clouds would make it harder to watch for crevasses on the Tahoma Glacier, the most dangerous part of their journey. For that matter, she had no idea what was left of the Tahoma or the Puyallup. It might take some creative hiking to get them off the mountain. She stared at the ice cliff below. First, she had to figure out how to get Zayden down a sheer cliff.

After she helped him out of the tent, she opened her pack, extracted a thick coil of rope, and threw it on the ground. "We need to get you out of here. As soon as I get the tent packed up, I'll lower you down with the rope."

She handed him a granola bar.

He didn't take it. Instead, he sank to his knees beside her. "I'm not hungry."

She tossed it back in the bag. She didn't feel like eating, either.

Five minutes later, she'd folded and stowed the tent in her pack. She picked up the rope and searched for a place to anchor it, finally deciding on a thick chunk of ice sticking out from the ground behind them. She wrapped the rope around it several times. "It will be easier for me if we tie this around you at the bulk of your weight, which is your chest, but I'm not sure how the wound in your shoulder will handle it."

"Tie it at my waist instead. I'll try to help with my good arm."

She bent down and wrapped the free end of the rope around his waist. After tying it off in front, she tugged hard on it. "Okay?"

He nodded. "You're sure you can do this? I don't want to pull you over the edge."

"Just go slow and try to use the ice screws to support your weight, as much as you can." She returned to the other end of the rope and untied the knot. If not for the ice knob's support, she'd never be able to hold him. Digging her spikes in, she spread her feet wide and braced for his weight.

He dangled his feet over the edge for a second before swinging off. The rope went taut in her gloved hands. The muscles in her back and shoulders strained to keep his weight suspended.

She fed the rope out a little at a time. Her hands burned with the effort. The rope bit into the ice, carving a small trench. Hopefully, that wouldn't become a problem.

She struggled with the rope until only ten feet of rope remained. He had to be at least three-quarters of the way down.

A noise, like the creaking of a door, made her stomach clench. "Rope fall," she yelled.

The ice knob splintered, then cracked in half. The pull of the rope dragged her toward the cliff.

She held on, trying to slow Zayden's fall as long as possible.

Three feet from the ledge, she had to let it go, or she'd fall over herself.

A loud grunt echoed up from below. She scrambled to the edge. He lay on his back, his legs splayed out. "I'm fine."

"You don't look fine."

He lifted his head. "Well, that did hurt a bit."

"Sorry." She scooted back from the edge and grabbed the backpack. "Look out below." She threw the pack down well away from him.

Now, it was her turn. Her gloves would likely slip off as she climbed, so she shoved them in her pockets. She went to the edge, swung her feet out and looked down. Although, she wasn't afraid of heights, she'd never done any mountain climbing without a rope as a backup. If she slipped, she'd fall thirty feet.

Twisting her torso, she grabbed the edge of the wall and used Griffin's ice ax and her bare hand to hold her weight.

She searched with her feet for an ice screw to stand on and found one just as her grip was giving out. She leaned on it, dug in her other ice spike for a base, and then moved the ax down. She felt her way along with her feet, moving her hands and the ice ax when necessary. Her progress was slow, but she made it down with less drama than Zayden.

By the time, she set her feet on the solid glacier again, he had fallen asleep still splayed out on the ice. Was he unconscious or resting?

"Zayden." She tapped him lightly on the face.

His eyes jerked open. "Will you stop doing that?"

"I will." She glared at him, hands on her hips. "If you'll stop passing out on me."

"It was just a nap."

"Come on. Let's go."

She put out a hand to help him up, but he rolled over and dragged himself up without her help. She tied them together with the rope and they started hiking again. Downslope seemed the hardest for him, probably because he had trouble controlling the pull of his body against gravity. Climbing up took more time but was easier.

The mist stuck with them like a white shadow. The constant lack of color lulled her mind into a kind of waking sleep. She stared at her feet to make sure she didn't trip and cause him to run into her. His pace had steadily declined for the last hour. He might not make it much longer. Could he handle another night out here?

An instant before the void, she saw it. A gray nothingness that marked the empty space of a crevasse.

She backpedaled, running into Zayden and knocking him over. His falling body acted as a ramp, sliding her toward the edge.

She dug in with her ice spikes, but it wasn't enough.

Cold fingers of fear wrapped around her heart. She was going over.

Her scream was choked off by a sharp squeeze to her abdomen. The rope yanked her back from the edge.

She fell backward on top of him, shaking with relief. His quick reflexes had saved her. He held her with his good arm, but she quickly realized from his squinted face the price he'd paid. He must have pulled her back with both hands. "Are you all right?"

He narrowed his eyes and raised his voice. "No. Everything hurts, I feel like I'm on fire, and we almost walked unknowingly to our deaths. Why would I be all right?"

Laughter bubbled up from her chest like a refreshing spring, bringing with it all the tension and stress of the last two days. "Now, that's the Zayden I used to know."

He bent his head sheepishly. "Sorry."

"Don't apologize for being yourself." She climbed off him.

They both sat and gazed out at the crevasse.

"What now?" he asked.

She blew out a breath. "Yeah. What now?"

The crack in the glacier was four feet across and deeper than she could see from the top. He couldn't possibly jump that far in his condition. She and Griffin had walked around it, but the trip had taken more than an hour. Zayden didn't have the stamina to add another hour to their trip. There had to be another way.

Her eyes fell on the rope. It should hold his weight if she could get it anchored well enough. She rummaged through her pack. Only two ice screws, but she could make it work.

She turned to Zayden who gave her a curious look. "I'm going to anchor the rope with an ice screw on this side and jump over. I'll dig an ice anchor on the other side, then toss the rope back to you. Anchor it again when it comes over by tying it to the other ice screw."

"Do you expect me to tightrope walk over?"

Jabbing one screw into the ice, she tied the rope securely around it. "No, you'll sit on the ropes and scoot."

"Uh, I don't scoot."

She tilted her head and glared at him. "You will if you want to keep from falling into an ice crevasse."

He stuck his head over the edge, looked down, then nodded. "Gotcha."

Two feet from the first, she stuck the other screw into the ice. All he'd have to do was tie the rope when she threw it back. She tossed her backpack over and it landed with a thud.

She grasped the rope in her gloved hand and backed up a few feet to give herself a runway for building up speed.

She focused her eyes on the other side. After backing up a few more feet, she ran as hard as she could toward the edge. At the last possible second, she jumped.

Her body flew through the air like a monkey leaping for a tree. The mouth of the crevasse gaped open and hungry beneath her feet.

The landing knocked the wind out of her. Her legs collapsed and she fell to her knees. She leaned forward and pressed her face into the snow, savoring the cool wetness. She'd made it across.

When she'd caught her breath, she sat up, wiped the snow off her face, and got to work on the anchor. She swiped away a layer of snow and then attacked the ice, carving a circular groove for the rope. Using her spikes, she cut as deep as possible. Her hands ached beneath her gloves, but she didn't stop until it was six inches deep. She curled the rope around it twice and tugged. It should hold.

She threw the rope to the other side. Zayden caught it on the second try.

The rope went taut as he took up the slack and tied it to the second ice screw. He gave her a thumbs up.

"Come slowly so I can watch the rope."

He moved to the makeshift rope bridge and, sticking his feet into the abyss, inched his way onto the supporting rope. It sagged with the extra weight.

As long as he'd tied a good knot, the ice screws should hold. But she had concerns about the anchor on her side. The rope had already cut an inch into the ice from his weight.

Half-sitting, half-leaning, he shuffled between the two sides of the rope. He pulled with his good hand and swung his legs to drag along the rest of his body. Minutes ticked by as a mere four feet seemed to stretch for miles.

The rope dug deeper into the ice. She glanced up.

Zayden had made it about halfway.

A crack appeared along the base of the anchor. At any point, it could break off completely like the knob on the ledge had.

She jumped on top of it, hoping her weight would be enough to hold it. The rope pulled and strained. The ice shifted under her.

He didn't have much time, but he just needed a few more seconds. She grabbed her pack and lifted it to her lap to add more weight.

His feet touched the edge. He swung around to grab the ice, and she felt the rope slip and swing out from under her.

He had one knee and one hand on the ice as the rope disappeared into the chasm. He clawed his way onto the glacier beside her.

She dropped the pack, lowered her head between her knees, and breathed deep. He was safe.

He blew out a large breath. "That was close, wasn't it?"

"Yeah. Are—"

In a quicker motion than she'd thought possible in his condition, he rose to his knees and brought his lips to hers. She froze, swallowing her words.

His lips were warm and gentle. Her body responded on its own. This felt familiar, almost right—but not quite.

She jumped away. "Don't do that."

"Sorry." He grinned. "I had to stop you from asking me if I was okay."

Her eyes fell to his chest. His unzipped jacket gave her a clear view. The sweatshirt bandage was wet with blood. How much blood could he lose without passing out? "Let's go. We need to get you some help."

She picked up the backpack and started out at a quick pace, but she soon scaled it way back so she could stay with Zayden. His steps were getting slower by the minute and they still had hours of hiking before they made it to the road where she'd left the four-wheeler.

A slow hour later, the peak of St. Andrews Rock came into view. "We're almost off the ice."

She glanced back and stopped. His face had gone pure white, like the ice surrounding him. His eyes were sunken and bloodshot.

He met her gaze for a second with pain dulled eyes, then his eyes rolled back into his head. He collapsed forward, hitting the ice with a thud.

She crouched next to him. "Zayden!"

She heaved him over onto his back. The soaked bandage had left a crimson stain on the ice. She had to stop the bleeding. After searching through her pack, she came up empty.

He needed a hospital. She had to get him there.

"Wake up!" she screamed. "Zayden!"

Her eyes dropped to the bandage again as she continued to scream his name. She needed help, but she couldn't leave him. He might die before she came back.

CHAPTER 31

Travis led the group of men as they hiked up the cleaver between the two glaciers. They knew the area better than he did, but he was too anxious to follow behind. Every once in a while, he would glance back at the sheriff who would nod to say he was on the right track or point his thumb in a different direction.

To their right, the Tahoma Glacier was shrouded in mist. To their left, with a somewhat clearer view, lay the broken remains of the Puyallup Glacier. Dark mud and rock trailed out from the ice that had sheared off with almost surgical precision.

He had no way of knowing if Lenaia had been trapped in the mudflow or if she'd made it through, but he wouldn't give up until he found out. Not far ahead, he spied a small peak with an apparatus holding solar panels on top. "Is that it?"

Sheriff Conklin stepped in front of his deputy to look. "Yep. The STAR station. I'm amazed it's still there."

The lahar had scoured from the base of St. Andrew's Rock and down through the river valley, but the majority of the dark, rocky peak remained intact.

"Zayden called from there." Travis scanned the remote area. "Hard to believe cell phones actually work out here."

The deputy, a large man whom the sheriff had described as an avid outdoorsman, spoke up. "Sometimes you get lucky."

Sounded more like blessed by God, but Travis kept his mouth shut. If this part of the mountain had been preserved, he could hold out hope that Lenaia was up here somewhere.

After a short, steep climb, Travis stepped onto St. Andrew's Rock, huffing and puffing. He'd never climbed this high on a mountain before. Paleontologists didn't usually have a reason to visit volcanoes. His stomach clenched. Unless of course one of their girlfriends was missing. If only he knew for sure where to look for her.

Dear Lord, I don't know what to do. What if she's dead? I couldn't handle it. Please, don't make me handle that. You brought us together and I know in my heart she's the one. Don't take her from me.

The sheriff set down his backpack, pulled out ice spikes, and strapped them to his boots. "We've got proper gear, so we'll do the searching."

"No way," Travis said. "I'm coming with you."

"In hiking boots? You'll slip and fall on the ice." The sheriff pointed to the splint on Travis's wrist. "You're already injured. If you get hurt again, I've got no choice but to take you back down and suspend the search until tomorrow. You don't want that, do you?"

He ground his teeth. "No, but I can't just wait here."

Sheriff Conklin put a hand on Travis's shoulder. "If you want us to find her, then you will."

Travis sighed in defeat. The sheriff and his deputy had experience at this. He'd have to trust them to bring Lenaia back to him.

Sheriff Conklin tugged a ring of nylon out of his pack. "Let's use a rope, since the clouds are heavy."

The deputy tied the rope around his waist and gave it to the sheriff who did the same. The sheriff turned to Travis one last time. "Sit tight. We'll search for a while, then check back in with you."

The two men headed out onto the ice, moving together in an easterly direction. Travis watched them until they disappeared into the mist. At least, the sheriff had agreed to come with him to search. He knew the man could have easily refused to hunt for a woman who might be buried in mud. But Travis couldn't accept the unknown. Even if she was dead, he had to know.

He paced along the only level spot. When that grew old, he climbed up and down the slope.

After half an hour, he'd worked out enough nervous energy to be able to sit down on a nearby ledge and pray. His lips moved with the desperate words, but he kept silent, preferring to listen for the returning of the men.

A distant noise pulled him from his prayers. It sounded like a faint birdcall, high-pitched and thin. He strained to listen. It grew louder, insistent, until it morphed into something more distinct. More human.

Could it be her? He got to his feet and moved to the edge of the ice. The thick fog limited his vision. He turned his head and listened.

The sound came again, a little north of the line the sheriff and the deputy had set out on.

"Lenaia?"

He fought the urge to pace again. Instead, he stood perfectly still, listening. The light whoosh of the wind brushed past his ears, but nothing else.

Was it her? If not, then it sounded like somebody else needed help. Should he wait for the sheriff or investigate on his own?

The sheriff might not return for hours. He couldn't wait. Not if there was any chance it was Lenaia. Stepping onto the ice, he kept a wide stance. Although it felt slippery underneath, this area was covered by enough slush that he could move ahead slowly. He slid his feet as fast as he dared, finally coming to a small rise. He spread his feet even wider, duck-walking up the slope. As he came down the other side, his foot slipped. He spun his arms, trying to keep his balance. Gravity won out. He thrust his sprained wrist under his armpit to protect it as he rolled down the hill.

Toward the bottom, he slammed into something that toppled over and landed on top of him.

Someone shouted. He looked over at Sheriff Conklin who lay on the ground to his right, glaring at him. "What are you doing out here?"

Travis pushed up from the snow. "I heard something. A voice."

Sheriff Conklin's glare turned skeptical. "Male or female?"

"I think female, but I couldn't tell for sure."

"Which way?"

Travis pointed to the northeast. "That way and I'm coming with you."

The sheriff raised his eyebrows. "Didn't you learn your lesson from your tumble down the hill?"

"Nope. I can't sit still anymore."

Sheriff Conklin shrugged. "Deputy Carlson, please allow Mr. Perego to hang on to your arm for stability, but ... " He stood, turning to Travis. "If we run across anything dangerous, like a crevasse, you stay on this side of it. Understood?"

Travis nodded and grabbed the deputy's arm.

They hiked for a few minutes in silence. Travis shuffled his feet along. He was slowing them down, but he couldn't stay behind. Not this time.

When Sheriff Conklin stopped and put a fist up to keep them quiet, Travis held his breath. A few seconds later, dark shapes emerged from the clouds. People? He bit his lip. Or was it rocks in the fog? "Lenaia?" Travis shouted.

A faint voice answered, too soft to make out the words. They moved faster across the ice.

"Lenaia!" Travis called again.

"Help. He needs help."

Travis's heart soared at the clear sound of her voice. She was alive!

Faster than him, the sheriff and deputy ran toward her. Travis slid along behind. As he came closer, he took in the desperate scene. Lenaia huddled next to a motionless man who had blood all over his chest. She wasn't crying, but her tears had left shiny trails along her cheeks.

He dropped to his knees beside her. "Honey, are you hurt?"

She focused on his face and her eyes went wide. "Travis? How ... ?"

"You didn't return my calls." He caressed her cheek. "I was worried about you."

She nodded like that made sense, but her eyes glazed over. She could be going into shock.

He dropped his hand and tried again. "Are you hurt?"

"No, but Zayden is. We've got to get him down the mountain."

Travis looked over at the unconscious man. So, this was Zayden. Her ex-boyfriend. He shouldn't be jealous of a wounded man, especially given his relief that she was alive, but the desperation in her voice shook him to the core. How much did she care for Zayden?

Sheriff Conklin pressed his fingers to Zayden's neck. "He's alive, for now."

Deputy Carlson tugged a canvas square from his backpack and unfolded it into a stretcher with handles on both sides. The two men rolled Zayden onto it, securing him by the straps.

Sheriff Conklin then knelt down and peered at Lenaia. "Can you make it down the mountain with Travis?"

"Yes. Please, take Zayden. He saved my life. Don't let him die."

"We'll do our best." The sheriff nodded to his deputy who grabbed the handles and lifted.

Lenaia's eyes followed the two officers as they carefully made their way off the ice. Nerves pulsed through his stomach. She cared for Zayden, that much was clear, but how deep did her feelings run?

Travis placed open palms on both of her cheeks. This wasn't the time for worrying. He needed to get her off the mountain. "Can you walk?"

She met his gaze with the fiery look he'd come to know as a symbol of her indomitable spirit. He was overjoyed to see it. "I can make it. The keys to the four-wheeler are in my backpack."

"Where did you park it?"

"Off Westside Road. At the base of the Wonderland Trail."

He wrapped his arms around her. "Honey, that road is mostly gone. It was swept away by the mudflow."

"Oh, no."

"Hey, it's just a vehicle. Your rental car is still near the highway." He tugged on her arm. "Let's get you out of here." He pushed unsteadily to his feet. In that short time, he'd forgotten how hard it was to move on the ice.

Lenaia got to her feet before he could help her. "You're not wearing ice spikes."

"Well, I don't exactly own a pair."

"You shouldn't have come out here without them. What if you'd have gotten hurt too?" The mist in her eyes reassured him that she still cared about him. He bent down and kissed her on the forehead. "That's why I was smart enough to bring people with better equipment than me."

She met his gaze, her dark eyes going cloudy like the mist surrounding them. "I couldn't save him. I thought I could. I mean, he was doing okay, but then ... "

"You did everything you could."

"No, I stayed here too long." She hung her head. "I should have gone for help sooner. I just couldn't leave him to die alone."

If only he could tell her it was okay, that Zayden would be all right, but he couldn't. Zayden's injuries seemed critical. Instead, he lifted her chin and said the only thing he could. "You need to trust that Zayden is in God's hands now."

She blinked several times, then looked at him as if she was refocusing. A single word escaped from her lips. "Trust."

CHAPTER 32

Lenaia sat on the edge of Zayden's hospital bed, holding his hand and watching him sleep. The doctors had said he'd make it, but he'd lost a lot of blood. Regaining his full strength would take time. After Travis had helped her down the mountain, he'd taken her to the hospital to get checked out as well. Her only injury was in her calf, now stitched up and covered by a bandage. But then Travis had left, saying he had to talk with the sheriff right away, and she'd stayed to check on Zayden.

His skin looked like gray parchment. A clump of dark, wavy hair lay across his forehead. Once upon a time, she would have smoothed the hair away in a familiar gesture. Part of her still cared for him that way, but it was a love she'd outgrown.

Zayden blinked a few times before focusing his half-lidded gaze on her. "Hey."

"Hey. The doctors say you'll live this time, but your days in mountain rescue are numbered."

He laughed, then winced at the pain. "I can accept that. I might have to move anyway."

"Actually, you won't. Morgan is no longer on the planning committee. I'll let someone else fill you in on how it all happened."

His brow furrowed. "You have to go, don't you?"

She gave a slow nod and a small smile. "It's been good to see you, and while it's been exciting saving your life and all—"

"Um, who saved whom is up for debate."

She chuckled and patted his hand. "Definitely." He flipped his hand around to capture hers, but she pulled away. "Zayden, I've made my choice."

"Lenaia?"

She jumped off the bed and spun around. Travis stood in the doorway. "I'm sorry. You startled me. I didn't hear the door and I thought you were still talking to the sheriff."

"All done. I've got what I need."

"Did you ask him if Christ's Devoted Church had evacuated?"

"Yes, most of the parishoners did. Unfortunately, the pastor, I believe his name was Marty, didn't listen when he was warned. They found him in his car. He probably heard the sirens, tried to escape, and drowned when the mudflow swamped his car."

She shook her head. In the end, Griffin had gotten some measure of vengeance.

"There were only two other casualties in Mayim." Travis shifted his eyes to focus on Zayden. "You saved a lot of lives, including Lenaia's. Thank you."

Zayden pressed his lips together and nodded.

"What about Randy?" she asked.

Travis turned back to her. "The sheriff is sending a recovery team."

She let out a heavy sigh. Randy didn't deserve what had happened to him. She'd have to visit Marge before she left town to express her condolences.

"Also, the sheriff still needs to get a formal statement from you." Travis glanced again at Zayden. "That is, if you're ready to leave?"

She nodded, then looked over at Zayden to give him one last smile. "There's someone else waiting to see you."

She swung open the door and motioned for Summer to come in. When Travis had told her on their way down the mountain about how he'd saved Summer, tears had gushed down Lenaia's face both from the realization of how close she'd come to losing Travis and from the joy of knowing little Arielle still had her mom. God had really come through for them.

Zayden's eyes lit up when he saw his sister-in-law. "You're safe."

Summer briefly touched her face where scratches marred her perfect skin. "No worse for the wear, thanks to Travis."

As Summer went to sit on the bed, Lenaia put a hand on Travis's chest. "I'm ready."

Travis grabbed her hand and dragged her into the hallway. He ran his other hand through his hair, causing it to stick straight up in front, and turned a tortured gaze to meet hers. "I have to ask. Do you still have feelings for him?"

The question didn't surprise her. He was the most perceptive man she knew. "I did."

His eyebrows knitted together, but he merely waited for her to go on.

"Zayden and I had something long ago. It had faded but hadn't died completely."

Travis stiffened and dropped her hand. "Do you need time to ... " He cleared his throat. "To explore your feelings?"

She had needed time. And that's exactly what God had given her on the way down the mountain. Time with Zayden. Although he'd changed into the man she thought she'd wanted, it was no longer enough. From the moment Travis had risked his life to save her in the Costa Rican jungle, she'd been head-over-heels in love with him. His rock-solid devotion to her, his curious mind, and even his intrusive nature when he knew she needed help—she loved it all. He'd refused to leave her alone in her pain because he cared. Apparently, it took a mudflow and some ice caves to make her finally appreciate that.

"This isn't about Zayden." She moved closer. "I took all that I was struggling with and put it onto us. No relationship can bear that kind of weight."

He pointed toward the hospital room. "But you still care for him?"

"Yes. I think God knew I needed to come back and deal with it."

She and Zayden had a connection, complicated by unresolved feelings from long ago, but when she'd seen Travis on the glacier, the truth poured over her as pure and as shocking as a bucket of ice water. Travis was much more than a physical attraction. He was her best friend. The one man who would accept her for all she was and try to help her be better than she was, if she would just trust him.

His hands trembled by his side. "What do you want, Lenaia?"

"Zayden was a part of my past." She took one of his hands between hers, pressing gently. "You are my future."

He closed the distance between them and bent down until their lips were inches apart. "You're sure?"

"Positive."

Running his fingers down her cheek, he whispered, "Here's to the future."

His lips met hers, and sparks raced through her entire body. The scent of earthy pine still clinging to his clothes surrounded her. She grabbed the front of his shirt and drew him closer, deepening the kiss until every thought was burned away by the fire raging between them.

When Travis pulled back, he rested his forehead against hers. "We need to find the sheriff and tell him we're ready to go. Then, we can take my rental car to the airport." He squinted at her. "Thankfully, the sheriff found it."

"Found it? You lost it, like the one in Costa Rica?"

"Hey, this time wasn't my fault. I didn't lose it. Morgan stole it."

"Oh." Another reminder of how close she'd come to losing him. *Thank you, Lord, for protecting him.*

He grimaced. "At least, Morgan Marshall will be entangled with the legal system for pretty much the rest of his life. But I needed to get this car back because I had something in my luggage that I would have hated to lose."

She studied his face. Nervous lines appeared around his mouth. He looked like he wanted to pace back and forth for a mile. She placed a hand on her hip. "What?"

He grabbed her other hand and tugged her down the hallway. With barely a nod to the nurses, he led her to the elevator and out the front door of the hospital. The mysterious silence was so unlike him that she followed placidly behind, equal parts curious and confused. Finally, he stopped near a small waterfall in a peaceful garden set up for the patients. "Travis, what's this about?"

He met her gaze and swallowed before answering. "In my rental car, I had a little box with a piece of jewelry in it."

Her breath caught in her throat.

Travis tugged at his back pocket and pulled out a small white box. Did he mean ... ?

Lowering to one knee, he placed the box on his other knee and took both of her hands. His bright blue eyes radiated with love. "Lenaia Talavera, I know this might not be the ideal place, but I can't wait anymore. I've never met anyone like you. You make me laugh. You make me feel alive. Sometimes, you even make me crazy." He picked up the box, opened the top and held it out. "I've loved you from the first second we met in the jungle and I can't live without you. Will you please marry me?"

She placed a hand on his stubbly cheek, her heart bursting with so much joy there was no more room for fear. "I love you, too. And yes, I will marry you."

Travis jumped up and wrapped her in a strong hug. She buried her face in his chest and breathed in more of the earthy pine scent. Nothing could get her to move from this spot. Well, except for maybe one thing ...

She pulled back and gave him a beaming smile. "So, do I get to wear the ring now?"

He laughed and handed her the open box. She gasped at the beautiful clear emerald cut diamond set in white gold.

Travis plucked it from the box and slid it onto her finger. She held it at arm's length, rotating it to allow the light to catch the stone at different angles. A flawless diamond. But more importantly, *her* diamond.

"I didn't know what you'd like. Will you be okay wearing that one?" His voice sounded more insecure than she'd ever heard.

She threw her arms around his neck and looked up into his eyes. "It's perfect. I'll wear it forever."

Travis had stuck by her through the jungles of Costa Rica, the dangers of Mt. Rainier, and her own misguided stubbornness. She knew in her heart, together forever was exactly what God had planned for them.

Dear Reader,

At the end of this story, I feel I must say to you two heartfelt things:

1) Thank you for taking this journey up the mountain (and down again) with Lenaia. Her stubborn spirit, courageous heart, and continual arguments with God have made her very special to me. If you enjoyed her story, please consider leaving a quick review. In today's world, reviews help readers and authors find each other, so keep the book love flowing by leaving reviews. Even a few words makes a difference.

2) Please don't try this at home. I spoke to one geologist who was horrified that I would write this book for fear of giving someone the explosive idea, so I officially want to say, it's very hard to blow up a glacier, and if you give it a try you will probably harm yourself.

That being said, figuring out how to blow up the mountain was great fun for me—in a fictional world. And yet, my heart goes out to those affected by volcanism around the globe, including Hawaii's recent activity. We should always respect the raw power that God placed at the core of our planet and take whatever steps we can to protect those who live nearby.

It is a very small world after all.

Blessings,
Janice

If you'd like to experience the beginning of Travis and Lenaia's love story, check out Earth Hunters Book 2:

Created (Earth Hunters Book 2)

When Paleontology Professor Travis Perego's fragile new faith leads him to question evolutionary theory, the dean tells him to get it together soon, or he's fired. Then, Travis learns of a biology experiment designed to prove evolution true. He searches the Costa Rican jungle for the result —a mysterious creature. But how far should he go to track down the truth?

Crevice (Earth Hunters Book 1)

Desperate to save her family's gold mine, Elery Hearst gives an order that results in the tragic death of one of her men. But before she can come to terms with the guilt consuming her, her brother disappears. To find him, she must find the legendary Lost Dutchman gold mine. And the one person who can help, has every reason to want her to fail.

If you enjoyed *Cascade*, I would love to give you another story for FREE!!

Join my VIP list and you will be the first to hear of new releases, giveaways, and free books! PLUS, you will immediately receive a Free Ebook copy of *Gem Hunter*.

No spam (I consider it a privilege to interact with you) and you can unsubscribe at any time.

Gem hunter Alyna Elkins is determined to prove her father didn't waste his life on a fruitless dream. Only days away from running out of money to continue his archeological research, Alyna's prayers are answered when she discovers a box of rare gemstones. But Alyna soon finds out there are others—with darker motivations—hunting for her treasure.

ACKNOWLEDGMENTS

Even for an author, it's hard to put into words how much it means to have the support of friends and family on this journey. Sometimes it takes years, as it did with this book, before it's ready to be published and during that time, these people continued to encourage me and push me forward. These few words are not thanks enough.

My rock-solid husband, Todd—without you, this writing dream would still be all in my head. Thank you for believing in me.

My three spunky kids, Zach, Jenna, and Riley—thank you for giving me such great material on how to wrestle with God. Keep the questions coming, while trusting He will answer every one in time.

Crystal Joy—your edits are always exactly what I didn't think of, but needed to. Thank you for enriching this book in your sweet and humble way.

Amelia Judd—your friendship has been a wonderful blessing. Thank you for always being ready to brainstorm (and especially for the last line of this novel).

Early readers extraordinaire, Carol Brandon, Donna Feld, Mary Johnson, and Charlotte Sanchez—each of you brought such insight to the characters and plot of this book. I'm grateful for your intuition and your passion for this series.

Lauren Dee (Daisycakes Creative)—for proofreading and fixing all my comma issues (whew).

Elijah Toten—for an updated book cover with a romantic and mysterious flair.

To you, dear reader—thank you for spending time with these characters that I've come to call friends. I pray God blesses you as much as you have blessed me by being here.

To my God—I'm honored to give you the praise from my lips because You already know how grateful I am in my heart. Thank you for allowing me to create with You.

Blessings,
Janice

ABOUT THE AUTHOR

Janice Boekhoff is a former Research Geologist who pours her love of science and the outdoors into her suspense novels. Janice is a three-time finalist in the ACFW Genesis Contest and a finalist in the Utah Great Beginnings Contest.

She writes from Southern Louisiana where she enjoys having only three seasons (cool, warm, and blazing hot). When she's not writing, she's hanging out with her amazing husband and three feisty kids or patrolling her backyard to keep her predator Vizsla (that's a dog, in case you weren't sure) from eating all the cute little geckos.

If you'd like to receive an email each time Janice releases a new book, please join her VIP list.

Connect with Janice Boekhoff online:
www.janiceboekhoff.com

9 781948 003049